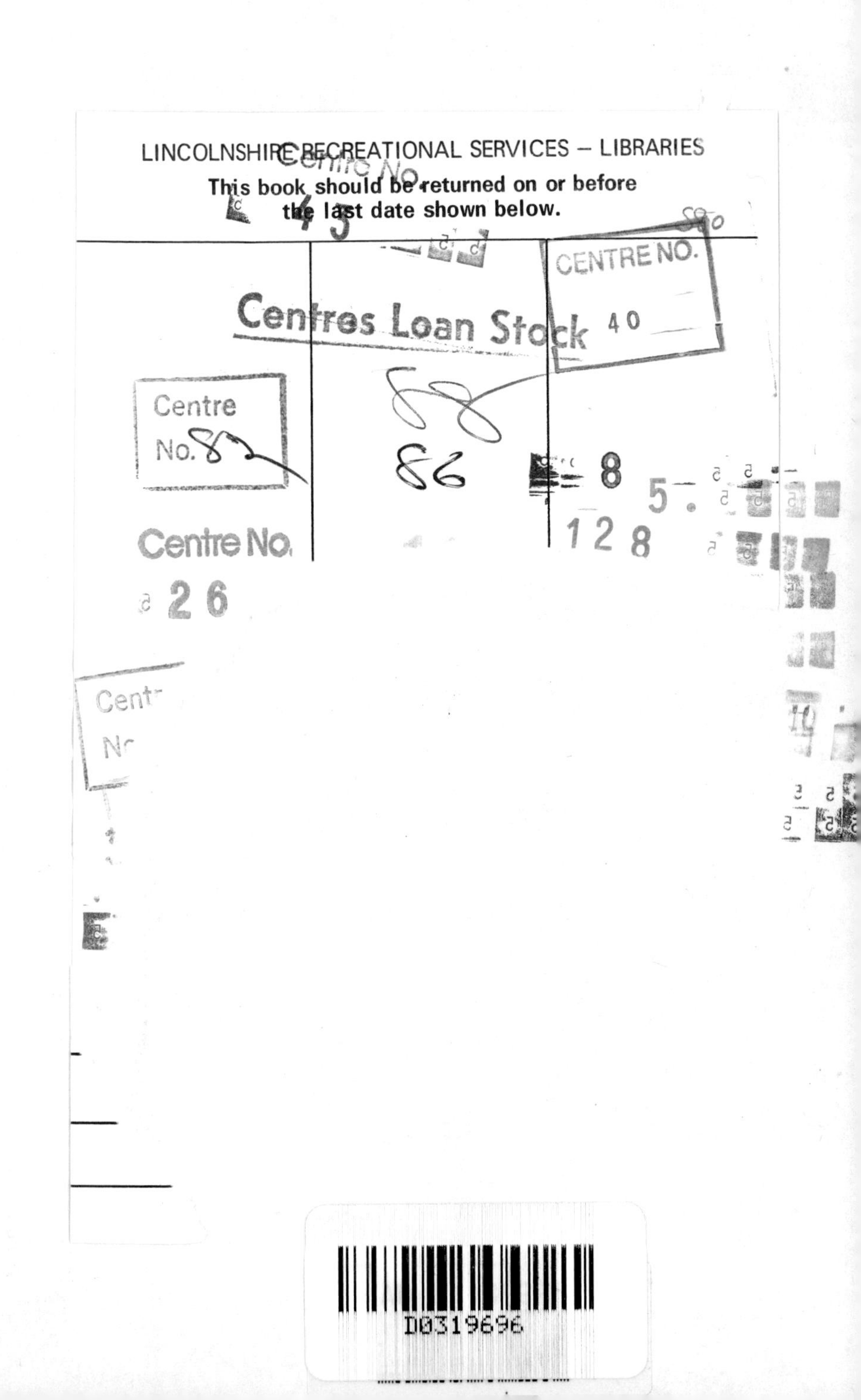

# UNBECOMING HABITS

When agent Collingdale was found dead, lying face down among the potatoes, Simon Bognor is lumbered with the case. Bognor couldn't see why Collingdale found it necessary to become a monk in order to check out suspicious goings-on at the friary. Collingdale had been leathery, tanned and taut, and assigned to dangerous foreign missions. Bognor was soft, rumpled and happy at his desk. But even Simon had known that one day life would become perilous, and that day had come. Simon Bognor was to succeed where tough, experienced Collingdale had failed rather spectacularly. God help him.

# UNBECOMING HABITS

Tim Heald

*A Lythway Book*

CHIVERS PRESS
BATH

First published 1973
by
Hutchinson
This Large Print edition published by
Chivers Press
by arrangement with
the author
1990

ISBN 0 7451 1056 8



**British Library Cataloguing in Publication Data**

Heald, Tim *1944–*
Unbecoming habits.
I. Title
823′.914 [F]

ISBN 0–7451–1056–8

In memory of my father

# UNBECOMING HABITS

August 14 was a hot heavy day on which the sun appeared through a hazy sky, looking dull and irrelevant, as if it had opted out of its duty of providing light and heat. The warmth, which was oppressive, seemed almost to come from below the earth's surface and from the top of Beaubridge Hill you had difficulty in distinguishing the individual houses of the village a couple of miles away on the other side of the valley. They were blurred shapes half hidden by the mist, but a mile nearer, the neat barracks round the old farmhouse were quite distinct.

All morning the sheep lay ruminatively under the gorse, scarcely bothering to chew at the short cropped grass which bore parched brown witness to a dry summer. The men in the valley were more energetic, hurrying about their work in the fields and gardens until shortly after twelve a sharp high-pitched bell started to peal a rapid summons from the farmhouse belfry. After five minutes the bell slowed to a strike of one every five seconds and the last of the Community's thirty-four members walked as rapidly as his habit would allow into the low rectangular building where the office of Sext was to be celebrated.

The friars sat in hierarchical order. Abbot on the left, Prior facing him across the flagstones. On the right of one and on the left of the other, brown-robed men huddled close in the pew, descending in seniority to the novices. Then a gap to tubular steel chairs at right angles to the pews. Today at Sext they were empty. They were for guests and visitors.

There was one other empty place, the most junior of all, to the right of Brother Rollo. Brother Rollo glanced across at Brother Bede opposite and raised his eyebrows. Since he had arrived three weeks before, Brother Luke had been late for practically everything which he had not missed altogether.

Brother Luke's excuse for missing Sext was the best possible. As his brothers raised a low plain chant to the glory of their Maker, Brother Luke remained in the vegetable garden where, hours earlier, he had been sent to gather potatoes for the Community's lunch. His rich brown habit merged with the rich brown soil; the white cord round his waist could easily have been confused with the bright white flowers of the plants. Only the livid purple of the back of his neck failed to blend.

He had been lying face down among the potatoes for quite some time when Brother Bede found him, turned him over and noticed that the deep magenta marks around his neck corresponded rather accurately with the pattern of the crucifix chain which he always wore. He was, of course, extremely dead.

# CHAPTER ONE

Simon Bognor finished the Beaubridge Friary file for the third time and threw it viciously on to the seat opposite. A piece of paper fell out on to the floor of the carriage and he cursed. It was a bit much. After three years at a desk in the bowels of the Board of Trade and an amazingly tedious assignment at the High Commission in Canberra he had suddenly been lumbered with this.

He had arrived for work early that morning, looking forward to lunch at the club, mindful as ever of the idiocy of his job, when a flustered Parkinson had dropped the thin brown file on his desk. The words had been rather hurtful.

'Right, Bognor,' he had said. 'Off your fat backside. Grab a voucher and sort this out sharpish. Collingdale's dead. Don't ask questions, it's all in the file.' Which was why he was sitting in a tatty first-class compartment bound for a religious community in the rural midlands. It was the story of his life.

The file told him very little. The Society of the Sacred Brotherhood had been founded at Beaubridge in 1912. It was a respectable Anglican Order, approved by the Church of England and famous for its honey. It ranked below the Community of the Resurrection at

Mirfield or the Benedictines of Nashdom, the Cowley Fathers or the Dorset Franciscans, but above the more esoteric societies of hermits and probation officers manqués which sprang up continuously and usually died with their founders. There were seventeen and a half acres of land with it. Most of it was vegetable garden, though there was some timber and space for the celebrated bees. The farmhouse acquired by the founder, an ascetic and very wealthy eccentric who had died twenty years ago, was seventeenth century with Victorian additions. The rest of the buildings had been built after the order's foundation, sometimes, as their rudimentary nature suggested, by the friars themselves. Woodstock was sixteen miles away by road, Great Tew about three.

On the second page of the file was a bare list of the thirty-three genuine members of the order, with the name of Brother Luke pencilled in at the bottom. The friars also entertained a few permanent guests—a concession to the charitable principle. These men were not identified in the file though Bognor understood that most were alcoholics or derelicts rescued from the benches of London's parks or main-line railway stations. On the final page was the single sentence which confirmed that each of the eleven Expo-Brit operations had included products from Beaubridge.

Bognor sucked his teeth. He still didn't quite

see why it had been necessary for Collingdale to actually become a friar in order to discover what was going on at the place. He remembered Collingdale well. He was usually assigned to dangerous foreign missions and would pass through London once every two or three months, lean, leathery, tanned and taut. Not a bit like Bognor who was distinctly chubby, and slightly florid.

Parkinson had said the police would meet him at Woodstock station. Bognor prayed they would be efficient and meticulous. He knew that he suffered from an inattention to detail. He was good at broad issues, but poor on minutiae. Also this was his first piece of real field work. He realised, of course, that it would have to happen, that he couldn't spend the rest of his life drawing up briefs and unscrambling codes and ciphers. Ever since the man at the University Appointments board had leant across the table and whispered 'There is *another* branch of the Civil Service, Mr. Bognor . . . a rather special branch . . .' ever since that moment and the series of curious encounters in pubs and country houses which had followed, Bognor had known that one day life would become dangerous. And this was it. He had been thrown in head first. He was to succeed where tough experienced Collingdale had failed.

* * *

It was not yet mid-day when the train reached Woodstock, and Bognor was surprised to see the purple-visaged shape of Sir Erris Beg proceeding down the platform in his direction.

'Cops,' he said noisily, 'are all busy.' He extended a fleshy hand, the other clutched a shooting stick. His Old Etonian tie heaved under the impact of asthmatic, alcohol-assisted coughs. 'Come and have a snifter at the Owl,' he said, 'before we dump you with the God-brothers.'

Bognor said he'd be delighted. He'd first met old Beg a couple of years before when there had been some question of the Chinese trying to plant foot and mouth virus in Lord Sodbury's dairy herd.

Since then they had lunched together occasionally and Bognor liked him. His imbecilic appearance was misleading, besides which he commanded considerable respect within the department and from Parkinson in particular. A great deal more than any other Chief Constable.

'Your boss rang,' said Sir Erris when they were ensconced in the saloon bar of the Owl and had embarked on a brace of large pink gins. 'He asked if I'd keep an eye on you. Thought you might need a bit of moral support.'

'Oh.' Bognor was pleased to have the support, but not happy at the thought of

Parkinson breathing down his neck. 'I don't,' he said, coughing slightly on the gin, 'anticipate any great problem. I've a fair idea of what happened already. But it'll be nice having you around.'

'You do understand the significance of this Expo-Brit connection, don't you?' asked Sir Erris.

This, Bognor had to concede, was worrying him more than somewhat. He had understood from the file that the brothers always sent their honey abroad on Expo-Brit expeditions. These were export jollies in which a number of small independent manufacturers banded together to form a mini-export drive, and although most of them remained intoxicated throughout the journey some succeeded in selling considerable quantities of such things as revolutionary bicycle pumps or pre-fabricated hen-houses.

'Er . . . well,' he said, 'I do realise that the Sacred Brotherhood have been on every Expo-Brit so far, which in itself is, naturally, highly significant.'

'More gin,' said Sir Erris dogmatically and Bognor bought his round. 'I'm willing to bet,' continued the Chief Constable, 'that every single agricultural secret that has gone behind the Iron Curtain in the last dozen or so years went out in a jar of Beaubridge honey.'

'I go along with that,' said Bognor, who had seen none of this on the file. It was typical of

Whitehall. He began to suspect the whole thing was simply an initiative test dreamt up by Parkinson.

'Collingdale is dead, is he?' he asked.

'Oh very,' said Sir Erris, 'which I would have thought was conclusive proof that our sacred brothers, or one or more of them, are engaged in a peculiarly unpleasant game of espionage.'

'Possibly,' said Bognor. 'But it doesn't help to have too many preconceived ideas.'

'Indeed not. Now drink up and I'll drive you out to the bloody brethren, and introduce you to our Inspector Pinney.'

* * *

It was obviously distressing for Father Anselm. It seemed to the rest of the Community that he had taken it very badly. Particularly as their dead brother had only been with them for three weeks. They had hardly known him.

'He's aged overnight,' said Brother Barnabas to Brother Vivian.

'I'm not at all happy about the Abbot,' said Father Xavier to Father John.

True, Father Anselm was looking tired and drawn, but then he had looked tired and drawn since the days of his novitiate. Indeed he had been a tired drawn infant, a tired drawn schoolboy and a tired drawn undergraduate before he ever became a tired drawn friar.

His naturally angular, even haggard, appearance gave him a slightly spurious air of asceticism which he cultivated, and led some to suppose, quite wrongly, that he was frail. He had played stand-off half in a particularly good Marlborough XV and would almost certainly have won a blue but for an untimely attack of hepatitis, or yellow jaundice as it was then called. At fifty-two he preserved his fitness by felling trees in a Gladstonian fashion and once a week in winter he would drive into Woodstock for a game of squash with the headmaster, a friend from Christ Church days.

It was perhaps wrong of the Community to be surprised at Father Anselm's distress. Ever since he had taken over fifteen years before he had ruled with an authority that was almost paternal. Some resented it and among the more sophisticated there was a feeling that his time with the Society's mission in Papua had inculcated an attitude towards his fellow man which verged on the contemptuous.

His actions on hearing of the death of Brother Luke were distinctly headmasterly, almost as if planned on the squash court in Woodstock. The friars—not the 'guests'—had immediately been ordered to the refectory, on the grounds, presumably, that this was a secular matter. The rumour of sensation was spreading but only a handful of them knew what had actually happened and Father Anselm was evidently determined that they should learn from him.

Two or three minutes of silent waiting at the long narrow tables and he entered hurriedly, black leather bible tightly clasped in his left hand. Eyes watched with unusually real interest as he climbed the three steps to the lectern under the room's solitary stained-glass window (1930-ish, St. Francis with birds). He paused to polish spectacles on the billowing sleeve of his habit before glancing sharply at his audience.

'I had never thought,' he began, 'that it would be necessary to remind you of Exodus XX, Verse 13. Indeed I had always believed that of all the commandments, the seventh was the nearest to the hearts of the followers of the life contemplative. Alas . . .' He paused, both hands clasping the sides of the lectern. 'Alas, for the first time in its life our brotherhood has been visited by death which is violent and unnatural. I can not in conscience believe that the murder . . .' Again he paused. 'For make no mistake about it, murder it was . . . that the murder of our brother Luke . . . is the work of one of us. And yet the circumstances suggest that it was.

'It has naturally been my unhappy duty to telephone the county police and they will arrive shortly.

'I want each one of you to answer the police questions and to help them in their difficult work. But more important, much more important, I believe that someone here in this room knows what happened to Brother Luke. I earnestly pray that that person should come to me. I know that he will be deeply troubled and profoundly unhappy. I cannot pretend that it is not my duty to tell the secular authorities if any person should come forward, but our concern, our whole existence, is dominated by a greater reality. The perpetrator of this dreadful crime must answer to the State but he must answer also to God. And in the knowledge of Our Lord's infinite compassion and mercy may that man come to me and confess.

'And now'—he became brisk as he approached the peroration—'when we move as we now shall to the chapel, we shall offer our prayers not only for the soul of our departed brother in Christ, but also for whoever did this deed that he may have the strength to acknowledge his guilt before God Almighty.'

Even Father Xavier, the Community cynic and Father Anselm's principal detractor, was impressed.

Their prayers in chapel were almost anti-climactic.

They prayed for the soul of Brother Luke:

'O God, who alone was always merciful and full of pity we humbly implore Thee on behalf of the soul of Thy servant Luke which at Thy bidding has departed today from this life; that Thou mayest not abandon it to the hands of the enemy nor forget it forever but that at Thy command the holy angels may bear it up and bring it to its home in Paradise; where because of its faith and hope in Thee, it will not suffer the pains of hell but will rather possess eternal joy.'

And they prayed for the man who murdered Brother Luke: 'Almighty and merciful God, who desirest that amendment rather than the destruction of every soul that repents and makes confession to Thee: look upon these servants of Thine; and turn aside from them Thy anger and indignation and forgive them all their sins.'

Some were chanted and some were spoken in unison.

When they trooped out into the courtyard there were two cars parked in it. One was a white Jaguar, the other an old Morris. Two red-faced men in policemen's uniform and two less rubicund people in grey flannels and blazers were standing waiting.

For the rest of the afternoon the police worked hard but without apparent direction. Fingerprints were taken and each member of the brotherhood was asked to say how he had spent the morning; but no one who endured the brisk five minutes of questioning in Father Anselm's study seriously believed that the interrogation was more than the beginning of a very long haul indeed.

Just before Evensong at 6.30 Father John met Father Xavier outside the tailor's shop.

'The locals evidently can't cope,' he said. 'The Scotland Yard man's going to be on the nine o'clock tomorrow. Father Anselm isn't going to like that much. It'll be in the papers before long.'

Father Xavier dropped the stub of his cigarette on to the cobbles and ground it underfoot. 'Sooner or later,' he said, 'Father Anselm and the rest of you are going to have to get used to the idea that one of us has committed a murder. And anyway, where were *you* this morning?'

* * *

Sir Erris enjoyed driving. Particularly Land-Rovers. After a few gins the deep whine of the engine and the pervading khaki took him back to North Africa. Five miles out of Woodstock he took the right fork, pushed the vehicle to seventy and started to whistle 'Lilli Marlene'.

They had just swerved past an unforeseen tractor when they saw the hitch-hiker. He was sitting on a rucksack about fifty yards off. Sir Erris who was by then singing 'The White Cliffs of Dover' looked across at Bognor. 'Why not?' he said. 'He won't get another chance for half an hour.'

They had passed him by this time and Sir Erris reversed back erratically brushing the great stalks of cow parsley by the roadside.

'Hop in the back,' he said to the man. He was about twenty, with a round, optimistic face and sandy hair. He wore cavalry twills and a nylon roll neck; looked like a pre-war student.

'Thanks awfully,' he said, limping towards the back of the vehicle and climbing in with some difficulty. 'I'm sorry. I hadn't meant to cadge lifts. I'm afraid I just overestimated my powers of endurance. It's quite a long walk from Sherton station.'

'How far are you going?' asked Bognor as Sir Erris accelerated.

'To the Friary the other side of Great Ogridge. You can drop me off at the turning down to the village. It's only a couple of miles from there.'

'That's all right, we're going to the Friary too.'

'Oh. Great. That's terrific. I'm Brother Paul . . . I've been away on leave,' he added, sensing accurately Bognor's surprise.

'By the way,' he asked a few minutes later, 'what takes you to the Friary? You don't look a frightfully religious type if you don't mind my saying so.'

'You're very perceptive. No. I'm a policeman.'

'Oh.' The young man thought for a moment.

'Nothing's happened, has it? Nothing wrong?'

'I'm afraid one of your people has been found dead. Not to put too fine a point on it he was murdered. Strangled, I'm led to believe.'

They had reached the hill above Great Ogridge now, Brother Paul asked who the victim had been, and Bognor turned in his seat before answering, wondering if the reply would have any effect.

'Brother Luke?' There seemed to be relief but no real recognition. 'He was new, wasn't he? I'm afraid he'd only just arrived when I went away. It was my mother, you know. She died. Cancer.'

'I'm sorry.'

'That's all right. It wasn't exactly a surprise.'

Sir Erris grated the gears through the village with its low picture-postcard cottages and its towering church, then plunged recklessly across the main road and up the hill the other side. He was no longer singing and he stared out through the windscreen with all the inherited malevolence of generations of warriors. At the top, on the plateau before the descent to the Friary, he pulled over on to the verge.

'There,' he said, gesticulating to the north. 'Scene of the crime.'

Bognor looked down into the valley, assimilated the gorse and the haze and the sheep and inhaled the warmth of the English countryside, its silence and its somnolence. It seemed a million miles from urban violence and the impersonal butchery of international espionage—mellow and mild and unchanged, surely for centuries. And yet down in that Arcadian setting someone had throttled Collingdale with a crucifix.

'Oh God,' said Bognor, scratching his right ear. 'I suppose we'd better go and have a look.'

## CHAPTER TWO

Father Anselm was waiting. He had seen the Land-Rover approaching and had anticipated the arrival of the policeman from London. As the vehicle stopped sharply, scattering chickens and dust, Brother Paul jumped surprisingly nimbly from the back, shouted a quick thank you and was gone. Bognor was unable to follow because Sir Erris and Father Anselm were already shaking hands.

'I am sorry that we should meet again under such unhappy circumstances,' the Friar was saying. 'I hope Lady Beg didn't find the fête too much of a strain.' He lowered his voice. 'We made over £200 this year and although I would like to attribute it to the intervention of the Almighty I'm afraid it's largely Father Godfrey's doing. It pays to have a bank manager among us.'

All this was said with extreme rapidity, and there was hardly a pause as he turned towards Bognor and inclined his head. 'And this,' he said, 'must be the gentleman from Scotland Yard. Good afternoon, Inspector, and welcome to Beaubridge. I'm only sorry that your first visit should be in a professional capacity.'

'Not Scotland Yard actually,' said Bognor, and then saw Sir Erris nodding at him ferociously. 'I intend,' he continued, rallying, 'to treat my visit as a retreat. The real work will be done by my colleagues from Woodstock. I shall spend a great deal of my time in contemplation.'

'Ah,' said the Friar. 'That would be agreeable, but you're being unduly modest. One of our concessions to progress and materialism is, I am afraid, a television set. It's largely because of that, that we understand the significance of Scotland Yard. However, I am being flippant. You will want to unpack. Brother Barnabas here,' he indicated a short round man with extremely thick spectacles who had been shifting from one foot to another in an orgy of embarrassment, 'is our guestmaster. He'll look after you.' Brother Barnabas smiled broadly and executed a manoeuvre which seemed very like a curtsey. 'Perhaps you'll join Sir Erris and myself for tea when you're ready,' said Father Anselm. 'Anyone will show you the way.'

The two men turned away, leaving Bognor with his guestmaster. 'Got much luggage, then?' he inquired in a thick North Country accent.

'Just the one case, thanks.' He took the battered brown leather case from the back of the Land-Rover and followed Brother Barnabas.

'We've had to give you Room Thirteen,' he said leading the way out of the courtyard and towards a long low post-war building which looked like a sophisticated Nissen hut. 'Brother Luke's old room.' He turned and smiled as broadly as before. 'Hope you're not superstitious.'

'Sorry,' said Bognor. 'Not at all.' A crazily paved path ran down the length of the building to the main door at the far end. Thriving Virginia creeper gave the whole an artificial softness, concealing the cheap red brick which contrasted unfavourably with the older Ham stone which had been used in the original buildings. Inside the narrow door an equally narrow and unlit corridor ran down the centre of the house. Doors led off to left and right at frequent intervals—it was a bit like the tourist class on a cut price (very cut price) cruise liner. The odd numbers were on the left and Bognor's new home was therefore the seventh door.

'You should be comfortable here,' said Brother Barnabas, demonstrating the springs of the iron bedstead with the palm of one hand. 'Bathroom's the third door on the right.'

'Thank you,' said Bognor. 'How do I find Father Anselm's study?'

'It's in the Old House. Off the courtyard. I should ask there.'

Brother Barnabas seemed to be hovering and Bognor wondered if he was waiting for a tip. 'If you want any help,' he said looking at the linoed floor, 'I mean anything about poor Brother Luke . . . well you've only to ask. It's been a blow, you see, and no mistake.'

'You're very kind. I'll remember.'

'That's right. I don't mean to seem impertinent. It's my manner. And that's what the good Lord gave me. Thank you.'

Bognor thanked him again and then, left on his own, stood for a moment contemplating the room. Poor Collingdale. There were two frames hanging on the walls. One was Holman Hunt's 'Light of the World' in dingy sepia—the other was a text: 'Verily, verily I say unto you, except a corn of wheat fall into the ground and die, it abideth by itself alone; but if it die it bringeth forth much fruit. He that loveth his life loseth it; and he that hateth his life in this world shall keep it unto life eternal. If any man serve Me follow Me; and where I am, there shall also My servant be. If any man serve Me, him will My father honour.' 'He that loveth his life loseth it,' he repeated out loud. Poor Collingdale.

There was a single overhead light with a dirty cream shade trimmed in maroon, a small light brown chest of drawers, a wardrobe of similar design and the functional iron bed, out of Hospital by Public School dormitory. No carpet or rug. The walls were painted a light green and the curtains were unlined in a faded but once garish orange print.

He unlocked the case and unpacked. Pyjamas under the pillow, shirts, socks, underpants, handkerchiefs in the chest.

Shaving things, soap, towel, he put on top of the chest of drawers and then hung corduroy trousers and thick blue pullover on a wire coat hanger. After some thought *Wisden* and the current *Punch* went on the chest along with his file. That was it. He had come for no longer than a week, and he'd soon sort this out. He was confident that the explanation would prove quite simple and straightforward. He wished he wasn't so nervous.

The window looked out towards the old buildings and the hills beyond. At least he had a view.

But he must get on. His first encounter with the Abbot was about to take place. It would no doubt be extremely decorous, punctuated with donnish pleasantries and sips of Lapsang Souchong, or maybe Earl Grey. On reflection it would be Earl Grey. He had already formed an impression, based largely on his prejudices, of

Father Anselm. Even if he hadn't killed Collingdale he must be involved. He wondered if the heads of religious communities shouldered blame and responsibility in quite the same way as editors and battalion commanders. If so then Father Anselm was for the chop. You couldn't have your friars going round doing each other in, any more than an editor could go on allowing expensive libels to be perpetrated by his reporters. The idea of Father Anselm getting the chop from the Bishop rather thrilled Bognor, and he left his little room in a state of contained optimism.

Conversation between Father Anselm and Sir Erris had clearly been flagging. Sir Erris didn't like China tea any more than weak liquor, and he despised people who didn't 'get out and do something with their lives'. Added to which there was the over-riding disadvantage that Sir Erris's Christianity though real enough was primitive. He regarded incense, for instance, as effeminate and silly.

Father Anselm, for his part, thought Sir Erris a cloddish yokel. He also, evidently, felt that his current misfortune placed him at a disadvantage. He had always previously been able to assume a moral superiority over the Chief Constable. This time the situation was reversed. So conversation was limp.

'Ah, Mr. Bognor!' exclaimed Father Anselm jumping to his feet. 'Or may I call you Simon.'

Bognor was slightly non-plussed by this. Basically it seemed wrong for a suspect to call him by his Christian name, but he smiled weakly and agreed. 'We have a Father Simon in the Community already I'm afraid, so there may be a little confusion,' said Anselm. 'Never mind. It'll be purely transitory. Tea? Sugar? Milk or lemon? It *is* Earl Grey I'm afraid. One of my vices.'

They sat and drank tea and discussed monasticism, the essential differences between the Benedictine and Franciscan rule and the power of private prayer.

'I know you will want to study the way we work,' said Father Anselm. 'Who knows what hidden mysteries you may uncover by a simple study of the written words?' He pressed some volumes on Bognor. 'I think those should tell you much of what you need to know,' he said. After some minutes of rather one-sided talk Bognor asked his first overtly professional question: 'How well did you know Brother Luke?'

'I was afraid you wouldn't be able to keep your promise,' said Father Anselm, smiling patronisingly.

'I only meant that you wouldn't actually see me with a shorthand notebook cautioning people in all directions,' said Bognor, 'but I have to admit that I do have some professional curiosities. I am afraid there will have to be times when I allow them to get the better of me.'

'I didn't intend criticism—simply a mild and no doubt misplaced amusement. I'm sorry.' Father Anselm's apology made the initially rather feeble remark seem much worse. It probably had been intended as a joke but Father Anselm's humour was largely academic. He was intelligent enough to recognise what was funny without actually finding it funny himself. 'Brother Luke . . . No. He was quite new here. He wrote to me from his home and said that he had been prematurely retired from the Colonial Office—Tanganyika I believe—and he believed that he had a vocation.

'He gave the name of two referees. A don at Cambridge' (he mentioned the name of a prominent ministry contact) 'and his previous superior in the Colonial Office.'

'And you accepted him on the strength of that?'

'It's not quite so easy. The references were acceptable and we invited him for the week-end so that we could get to know one another. That was about eight weeks ago.'

Bognor finished his cup of tea and accepted a second. There had been nothing in the man's manner to suggest that he suspected Luke's alternative identity. His edginess was entirely plausible. It was natural to accept the cover story. It was a perfectly good one, adequately authenticated.

'The week-end was presumably a success?'

'He seemed to me and those of my colleagues who discussed it with him, to have a very genuine sense of vocation. He evidently believed that he could be useful here. We agreed that he should join us as a novice.'

'Which he did about five weeks later?'

'There are always some loose ends to be tied up, Mr. Bognor . . . Simon . . . even when the new brother is the loneliest of men, the most independent of characters, there are still leavetakings. Mundane matters have to be attended to. Bank managers to be interviewed, subscriptions to be cancelled. Above all a period of quiet contemplation is not undesirable before finally taking such an important step.'

Bognor frowned. Collingdale had had a reputation as a womaniser and a rake. His five weeks would undoubtedly have been extremely dissipated. The more he thought about it the more tasteless Collingdale's mission became.

'And he seemed to be settling in all right?'

'I think so. He was a little erratic in his personal habits. Often a little late for offices. But he was, I believe, a genuinely good and thoughtful man. I believe he could, in time, have become a very useful member of our family here.' He paused, as if as an afterthought, and said, 'He was strangely interested in the bees.'

'Oh.'

'Yes. I recall him saying on one occasion that his father had kept them. Father John was taking him in hand over bees. Perhaps you should talk to him.'

'Thank you, yes. You've no theories yourself then? No ideas about motive, for instance?' asked Bognor, making a mental note to investigate the bees as soon as possible.

'Alas, no. I am confident—with respect to your skills—that our prayers will provide us with an answer.'

'I hope so.' Bognor drained his cup. 'Thank you for your help, I look forward to having another talk before long. Sir Erris, could I have a word with you?' The two men said goodbye and went out into the courtyard. The sun was getting low over the hills. From the village they could hear a farmer chivvying his cows towards milking.

'Do you think it's time I met your policemen?' asked Bognor nervously.

'If you like,' said Sir Erris. 'But if you'll accept my advice you'll take it slowly. Try to be patient.'

'Oh,' said Bognor, 'I'll see.'

* * *

They found the men of the local constabulary pacing round the potato patch. Two constables were treading out distances under the supervision of Sergeant Chamberlain while Inspector Pinney contemplated the rich earth with his hands in his pockets. He took them out on recognising Sir Erris. Introductions once more.

'Have you got anywhere?' asked Bognor, trying to look impressed.

'Done what you asked for,' said the Inspector. 'More than that . . . no, can't say I have. Buggered if I know who did it. Or why. The reports are in the car.'

'Could we go and have a look?'

'Right.'

He told the others to go on with their apparently meaningless manoeuvres and led the way back to the courtyard.

The papers were locked in the glove compartment of the Jaguar.

'Best we could do in the time we've had,' said Pinney, half apologetic, half truculent. He didn't care for Londoners poaching on his territory, but he had a proper awareness of the structure of authority.

There was only one item Bognor really wanted. He turned over the first two pages and found it.

'The following members of the Society,' it said, in flowing and immaculate copperplate, 'have been in continuous residence at Beaubridge Friary for the past eleven years:

'Father Anselm
Father Xavier
Father John
Father Simon
Brother Aldhelm
Brother Vivian
Brother Barnabas
Brother Bede.

Certain inmates of the home attached to the Friary have been in continuous residence for a similar period. These are not enumerated as we are given to understand that this information is not relevant to the case.'

Eight suspects. Eight suspects, that is, if the murder was part of the espionage business. And if it wasn't, then it would surely have to be the work of a maniac. And if it was the work of a maniac then information about the inmates of the home might indeed be relevant to the case.

'Excellent,' he said, debating the extent of the confidence into which he was about to take the Inspector and opting for caution. 'I have a feeling,' he continued, 'that it will turn out to be one of these. Not, of course, that we can dismiss all the others. Do you have any hunches about any of them?'

'Not really, sir. Can't say I care for Father Anselm. Otherwise . . . well they're a rum lot, but I don't know I'd think any of them were murderers.'

'Do any of them have anything to do with the honey?'

Inspector Pinney looked at him as if he embodied all the vices he had ever associated with urban people, Londoners in particular.

'Father John looks after the bees,' he said. 'Is it important?'

'Could be.'

They went back up to the potato patch, neither man talking, and found the others still pacing about and frowning. The patch was behind a wall and therefore invisible from the main part of the Friary. Not a bad spot for a murder, particularly at that time of the morning when everyone was busy. 'Whoever it was,' said Pinney, 'came at him from behind and just pulled very hard. He never had a chance.'

'Which direction was he facing?'

'South.'

'So whoever did it just came round the north end of the wall, took him by surprise, killed him, and went back to whatever it was he was doing before?'

'Suppose so.'

'And even if the murderer had been spotted it would have been from quite a distance and as he would almost certainly have been wearing a habit he would have looked just like anybody else.'

'Wouldn't necessarily have been wearing a

habit. Not in the middle of the morning.'

'No.'

Sir Erris joined them and said he would be getting back. Bognor had his number, if there was anything he could do . . . Yes. Bognor wanted mobility, could a car be arranged? No problem, he could borrow the Land-Rover. Pinney would give him a lift home.

It was beginning to get dark and the four policemen agreed to go too.

Bognor watched them drive away—his last links with the outside world—and walked slowly back to his room. It seemed even drabber and more depressing than at first. With a sigh he flopped down on the bed and turned to the literature Father Anselm had provided. There were three volumes: a heavy book called *Benedictine Monachism* by the late Dom Cuthbert Butler, Abbot of Downside, and two pamphlets—*The Eyes of the Church or what is the Good of Contemplative Communities?* and a slim brown one which was *The Manual of the Order of the Society of the Sacred Brotherhood*.

There was a note pinned to the dust jacket of the book and Bognor read it first. '*Benedictine* I know, but the principles are not dissimilar, and you will find Dom Cuthbert *most* stimulating. A.' There was a lot of the schoolmaster in Anselm—he half expected to be examined on the contents of these things when they next met. He put the book on one side and turned to the manual. Its brevity was attractive.

He opened it at random and found a section headed 'Works.'

'The active works by which the Brothers seek to serve their Master begin with the house and in the garden,' he read. 'The sweeping, dusting and other menial offices, as well as certain forms of manual work, are apportioned among them so that each may contribute his share to the work of the household and the cost of his own living. All Brothers must be capable of engaging in some form of manual work.

'All must consider the interests of the Community in its work for God and study strict economy. Brothers will do their own work as far as possible. The idle Brother has no place in the Community.'

Just like school, thought Bognor. He shivered slightly and glanced at the Holman Hunt. Flipping through the manual he suddenly came to a type-written supplement at the back. 'Notes for the laity' it was headed. There followed a paragraph about the abiding love and charity of the Sacred Brethren, their perpetual and unstinting hospitality and the very natural curiosity of their usually ignorant guests. 'It is the purpose of these notes,' wrote the anonymous author, whom Bognor guessed to be Anselm himself, 'to attempt answers to some of the more frequent and commonplace queries which are made. Nevertheless the

Brothers are here to help in whatever way is possible and so guests are asked not to shrink from approaching anyone in their quest for knowledge.' Bognor was suitably encouraged. He laughed at the final sentence, confirmation, in his view, of authorship. 'Contrary to secular belief,' it ran, 'curiosity is never idle.'

The next page contained an account of the regime, which certainly looked spartan. The first service, a combination of Matins and Prime, began at 5.45, and the public celebration of belief continued at irregular intervals through Communion, Terce, Sext, None, Evensong, to Compline at nine. At nine there was a rule of silence till morning when the cycle began again.

However, there was more to the Community than communal prayer. Bognor, who was conscientiously annotating as he read, found that 'the Brothers must guard with jealous watchfulness the times of private prayer. They must remember that corporate worship is not a substitute for the quiet communion of the individual soul with God, and they must strive to go forward to ever fuller enjoyment of such communion, till they are living in so constant a remembrance of God's presence that they do indeed "pray without ceasing".' Bognor, who was a cheerful agnostic, wondered what it meant. Further on he got some sort of reward. Although the brothers, being friars, were rather more gregarious than some of their monkish counterparts, their day seemed to include a lot of silence. From time to time there were silent lunches, silent breakfasts, teas and suppers as well as the all-night silence from Compline to Prime. During the meals if was evidently the custom for some book of an improving nature to be read out loud by one of the brothers. As if this frequent though spasmodic ban on conversation was not enough there were special week-end retreats and quiet days when there was no talking at all. Bognor wondered what happened when the telephone rang.

Then there was work. Most of this seemed to happen between the end of breakfast at nine and the beginning of Sext at 12.15. The majority of the brothers formed a pool of basic labour—gardeners and cooks, hewers of wood and fetchers of water. A few had specialist jobs like honey or library which exempted them from the more menial functions. The only time in which they were really encouraged to take any relaxation seemed to be the period immediately after lunch. As far as Bognor could make out this consisted principally of walking about and communing with nature.

It wasn't the life for him and it couldn't have been much of a life for Collingdale. So much prayer and introspection, so much heartiness and outdoor living, although obviously there were diversions. Those who drove made occasional excursions in the van to Woodstock, those who were able sometimes went to local parishes to preach or conduct retreats or perhaps to help out a vicar or curate who was sick or needed a holiday, but in the main it seemed to consist of a primitive struggle to live off the soil and a little charity, coupled with incessant conversation with God. Bognor wondered if He often got bored. The aspect which he found most sympathetic was the establishment of mission stations round the world, which presumably provided education for the underprivileged even if it was accompanied by a certain bias.

His eye stopped briefly at the final paragraph on page 16. 'It is the purpose of Christ our Master to work miracles through His servants; and, if they will but be emptied of self and utterly surrender to Him, they will become chosen vessels of His Spirit and effective instruments of His mighty working.'

He looked again at the appalling sepia of the Light of the World and pondered. Reading through this comfortable though curious religious exposition, he had almost forgotten that he was here on a murder hunt. Someone, he reflected, was going to have to be emptied of a little more self, and, compounding the sacrilege, would be surrendering to him, not his Master. For the time being the written word had yielded enough. He decided to take a walk. There was plenty of time before Compline. He turned out of the Friary grounds and started to walk down the lane away from Great Ogridge. He must have been going for more than half an hour when the steep hedges on either side of him fell away and he was in a small jumble of houses with a post office and a pub uncompromisingly named the Boot. The rich smell of cowdung was all about him and the dung itself plastered the road with a thick layer of brown. The door of the Boot, from which most of the paint had long since vanished, was also splattered with the stuff and the pub (licensee one Geo. Hey) was a picture of meanness and decrepitude. However, the walk had made him thirsty and a pub was a good place for gossip.

Inside it was dark and the very definite smell of cow mingled with stale beer and cigarettes. Two farm hands in caps and light khaki trousers conversed in incomprehensible dialect. They wore braces and shirts which had been designed to go with stiff collars, and might have done on Sundays long ago. He ordered a pint and asked the barman (who soon transpired to be none other than Mr. Hey himself) to join him. Mr. Hey said he didn't mind if he did and his was a mild-and-bitter, thank you very much, and was he staying in these parts or just passing through.

The idea of this particular hamlet on the way anywhere hadn't occurred to Bognor who admitted staying at the Friary. Mr. Hey looked at him with suspicion. After a bit he said, 'You don't look like one of them.'

'That's the second time today someone's said that. You're right. I'm not.'

'You don't even look as if you're on what they call "retreat",' said Mr. Hey, his initial approval slowly returning.

'Not in a very full sense. I'm studying.'

'Ah. Studying what?'

'Oh, you could say I was researching into the significance of monastic life in Britain.'

Mr. Hey's eyes narrowed and he appeared to be cogitating.

'Could tell you some funny things about that lot. If you were interested.'

'What sort of things?'

Mr. Hey leant across the bar and lowered his voice.

'Not all they might be, them,' he said ambiguously. 'Not some of them, anyway.'

'Oh.' Bognor implied interest.

'Oh yes. I could tell you a thing or two. Take those vows, for instance. What is it? Chastity and poverty and obedience, well . . .' He was lowering his voice to new depths when the door opened and a middle-aged man in light-weight cotton jacket and open-neck shirt came in.

'Usual, please, George,' he said, adding a terse but not unfriendly 'Evening' to the company in general. He put the canvas duffel bag he'd been carrying over his shoulder on the floor beside the bar stool. Mr. Hey poured a double whisky and added a single measure of water. The newcomer took a considerable sip.

'Busy?' he enquired, without appearing to be interested in the reply, which also had the tired air of oft-repeated ritual.

Mr. Hey clearly regarded the duffelbagger as a valued customer, which judging by the rapidity with which the second Scotch followed the first he certainly was. Bognor practised the unaccustomed art of detection. The man was comfortably off. The shirt was silk. The pound notes peeled off in a thick roll and he was smoking Perfectos Finos. Rather a lot of them. He and Mr. Hey talked about the weather and cricket and the price of whisky.

After a few minutes Bognor finished his pint, told Mr. Hey that he was looking forward to a chat some other time, and set off back to the Friary for Compline.

He made it with time to spare and was sitting in his tubular steel chair before even the first of the friars came in. The chapel had atmosphere, of that there was no question. The low rafters, the little niches with statues of the saints and the dull plain wooden crosses—fourteen of them—signifying the stations of the cross. Bognor tried to remember them. Condemnation was the first, then actually being given the cross, then falling for the first time under the weight of the cross—he got stuck around the middle and couldn't remember which came first, the cross being given to Simon of Cyrene or Jesus' face being wiped by Veronica. He was wrestling with the problem as the first of the friars entered. He was an old man with a stick and Bognor switched anxiously from the problems of Veronica's handkerchief to the more immediate ones of murder and espionage. He wondered if this was one of his suspects. The old man shuffled in past him and then reaching the middle of the chapel turned to face the altar on his right, made a fumbled genuflection and went to his place in the stalls. A few seconds later another younger man followed whom Simon recognised. It was Brother Paul. He smiled briefly and then performed an altogether crisper obeisance towards the altar before kneeling in his place. After Paul the friars came faster. Old and young, fidgety and arthritic, decisive and athletic, faces that suggested a Victorian missionary zeal and others than seemed totally introspective and withdrawn; clever-looking men and stupid, men with vacuous expressions and men with darting observant eyes. Only two that he knew—Brother Barnabas, gauche and almost tripping on the step into the stalls. Brother Barnabas, reflected Bognor, could never have pulled a man's crucifix with his bare hands until the man wearing the crucifix choked and died. He shuddered at the thought. And Father Anselm, the last to arrive, his coming signalling the beginning of the service. Bognor still found him irritatingly obsequious, but he had a presence of sorts. As he sat at his place nearest the altar a brown-clad figure rose from the stalls opposite him and intoned in bass 'The Lord Almighty grant us a quiet night and a perfect end.'

As he sat, a friar almost immediately opposite him stood and chanted, this time tenor, 'Brethren, be sober, be vigilant, because your adversary the devil, as a roaring lion, walketh about, seeking whom he may devour; whom resist steadfast in the faith.' Bognor was entranced. Despite the actual modernity of the chapel itself and the fact that he had seen one of the men in front on him riding in a Land-Rover that same afternoon the whole effect was medieval. If it made industrial espionage seem less likely it gave murder a greater probability.

The Community progressed in plainsong through a variety of prayers and responses and then four different psalms concluding with the Nunc Dimittis, a confession and a Lord's Prayer.

For Bognor, whose recollections were exclusively of hymns like sea-shanties sung by five hundred schoolboys, it was a strange experience. He wondered if the tenor who sang of the devil as a roaring lion had a murder on his conscience. He was a square robust man, about Bognor's own age. Or the bass, tall, stooping, late forties, who had asked for a quiet night.

There was a lull and he realised with a start that the friars were kneeling in silent prayer; then silence was broken by Father Anselm's voice calling on 'Our Lord, who at the hour of compline didst rest in the sepulchre and didst thereby sanctify the grave to be a bed of hope to thy people.' Another pause and then a rustling as every man stood and pulled his cowl about his head and slipped his hands into his sleeves. A clip of Eisenstein passed through his mind as he stood watching. Slowly the men, faces hidden, hands unseen as if in muffs, filed past him and into the dark outside. They were no longer recognisable as individuals. Each one looked like his brother and the high point of the cowls gave the normally comfortable brown habits a new and sinister dimension. They looked like a rural English Ku-Klux-Klan.

He waited a few moments after the last figure had shuffled past him into the night and got up to go. Outside he stood in the courtyard and stared up at the clear sky. He picked out Orion and this time remembered his Hardy. Betelgueux and Aldebaran were there shining brightly. Obviously a good part of the country for stars. The reminder that things didn't change and the occasional sight of a shadowy friar performing some final task before bed made him uneasy. He rather wished he had decided to stay nights in a local pub, but he would never solve a crime unless he was on the scene itself.

Turning away from these depressing thoughts he headed back to his poky cell. As he passed the building he noticed that most of the lights were on and thought nothing of it. Turning down the corridor he stopped outside his room and was mildly surprised to see that there was light coming from under the door. He must have forgotten to turn the light off. Unlike him. Usually so punctilious.

Still only half apprehensive he opened the door.

* * *

The brown figure on the bed exhaled a small balloon of expensive cigarette smoke, and Bognor noticed the packet of Perfectos Finos open on the chest of drawers.

'Good evening,' he said. 'I'm Father Xavier.'

'Good God!' said Simon shutting the door slowly and standing in front of it.

'It occurred to me,' said Father Xavier, 'that when you eventually identified me as the solitary drinker in the Boot you might perhaps begin to harbour some unworthy suspicions. So I thought I'd better seek you out and explain myself before you started to attribute poor Luke's death to some drunken excess on my part. So here I am. Do sit down. Would you like a drink? I took the precaution of buying a bottle from our friend Mr. Hey—who incidentally will provide you with a great deal of rumour and speculation but very little in the way of fact. I would personally treat his information with caution but then you'll hardly need me to warn you about that. I'm sorry. I'm talking too much. Would you like to ask some questions? Fire away.'

He leant back against the wall behind the bed and waited. He was enjoying the situation, the eyes half shut showed deep crow's feet at the corners. Bognor poured a slug of whisky into a tooth mug and decided against going down the passage to get water. He sat down.

'I thought,' he said, 'that there was a rule of silence between Compline and Matins?'

'I have an idea there's a rule about drink.'

'I would have thought so. You don't seem to be awfully good about rules.'

'No.'

There was a pause. Eventually Bognor said, 'How exactly do you think you can help?'

'I suppose primarily by eliminating myself as a suspect and then by giving you a certain amount of accurate and truthful information. You won't get a great deal from that tight-lipped hypocrite Anselm.'

'O.K.,' said Bognor, groping. 'Tell me what you think I ought to know.'

Father Xavier stubbed out his cigarette and took another drink. 'People in intelligence organisations always work in curiously elliptical ways. I came across a few in North Africa. There's an opaqueness about them which can be irritating. Most of them were dons on sabbatical. Fancied themselves to death. Nowadays I suppose you're career men.'

Bognor smiled and said nothing.

'Anyway,' the maverick Friar continued, 'you will not, contrary to the protestations of our respected Abbot, find this a happy or indeed a noticeably religious community. I don't for myself believe that there are more than half a dozen of us with a genuine sense of vocation. I know one who's wanted by the French police on a pederasty charge but other than that I don't believe there are any actual criminals here. Or weren't until the Brother Luke business. Now that was interesting. No sense of vocation. No apparent need to escape from anything. No obvious weakness. He was one of yours, wasn't he?'

Bognor was entirely unprepared for the observation.

'I couldn't tell you even if he were, which of course he wasn't,' he said. 'I'm afraid our operations aren't as cloak and dagger as that. We're much more conventional.'

'Have it your own way,' said Father Xavier, 'but if you don't admit that he was one of yours we do get rather bogged down on motive.'

'In this instance,' said Bognor, 'I expect the motive to come last of all. In any case.' He tried to be brisker. 'Where were you when Luke died?'

'Do you have a precise time in mind?'

'Some time that morning. We can't be certain.'

'I was in the library and then I slipped down to the Boot for a quick one. George Hey will confirm that.'

'Anyone with you in the library?'

'Anselm for about five minutes, changing a book. Brother Bede for an hour.'

'What were you doing?'

'Cataloguing. It's my job. Bede helps.'

Bognor struggled with the alibi which seemed insubstantial. He admitted to an excursion to the village. Since it was a twenty-minute walk each way that gave him plenty of time for a quick murder. But it would do for the time being. The two men were silent for a moment, it was very still outside and Bognor, used to the traffic and the aeroplanes of London, found it unnerving. He started to remark on it, but Father Xavier waved him quiet.

'Shhh,' he said. 'Listen.' They both sat silently straining for a noise, but there wasn't a sound. Somewhere, probably up on the hill, a car changed gear. It was a long way away.

'Funny,' said Xavier. 'I could have sworn I heard something.'

'Probably a cat,' said Bognor.

'More likely the whisky . . . anyway, can't I tell you something useful? Like who's sleeping with who.'

For the first time Bognor was genuinely shocked. He must have shown it because Father Xavier laughed.

'A prudish policeman. Dear oh dear. Well for a start there's Brother Barnabas—you've met him, comes from Leeds and stammers, poor soul. He's with Vivian, has been for about six months now. Before that I think it was Bede though I'm not too certain about that . . . ah . . .' A thought suddenly appeared to strike him. 'Perhaps that would be a motive. Maybe your Brother Luke was trying to cut in on that cosy relationship and someone didn't like it.'

'He wasn't queer,' said Bognor.

'And he wasn't one of yours either. I know. For a policeman you're either very slow-witted, or very on edge, or extremely crafty.' He smiled. 'Don't worry. You'll find me a great source of comfort in the hard days ahead.'

Again he suddenly held up his hand and listened. This time there was no mistake about it. It wasn't from outside, but from the corridor, and it sounded like a foot on a floorboard. The two men paused a moment and then both made for the door, but they had paused too long. By the time they were out in the corridor the outside door was slamming shut, and by the time they had got to the outside door the intruder was invisible in the darkness. They could hear running footsteps hurrying away, clipping a staccato pattern on paving stones. Then another door slammed and there was silence.

'Someone from the farmhouse,' said Xavier.

'Who lives there?'

'About half the community. It could have been almost anyone.'

'Let's have another talk tomorrow,' said Bognor. He was tired and cross. He had an uneasy feeling that someone was trying to make him look silly, and it was beginning to get him down.

He slept badly. The walls between rooms were wafer thin and he could hear his neighbour snoring with a deep monotony. At 5.15 Brother Barnabas woke him with a stuttered quasi-religious greeting. He turned over and tried to get more sleep. Breakfast was silent and he had to endure not only lumpy porridge but a biography of the prison reformer, Elizabeth Fry, read stumblingly by an elderly friar with a squint. His depression increased as the morning went on. His colleagues from the local police reappeared and together they ran through the list of suspects. It was, he said to himself, ridiculous. None of them had alibis which could be corroborated because each one had been working on his own. Anselm had been in his office going through accounts and bills, except for the brief excursion to the library. Xavier had been in the library. John with the bees, Simon working on Expo-Brit, Aldhelm weeding the herbaceous border outside the recreation room, Vivian tinkering with the van, Barnabas cleaning out the washbasins and baths, Bede in the library with Xavier for an hour, then cooking. Everyone had seen everyone else some of the time—and of course at the 11 a.m. cocoa break. Except that none of them seemed able to remember the cocoa break with any precision. Or indeed anything else much.

The cocoa break was part of the community ritual. Bognor and Inspector Pinney helped themselves to mugs of watery chocolate from the chipped urn on the trestle table and looked round.

Hardly anyone except for Anselm was wearing a habit. Paul was wearing the same outfit as the day before, hitch-hiking. Barnabas was in baggy grey flannels with bicycle clips; Father John in khaki shorts and a faded blue Aertex shirt, Brother Giles, an ex-naval Petty Officer, demonstrated press-ups in the middle of the courtyard, to the considerable amusement of a small group of guests, friars and pigeons. Interspersed among the friars themselves were the various inmates of the home, usually, though not always, distinguishable on account of some physical or mental handicap. All this was described and interpreted for Bognor and Inspector Pinney by Father Xavier, himself looking like a cross between a tea planter and a don, in faded white trousers, sandals and cream silk shirt.

After he had pointed out everyone present, each man accorded a more or less rude epithet, he took Bognor by the elbow and led him away from the crowd towards the well which stood in one corner of the courtyard.

'Funny thing happened this morning,' he said, quietly.

'Yes.' Bognor was not in the mood for funny things.

'Yes. Old Anselm came into the library about an hour ago. Very uptight. "Xavier, a word, if I may," he said. He's always at his most punctilious when he wants to say something unpleasant. Anyway he warned me off.'

'Warned you off?'

'He said that while we were to give the police every assistance it was not part of our duty to start playing at Peter Wimsey, and that we should on no account approach the police without first being approached, and that the situation was bad enough already without irresponsible brethren putting wrong ideas into policemen's heads. And then he said he hoped he made himself clear.'

'To which you replied?'

'That I'd no idea what he was going on about but that I personally had a great deal more experience of the police than he had, and I would use my own judgement.'

'You think it was him last night?'

'It's your job to do the thinking,' Xavier smiled. 'I'm just giving you the facts. I'll be seeing you.' He drained his cocoa and walked off briskly grinning broadly and bowing in the direction of Father Anselm who had been watching with unconcealed irritation.

Bognor was wandering towards Inspector Pinney and wondering what new line of enquiry to pursue when there was a tug at his elbow. He turned and saw a man of about thirty in a plastic mac and a brimless panama hat; he recalled Xavier's description. 'Lord Camberley's son and heir,' he had said; 'the rest of them call him Batty Tom. Nutty as a fruit cake. Or so they say. I'm rather fond of him actually, and I'm not so sure. Anyway I always call him Thomas, just in case.' Bognor looked into the piercing pale blue eyes and wasn't sure himself.

'Do you know who lives at Balmoral?' asked Thomas urgently. And before Bognor could answer him he embarked on a catalogue of royal names.

'Not all the year round,' said Bognor seriously. 'Only on holidays.'

Thomas looked at him with interest. 'The capital of Mali,' he said slowly, 'is Bammaku.'

He waited for the information to sink in and then went on, 'You see. I'm not as stupid as I look. Not by a long chalk I'm not.'

'No,' said Bognor.

The blue eyes glazed. 'I can help you.'

'How?'

'You'd like to know who did it, wouldn't you?'

'Did what?'

'Strangled him.' He drew his hand across his throat expressively. 'Throttled him. Did him in. You'd like to know about that 'cos that's what you're here for. You're here to find out who did the murder. See. I'm not stupid.' He pulled clumsily at the sleeves of his mac, waiting for approbation.

'No,' said Bognor, 'I can see that. But who do you think did it?'

'I don't think, I know. I know for certain. Just like I know the Queen lives in Buckingham Palace when she's not in Balmoral. Did you know who the Emperor of Ethiopia was?'

'Haile Selassie.'

Lord Camberley's son smiled. 'That's what you think,' he said. 'But I saw him the day of the murder. I said "Good morning" to him too. Never said anything to me though. Told him he wasn't supposed to be there too.' He smiled vacantly and the eyes went more empty than before. 'Here comes Father Anselm. I'll see you here after lunch. At one.' He raised his voice, on what Bognor supposed must have been purpose. 'Haile Selassie doesn't just have lions. He has bulldogs too. Big fat bulldogs from Britain.' He giggled and turning, smiled inanely at Father Anselm who was on the point of interrupting them.

'Morning, Thomas,' said Father Anselm with less than friendship. He was obviously in a foul temper. His mouth was tight and he seemed to be shaking. A thin line of cocoa stained his upper lip and he was not as impressive as earlier in chapel.

'Good morning, Simon,' he said as Batty Thomas made his way back across the yard.

If it hadn't been Anselm last night then he clearly knew all about the encounter.

'Look,' he said breathlessly, 'I know you have a job to do, but so have I. Mine is preserving the good order of the Community and preventing any unnecessary things which interfere with its smooth running. It's bad enough already, without a lot of cloak and dagger stuff. For instance I don't like you talking to poor things like Thomas. He can't help himself, and he doesn't know what he's saying. You'll be bound to get false impressions from him. And . . .' he lowered his voice, though there was no one within yards. 'There are other people who are less than reliable. I see, for instance, that you have made contact with Father Xavier.'

He laughed a laugh that was intended to sound weary but was really just brittle. 'I was afraid this might happen. He's a wonderful man in many ways, a man of massive spiritual integrity, a fine preacher . . . many things like that. But he's the last person to be talking to at a time like this. He's an incurable romantic. Everything is adorned. Of course he wouldn't actually lie but he can't help exaggerating; and his war wounds have, I am afraid, left indelible scars. Sometimes he scarcely knows what he is saying.'

'War wounds?'

'He didn't tell you?' Father Anselm looked at him with surprise. 'Oh dear, then I'm afraid that he's been less than honest. I can hardly blame him. He finds it distressing and there are only a handful of us here who know anything about it. He was in a tank on the North Africa campaign. Not an unusual story in its way. There was a direct hit and he was the only man to survive. It affected him terribly. Amnesia, hallucinations, paranoia. He seems so dreadfully normal so much of the time, and yet there are times when . . .' Father Anselm put his hand to his forehead. 'It's peculiarly unfortunate that you should have encountered him so early. I blame myself.'

'He seemed all right to me,' said Simon.

This remark irritated Father Anselm still more, and he said something semi-coherent about policemen being trained to recognise that sort of thing. They were alone in the courtyard by now, and only the cawing of rooks and the sporadic whine of a circular saw up on the hill disturbed them.

'It would be better,' said Father Anselm, 'if your interviews were arranged through me in future.'

Bognor demurred. 'I'm sorry,' he said. 'I'll co-operate as far as possible but I do have a job to do.'

This seemed to alarm rather than irritate Anselm.

'What do you propose doing next?' he asked.

'I've got nothing much on before lunch,' said Simon, who was pinning a lot of hope on his interview with Batty Tom. Any other progress was difficult. The alibis were all essentially similar and an overt admission that he was suspicious about the Expo-Brit scheme might ruin everything. At the moment the murderer couldn't be sure that his motive was known. It had better stay that way for the moment. He remembered Sir Erris's advice about not trying too hard.

While he was thinking this he was being talked at. 'I'm sorry,' he said. 'What?'

'I said I'd like you to meet Father Simon. Thoroughly sound and helpful. I think he'd help you get things back in perspective after Xavier and poor Thomas.'

Father Simon was in charge of the administration side of the honey export drive. A prime suspect. If Anselm was involved in the intrigue and the murder he was being exceedingly cavalier, or perhaps cunning. Bognor's mind flickered between the two possibilities. 'I'd be delighted to meet Father Simon,' he said. 'In what way is he so sound?'

'He joined the Community the same year I did. I've known him for most of my adult life. You'll see what I mean when you meet him. The concept of inner peace probably doesn't mean much to you, but if you think it's a cliché, you'll be reformed after meeting Simon.'

'Good.'

They walked into the main building and stopped outside a door in the same corridor as Father Anselm's own office. Anselm knocked and entered in the same movement.

'I've been looking for you everywhere,' said Father Simon in tones which betrayed little inner peace. 'The labels have disappeared. I simply can't find them anywhere. You haven't taken them off, have you?'

'Later, Simon, later. I'd like to introduce you to a namesake from London, Simon Bognor. I'm afraid he's here about something rather more serious than labels.'

Father Simon was having none of this. He was an extremely small man with a grey, office-bound face and rimless glasses, and he was agitated.

'I'm sorry,' he said. 'But the labels are important. They ought to be on by next week if we're going to get everything packed in time. I've tried everything else. Have you no idea where they are?'

Anselm was discomfited. 'I'd really prefer not to discuss domestic trivia at a time like this,' he was saying when Bognor waved him on, with well-assumed languor.

'I'm not fussed,' he said. 'It's obviously very important to Father Simon. My business can wait.'

The little man smiled at him quickly and mechanically, and Anselm looked even more ill at ease. 'It's simple,' he said. 'As you yourself must have noticed, the quality of print on those labels was woefully inadequate. I've sent them back to the Press. They say they'll have them re-done by the week-end. There's no reason for all this distress.'

Father Simon subsided. 'Thank goodness for that,' he said. 'They get most upset if anything's late, and our relationship with the *Globe* has always been so good. I'd hate to spoil it.' A thought occurred to him. 'I never noticed anything wrong with them,' he said, slightly testily, his mouth pouting in an unaccustomed gesture of insubordination. 'They looked all right to me.'

'But not to me,' said Anselm. 'Neither of us is getting any younger, I'm afraid. But still, I want you to help Mr. Bognor with his questions. He's been having a difficult time since he arrived.'

It was useless. Admittedly he had a sort of half-cock alibi because he'd made some phone calls that morning. Five in all and not one of them lasted more than five minutes. Bognor told him patiently that that left about an hour and three-quarters unaccounted for, if they accepted that Luke had been killed between the time he was last seen setting off for the potato patch with a sack over his back (just after ten) and the beginning of Sext which was 12.15. Father Simon said he'd been to cocoa break and Bognor conceded another quarter of an hour. Father Simon said that he hadn't noticed Luke at cocoa that morning and that fitted in with the pattern. Nobody could remember seeing him at cocoa that morning.

Which might have meant that he was already dead by eleven; or simply that he didn't feel like cocoa. Bognor shuddered at the recollection of his first cup and decided that Luke's absence from cocoa was unlikely to be significant.

'If time concerns you,' said Anselm, 'I think I should say that he had dug remarkably few potatoes when they found him.'

'Maybe he was a slow digger,' said Bognor, realising that it sounded facetious the minute he'd said it. The two friars looked at him with contempt. 'I'm sorry,' he said. 'It's interesting but not conclusive. Luke could have died at any time between ten and twelve-fifteen and I have to tell you that no one has yet produced a water-tight alibi. It could have been anyone.'

There was a silence after that. The heavy and functional alarm clock on Father Simon's mantelpiece ticked noisily and he shuffled through some of the scattered heaps of paper on his desk.

'Is there anything else I can help you with?' he asked eventually. He had, Bognor reflected, the same slight old-maidishness as his superior, Anselm.

'It's not really relevant, but very interesting all the same . . . and we've got half an hour before lunch . . . I wonder if you'd tell me a bit about the honey and exporting it.' Bognor hoped they wouldn't notice the entirely professional nature of his interest in their honey.

Father Simon was enthusiastic. Anselm less so, although he seemed relieved that the serious questioning was over and that a red herring could be indulged. Either innocent, decided Bognor, or he underestimates me.

Father Simon's was a virtuoso performance.

Starting in a low key with the historical beginnings, the arrival of the first bees, he painted a dramatic picture of the honey's growing reputation as a genuine gourmet's delight.

'What Frank Cooper became to marmalade, the Friars of Beaubridge became to honey,' he said in one well-rehearsed phrase. From the acceptance of the Beaubridge honey on the breakfast tables of the nation's connoisseurs he moved with enthusiasm to the day when the managing editor of the *Globe* had telephoned at Lord Wharfedale's personal request. Lord Wharfedale, he had said, has long been an admirer and consumer of your excellent product. He believes that yours is a gift which should be shared with other nations. Other great British products, too, must be introduced to less fortunate countries but amongst those which Wharfedale Newspapers choose to sponsor yours will ever be foremost. By the first post next day they had received a letter asking them to take part in the Expo-Brit scheme. It was an opportunity quickly grasped, and not just for the sake of Beaubridge's inestimable honey.

It was at this point that Father Simon himself had begun to take active part in the proceedings.

'For some years,' he said, 'I had maintained an interest in the plight of our beleaguered church behind the Iron Curtain, the oppression amounting sometimes to torture, the persecutions and the trials. All this made bearable by the heroism of our brothers. I had been in correspondence—a secret correspondence you understand—with many of them and I had come to know them well.' He lowered his voice for dramatic effect and continued: 'The minute I heard of Lord Wharfedale's idea I saw it as a golden opportunity. Under the guise of a somewhat materialist export scheme we could bring succour and encouragement to our Holy Mother the Church in countries where normally there was only a very little.'

Father Anselm, who had obviously heard this moving speech many times before, muttered an excuse and left. Quickly.

Father Simon, however, was delighted to have an audience and appeared not to notice that the Father Minister had left. He became increasingly fluent, dwelt at length on the joys of his first visit to Rumania and to Poland, and his meetings with the church people there. On the subject of his fellow exporters and more particularly on that of his official hosts he was more guarded. There had, he gave one to understand, been excesses: a great deal of slivowic in Rumania and vodka in Poland, and not every member of the party had behaved well. There had been women, unfortunate souls, no doubt forced to prostitute their bodies by their Communist masters. A hazard of dictatorship, feared Father Simon, but whatever the reason, they were prostitutes and some of the British had behaved less than properly. Naturally he regretted it as a man of the Church, but also as a patriot.

'It's all,' he said, lowering his voice to previously hidden depths, 'on microfilm.'

Bognor nodded. There were still ten minutes before lunch.

He asked if Father Anselm had ever been on one of these expeditions, and Father Simon said yes, of course, but that the two of them had never been together. It wasn't usual for any exporter to send more than one representative—something to do with the notorious meanness of Lord Wharfedale and the declining circulation and shrinking profits of his frightful newspapers. Usually it was Simon or Anselm but others had been occasionally.

'Poor Luke,' said Father Simon. 'He knew Bucharest quite well.'

'Oh.' Bognor knew that. As Collingdale he had had at least two spells there in the past five years, but how the hell did Father Simon know that? It sounded as if Collingdale had been careless.

'We had some very stimulating conversations,' Father Simon went on. 'He was interested in the honey . . . Like you.' He gave

Bognor a searching look and smiled.

'It's an absorbing subject,' said Bognor. 'How much do you produce?'

'John would have to tell you that. Not enough, I'm afraid. The season only lasts about twelve weeks.' He looked conspiratorial. 'There have been times when we here have been reduced to eating Canadian.'

Bognor looked suitably shocked. 'Well, thank you,' he said. 'I'll have a chat with Father John as soon as I can. I hope you find your labels before long.'

Father Simon immediately looked troubled again. The chance of delivering his speech on the export business to a new audience had produced a state verging on euphoria, but now he was back in one of twitch. 'We've never been late before,' he said. 'I do hope Anselm isn't going to upset everyone. I must stick them on by next week.'

They got up to go across to lunch.

'You stick them all on?' asked Bognor. 'That's a lot of spit.'

'Yes,' said Father Simon, not smiling.

'And then parcel them up and that's that.'

'Just about. After they've been checked by Father Anselm.'

'He checks them?'

'Yes. It's just a formality, of course, but it is his responsibility in the end.'

They were almost late for lunch. Heads

turned as they entered the refectory still talking, and Bognor was conscious of a sea of inquisitive pink faces looking at him with undisguised suspicion mingled with incipient dislike. Father Simon slipped away immediately to his place and Bognor himself was deftly propelled to another position by a smiling Father Anselm.

'Not too busy for a light lunch, I hope?' he enquired softly.

Bognor gave him a flattering smile and looked to see who his neighbours were. One was the nervous and rotund Brother Barnabas who favoured him with a jerky nod, but the other was unfamiliar. This was odd since he was a strikingly good-looking man in his early thirties, tall with thick black hair brushed back from a widow's peak. Bognor was wondering why he hadn't noticed him when there was a breathless coughing and the chubby figure of Father Xavier pushed into the room and took up a position immediately opposite him. Father Anselm stared at him for a moment with unconcealed dislike and said an expressionless grace: 'Benedictus, Benedicat Beniesum Christum Dominum Nostrum.'

There was a moment's pause and then as Anselm scraped back his high-backed chair at the end of the top table the room erupted into activity. Long benches were lifted back from the tables and friars girded up their habits, to straddle them before sitting down. He had a sudden glimpse of white calves and Clark's sandals before the whole community was sitting with its elbows on the tables talking to its neighbour. The silence of breakfast was broken in an outburst of noisy chatter.

'I don't know what people do to washbasins,' said Brother Barnabas pouring him water from a brown earthenware jug. 'The filth is fantastic. You need a lot of elbow grease and Vim to get that lot clean I can tell you.' He seemed to have acquired some overnight self-confidence. 'Oh, I don't suppose you've met Brother Aldhelm, have you?' He leant across Bognor to the handsome man with the widow's peak. 'Aldhelm, old cock, this is Mr. Bognor.'

'Oh, just Simon, please,' he said.

'Learnt anything?' enquired Xavier, tearing a homemade crust with both hands.

'Nothing spectacular . . .' he smiled. 'By the way. You said something about knowing Intelligence people in North Africa. Were you in Intelligence yourself?'

The bloodshot eyes looked across the table with mild curiosity, but, as far as Bognor could see, nothing approaching alarm or confusion.

''Fraid not,' he said. 'Footslog. I was with the Holy Boys, which was oddly prophetic, don't you think?'

'Holy Boys?'

'The Norfolks. They were in the Peninsula

and the idiot Spanish were misled by their cap badges. They had Britannia on it, and the locals thought she was the Virgin Mary. Rather a good joke actually.'

'It strikes me as being in remarkably poor taste.' It was Aldhelm who had spoken and he blushed slightly.

'I wouldn't have thought you were in any position to pontificate on the subject of taste,' said Xavier knowingly.

Brother Barnabas giggled. 'That's a bit below the belt, Father,' he said, and then giggled again. 'Oh dear. What an unfortunate turn of phrase!'

The situation was saved, momentarily at least, by the arrival of the first course. Food was being served by about half a dozen of the friars, chosen, Bognor presumed, on some sort of rota basis. They brought steaming enamel bowls to the head of each table and deposited them on the straw mats. Then the friar seated there started to ladle, and the bowls of hot liquid were passed along the table from hand to hand.

The first bowl reached Brother Barnabas in mid-giggle.

'Oh Cripes,' he said, sniggering and sniffing in unison. 'It's Brother Bede's Broth again. Time they took him out of the kitchen and put him back in the garden.'

He passed it on to Bognor who passed it on to Aldhelm. It looked all right to him, even if it did seem to rely rather heavily on potatoes. He said so.

'Oh take no notice of them,' said Brother Aldhelm sourly. 'They don't seem able to take anything seriously. Except for Barnabas and his permanent spring cleaning. Isn't that right, Barnie?'

Brother Barnabas giggled again, more nervously this time.

'I don't think it's a crime to take a pride in cleanliness,' he said, sniffing:

'A servant with this clause
Makes drudgery divine;
Who sweeps a room as for Thy laws
Makes that and th'action fine.'

He passed on another bowl of soup while the others digested this pearl. Bognor's principal thought was that the words sounded rather better in Barnabas's flat Yorkshire than the last time he had heard them, which was when he had heard himself singing them, along with several hundred other male voices. It must have been during his national service. The next bowl of soup he kept.

'Anyway,' it was Brother Barnabas again. 'When all's said and done, it's the likes of us keep the world going. You may be very well educated, but education on its own never buttered any parsnips. It's hard slog and grind that makes things tick, hard slog and grind.' He slurped at his soup and made a face.

Bognor started to eat and looked around at the community. Everyone to his own taste, he mused, and sighed wistfully for the sophistication of his London club.

Thanks to Xavier's cocoa break lecture, he could name quite a number of the brothers. And now that he had met Aldhelm, there were only two suspects he couldn't identify: Bede and Vivian. Bede presumably wouldn't be in the refectory at this moment since he was responsible for the soup. As for Vivian, all he had established from Inspector Pinney's notes was that he was responsible for the maintenance of the Friary's Dormobile. He had apparently worked in a garage before his conversion to the life monastic. It had been Inspector Pinney's opinion that the conversion had more than a little to do with the man's sexual proclivities, and Xavier's revelation about his friendship with Barnabas tended to confirm this, though what on earth he could find attractive about Barnabas was impossible to guess. He wondered which of the greedy soup drinkers was Vivian and would have liked to ask if he could have been sure of not antagonising Barnabas.

Conversation drifted away from prickly antagonisms and settled in to the everyday at which Barnabas was a past master. So indeed was Aldhelm, and curiously it was Xavier who was excluded. It was easy to see why Anselm had placed Bognor between these two as the talk shifted with remarkable lethargy from food (problems of low budget, high-protein catering) through bed-making (necessity or otherwise of hospital corners) to the weather (ritual amazement at vagaries of English climate). There was, despite the banality of what Aldhelm was saying, a sensuousness about him which Bognor found disturbing.

As noisy conversation filled the refectory the Community ate its way through the soup and toad-in-the-hole and a jam pudding composed almost entirely of suet. A singular meal considering that the temperature was still over 80.

Not until Bognor conceded victory to the absurd pudding did anyone say anything which interested him.

'Are we fully booked for this week-end?' asked Aldhelm.

'Couple of empty beds,' said Barnabas. 'Depends if the Visitor comes.'

'What have you got planned for the week-end then?' asked Bognor.

'Just a routine retreat,' said Aldhelm. 'You know what that means, I suppose?'

'Yes, thanks. What sort of people do you normally get?'

'You'd be surprised,' said Aldhelm.

'All sorts,' said Barnabas.

'Quasi-cosmopolitan riff raff with theological pretensions,' said Xavier.

Further discussion on this point was brought to an end by the insistent jangling of a small handbell. Looking up Bognor saw that it was being rung by the Abbot in an attempt to draw attention to himself and induce silence. When he had achieved both he coughed and began to speak from notes attached to a foolscap clipboard.

'Just one or two points,' he said. 'There will be a tree-felling party in Simpson's copse this afternoon during the rest period. Volunteers please assemble in the yard at 2 p.m. sharp.'

He rustled the papers. 'Brother Vivian will be taking the minibus in to Woodstock this afternoon. Anyone with letters to post or any requests for toothpaste or shaving things let Vivian have them before . . .' He peered round the room, looking for Vivian . . . 'before 2.30, that's right, is it, Vivian?'

A robust, rather swarthy man halfway down the second table said yes. 'Depending,' he added in a country accent Bognor couldn't place, 'on whether I can fix the petrol pump proper, or not.'

Father Anselm was momentarily nonplussed. 'Quite,' he said after a pause. He put his clipboard back on the table and looked earnest.

'A more general matter,' he said. 'I heard this morning from our Visitor, the Bishop of

Woodstock, and he has said that he will be attending this week-end's retreat and preaching in chapel on Sunday evening. I need hardly say that in view of recent unfortunate circumstances it is more than ever important that we put on a very good show indeed. Politeness, austerity, prayer, none of these in themselves is enough. It is vital that the inner sanctity which is the core of this community should make itself evident, and that we should at all times demonstrate our dedication to our Founder Wilfrid, and to God the Father, God the Son and God the Holy Ghost.' He shut his eyes for the final sentence and crossed himself.

It wasn't the end of the meal. Father Anselm sat down again and plates were piled up, jugs removed and conversation resumed. Bognor looked at his watch. It was almost time for his interview with Batty Thomas. He looked across the room to the far end of the third table where the 'guests' were sitting dominating the room with raucous conversation. He ran an eye up and down the line and failed to find Thomas; retraced more slowly and still didn't see him. He looked at his watch again. Only about a minute to go. Perhaps Thomas had managed to sneak out before the final grace. He looked towards Anselm and saw to his relief that he was standing up to bring the meal to its end. Another scraping of benches, a crisp 'Benedictus Benedicata' and a rather undignified jostle towards the door.

Bognor, despite an uneasy but irrational feeling that haste was necessary, refused to join in the scramble. Together with Father Anselm he was the last person to emerge into the courtyard. Once he did it was immediately clear that his unease was well founded. Something unpleasant had happened.

## CHAPTER THREE

'Shit,' said Bognor under his breath. It was a numbing feeling he hadn't had for years. It was the sudden recognition that a vital clue, the guarantee of a 'quiet night and a perfect end', had been snuffed out. Given ordinary luck he should have had the whole business solved and tidied up in ten minutes, after Batty Thomas had revealed the murderer's identity. That, however, was not to be because over in the far corner of the yard a milling crowd of friars was hauling frantically at the rope which hung down into the well. Intuition, as much as the sodden brimless panama hat which lay by the wellside, told Bognor what to expect. In seconds he had traversed the thirty yards of courtyard and was standing by the well just as the corpse of Batty Thomas was pulled, dripping with blood and water, from the shaft. A final heave on the rope and the body, together with the bucket, landed in a wet flabby heap on the paving stones. Like a big cod, thought Bognor, looking on with dismay. Any thought of sympathy for the dead man was far from his mind as he stood staring at the wet, bloody mess stretched out on the stone. He wondered what Collingdale or Sir Erris or even Parkinson would have done in his place. If only Anselm hadn't interrupted them at just that moment . . . He was lost in this self-recrimination when he realised that there was an awed silence and that everyone, even Father Anselm, was looking to him for a lead. The thought of death might have been a commonplace to the brothers, but the reality was still upsetting.

'He must have fallen,' said Bognor, kneeling down in the widening pool of blood and water. He turned the body on to its back and closed the eyes clumsily but effectively. Looking up, he saw that Anselm was hovering above him, hands clasped, apparently in reasonable control of himself.

'There's not much point,' said Bognor, trying hard to emulate him, 'but you'd better get a doctor. He could hardly be more dead than he is. If he wasn't dead from this,' he indicated the wounds on the head, 'he'd be dead from drowning. Or shock. But you'd better get a doctor all the same. And fetch Inspector Pinney.'

Anselm nodded and turned towards his office. Bognor straightened. He felt sick but he had a job to do. 'Who found him?' He addressed the crowd in general. There was a confused murmur and then Father Simon spoke.

'I think several of us noticed something was wrong,' he said. 'You see, normally the rope is kept wound tight and the bucket is easily visible. Well, when John and I got out of lunch we noticed that it had been left in a lowered position. So, anyway, Vivian and myself and two of the others came to have a look. We thought it was just a mistake . . .'

He looked at Bognor, eyes pleading for some easy way out, but Bognor could think of nothing to say. 'And,' he went on, 'when we looked down, we saw . . . well, we saw this . . . Poor old Tom.' He shuffled his feet and peered at his sandals.

'That's right,' said Brother Vivian. 'That's how it was.'

There was a silence. Bognor looked round at the brothers. Practically all of them must have been there. They looked embarrassed more than shocked. It was as if something mildly tasteless had interrupted their routine, as if a telegram had arrived in the middle of Matins or someone had dried up in mid-sermon. They were still standing there, Bognor looking at them, the friars looking anywhere but at him, when a car swept noisily into the yard and stopped. Inspector Pinney was back from lunch. The sun baked down, rooks cawed in the nearby beeches, and the Inspector's boots hammered across the stones.

'Trouble, sir?' His face, a few degrees redder after a largely liquid lunch, betrayed little concern, but he took in the corpse and the crowd in one unwavering movement.

'A little.' Bognor felt hugely relieved. He addressed the brothers again. 'I would prefer it if you could wait here a few moments,' he said. 'Just while I have a word with the Inspector here.' He motioned Pinney into the shade of an outbuilding, and the two of them bent their faces towards each other.

'Not nice,' said Bognor.

'No, sir.'

'Question everyone. Get statements. Same with the doctor.'

'I know the drill,' said Pinney drily. 'It's not *my* first corpse.'

Bognor looked hard at the solid Dorset face and wondered if the personality matched the appearance. Apart from the possible over-indulgence in beer he decided Pinney had better be trusted.

'The doctor,' he went on, 'will be as non-committal as possible. It doesn't matter. I'm fairly certain what killed him, and I doubt whether anything but a detailed post mortem will tell us whether he was pushed or whether he fell. As far as we're concerned, Inspector, he fell. It doesn't matter whether it's accident or suicide, I just want no suggestion of foul play. One murder is quite enough for the time being. So. Play it very very quietly.'

Inspector Pinney looked at him for a moment, then turned to take in the crowd of friars now talking eagerly and excitedly among themselves, and returned to his superior.

'Right you are, sir. Just leave it to me.'

'Good.'

The Inspector walked heavily across to the friars and the corpse. Someone had brought a sheet, and draped it roughly over Lord Camberley's son. The edge had soaked up the blood and well water like blotting paper, so that there was a rough rusty stain on it like a handkerchief after a nose bleed. Bognor shivered slightly. He'd better go and consult Sir Erris.

It was excruciatingly hot, he realised, as he walked down the path towards his room. He wiped the back of his hand across his forehead and was surprised to find that it was wet with sweat, not all of it due to the heat. Right now he envied Inspector Pinney his beer. He could do with a large Scotch, but there wasn't time and in any case it was time for some incisive, logical thinking.

Inside the room he took off his jacket and

flung it on the bed, then crossed to open the window, leant out for a second and inhaled country air rich with roses and silage, underlaid with something less usual, which after a moment's thought he identified tentatively as incense. Two murders in three days, he thought to himself. Two murders, two murderers? He wasn't so sure.

He drew his head back into the room and decided to make some notes. When he was more than usually perplexed he always made notes. They were usually inane but they comforted him, and sometimes he derived inspiration from them. It was only when he went to the chest of drawers that he saw the letter. God knows why he hadn't seen it before, because it was lying in the middle of the chest's surface on its own, a plain buff envelope with the words 'Mr. Simon Bognor' written across it in spidery semi-literate biro.

He picked it up, read the address through a second time, speculated a moment and tore it open. Inside, the letter was scrawled on lined paper which looked as if it might have been taken from a school exercise book. The writing was the same malformed stuff, puerile almost to the point of being contrived.

'Dear Mr. Bognor,' it said, 'I'm sorry about this only I couldn't live any more having done it. You see I killed Brother Luke. I don't know why. I couldn't help myself. Please tell my father and Father Anselm and everybody.' Underneath the one word 'Tom', underlined with a shaky flourish.

Bognor read it a second time, folded it, put it in his inside jacket pocket. Then he made some notes.

'1.' he pencilled. 'Fake. 2. Why? 3. To shift blame. 4. From whom? 5. From murderer.' He sighed and screwed up the paper. 'X murdered Collingdale and was seen by Batty Tom', he wrote. 'So X murdered Batty Tom before he could talk to me.' That was all right as far as it went. 'Batty Tom was killed during lunch,' he continued. 'Everyone eating lunch has an alibi.' That was better. 'Make a list of those without alibis.' Much better.

Outside be blinked in the brightness and walked back to the yard. In one corner a knot of men in the same motley dress that had characterised the cocoa break were standing about with axes and saws; in another a pair of feet, Vivian's presumably, protruded from under the Community Dormobile; by the well the body had gone, leaving a fast drying brown patch. Inspector Pinney sat on the wall nearby talking to Father Simon and making notes. As Bognor approached, the Friar turned and shuffled away towards the main house.

'Suicide,' said Bognor. 'I've had a little note. Spread it around but go on with the statements. Make a list of everyone who was helping cook or dish up lunch; but don't let anyone know what you're doing. I'll be back in a couple of hours. I'll be with Sir Erris if you want me.'

Inspector Pinney scratched at the brown patch with the toe of his shoe. 'Right you are,' he said. 'Suicide it is. Until you say otherwise. Bloody silly way to kill yourself, though.' Bognor flushed. 'They didn't call him Batty Thomas for nothing,' he said.

The tree-felling party was moving off as he walked towards the Land-Rover and a murmur of gentle conversation reached him across the stones.

From the chapel came the sound of inexpert fingers playing 'All Things Bright and Beautiful' on the piano; a fat friar with red hair padded across towards Inspector Pinney. He smelt the incense again, nearer this time, and stopped himself quickly as he realised that he was humming in accompaniment to the piano player. It was hardly appropriate.

The Land-Rover started first time and he swung it out of the gates and up the hill over-revving it dramatically as he waved at the tree-felling party standing out of his way, backs pressed against the high green bank. He caught a glimpse of Brother Barnabas's face grinning vacantly from among the buttercups and daisies, a handkerchief knotted at all four corners protecting him from the heat of the afternoon sun. Then they were gone, vanished in dust and exhaust fumes, as he lunged up the hill.

It was a remarkably steep hill, something he had hardly noticed on his arrival the day before, and he had to change down twice inexpertly before he reached the top and turned left on the road which led through Great Ogridge and then on to Woodstock. Poor Old Thomas, he thought to himself, realising guiltily that it was the first time his feelings had turned towards the dead person himself. He hoped it was a sign of professionalism to regard victims as ciphers but he couldn't help regretting it. Poor Thomas. A sad little life with a pretty squalid end, and almost certainly an end which was none of his own doing.

He was musing in this vein and driving the vehicle in a deplorably ham-fisted way when he glanced along the road, which at that point was clearly visible for almost a mile, and saw a brown blob in the distance. As it grew closer he identified it as one of the brothers sitting on a staddlestone under a chestnut tree. To have got that far since lunch, particularly having climbed the hill, he must have walked fast. He changed down and slowed, muttering to himself about friars who spent all their time hitch-hiking. It wasn't Paul however, but his new acquaintance Brother Aldhelm, like Brother Barnabas another man who couldn't have done the second murder, might have done the first and had been at the Friary long enough to smuggle secrets. He started a process of mental note-taking.

'Hop in,' he said leaning across and opening the door.

'Very kind of you, but I'm OK. Just walking.'

'Oh. You look shattered.' He did too. He was very red, and still panting slightly. The sweat stood out on his face in large drops and there were dark marks under his arms where more perspiration had soaked through on to his habit. Bognor was reminded of another stain he had seen only recently.

'You saw what happened to Batty Thomas?' asked Bognor.

'Yes I did.' He seemed nervous, impatient too. 'Look, if you don't mind I'd rather be left alone.'

'Sure you don't want a lift? You don't look as if you could walk much further.'

'Yes. Quite sure. Please leave me alone.' There was no mistaking the urgency in his voice this time. Bognor was intrigued.

'I did ask people to stay in the yard to help Inspector Pinney.'

'I'm sorry I didn't hear.'

'I'm sorry too. It might have been important.'

'Look, please. I'd like to be left alone. Please.'

Bognor was exasperated. 'All right,' he said.

'But Inspector Pinney or I will want a word later. We are dealing with a murder, you know.'

'Of course I know. Now please.' He slammed the door shut, and slumped back on to the staddlestone. Bognor pushed the machine back into gear, and shouted back, 'Later then. Don't kill yourself!' and drove off, realising too late the inappropriateness of his idiom.

Driving into Great Ogridge he noticed to his irritation that the petrol gauge showed empty. Sir Erris might have left him a full tank, it would have been embarrassing to have got stranded in the middle of the Oxfordshire countryside only an hour after a murder. He was just getting really apprehensive when, the other side of the village, he saw a modern service station, and turned in. They took Barclaycard.

'Fill her up, please,' he said to the attendant, a middle-aged bucolic figure looking absurdly out of place in the ostentatious white uniform provided by the petrol company. 'And check the oil and water if you could.' He left the Land-Rover to the inexpert attentions of this man and wandered idly across the forecourt to the side of the road, where he bent down to pick a long stalk of grass, put it in his mouth and chewed ruminatively. The road was empty and it was astonishingly quiet.

'Oil and water OK, sir. And she took more'n

ten gallons.' The strong country accents broke in on his thoughts and he turned back to the twentieth century.

'I'll pay by card,' he said handing it over. The man marched to the plate-glassed office while Bognor followed more slowly. His feet crunched on the gravel and he heard a car driving fast and noisily through the village. The brakes squealed distinctly though it must still have been a mile away. 'Sounds like an Italian,' he thought moodily. The man came out of his office with the form ready to fill in.

'Someone driving awful fast,' he said handing over the pieces of paper and shading his eyes to watch the Jehu drive past. Bognor paused, pen poised, and waited with him. It was certainly being driven very fast; there was another squeal as it turned the bend about a hundred yards away followed by a brief and a powerful roar as it was let out into gear and accelerated. The two men caught little more than a glimpse as it hurtled past, a red blur, and disappeared still accelerating.

'E Type Jag,' said the man with satisfaction, like a child who has just spotted a particularly interesting engine.

'Oh,' said Bognor who knew nothing about cars. 'Sure?'

'I'm sure, sir.'

Bognor gazed down the road frowning. He signed the papers and handed them over with a florin tip, acknowledging the salute which was almost a tugged forelock.

'Wish *I* was sure,' he said, as he levered himself into the driving seat and let out the clutch. He hadn't been looking at the car as it passed. He was more interested in the occupant, and as it turned out there were two. The driver had been obscured by the passenger, though he was almost sure it was a woman. But it was the passenger who intrigued him. He was wearing that rich brown with which he was increasingly familiar; and although the car had been moving at more than sixty he could have sworn it was Brother Aldhelm.

It was tea-time when he arrived at the Old Rectory, which was not in fact a particularly old Rectory and would have been more accurately described as the Former Rectory. It was large and Victorian but had good views looking across the valley to the south. Sir Erris was on the lawn in grubby white flannels, a red and yellow tie holding up the trousers and a wide-brimmed grey hat in felt keeping the sun out of his eyes. As Bognor approached he was bent, legs apart and rather stiff, over an ancient croquet mallet with which he was taking studious aim at a hoop some ten yards distant. He heard Bognor approach and motioned him to silence with an impatient flap of the right hand. Bognor froze. There was an agonising silence and then a sharp crack. The faded yellow ball sped across the lawn, hit a worm cast, veered to the right and struck the right hand post of the hoop off which it cannoned at right angles fetching up three feet short of a herbaceous border.

'Fuck,' said Sir Erris.

'Bad luck,' said Bognor.

Sir Erris straightened. 'Not at all,' he said, 'rank bad shot. Cup of tea?' He waved in the direction of a wooden tea trolley which stood under an ilex tree. The two of them walked over to it.

'Do you play?' asked Sir Erris, and continued without waiting for an answer: 'Then we'll take a turn round when we've had a cup. Nice to see you. How are things?'

'We've had another murder.'

'Have you?' said Sir Erris, looking only mildly surprised. 'Not Father Anselm by any luck?'

'A poor chap called Thomas. The Earl of Camberley's son, as a matter of fact.'

'Bert Camberley's son?' Sir Erris *was* surprised this time. 'Good God. I'd no idea he had a son there. That's bad. Are you sure it's murder?'

Bognor recounted the story as far as he understood it while they drank their tea. 'Anyway,' he concluded, 'I want to go along with suicide. It'll make life a bit easier if I can lull our villain into some sort of security. So if you could make sure there are no awkward questions. Not now. Not from the doctor or from Camberley or any of your people.'

'Have a mallet,' said Sir Erris, taking one from a long wooden box on the grass. 'You can be blue.' They walked back to the hoops.

'I'll do what I can,' he said, after a bit. 'I can see your point. I just hope we can get some goods before long. Bert Camberley isn't easily fooled. I can deal with my own people but he won't be so easy. He'll know it's not suicide.'

Bognor took aim and achieved a moderate shot, the ball ending up a few feet short of the first hoop but giving him an easy shot for next time.

Sir Erris' first shot hit Bognor's ball and on the second he knocked him yards off course in the direction of the border again.

They finished the game in about twenty minutes, Bognor's marginally superior eye not quite making up for Sir Erris's superior experience and considerable gamesmanship or, as most people would have described it, cheating.

Bognor told him most of what had happened so far, using the older man as a sort of verbal punchbag. Sir Erris came up with little new or even constructive but, as with the note-taking, it helped Bognor to get his ideas into some sort of order. 'If Batty Thomas didn't commit suicide . . .' he began.

'We've got three different crimes,' he pointed out. 'Any one of eight could have done the secrets. Any one at all could have done the first murder.'

'Except for the boy we picked up hitch-hiking,' said Sir Erris.

'Yes, but that still leaves thirty-two friars and the guests . . . then there's today's job. It could have been any of the cookers and servers, but I know this lot. They won't have noticed anyone slipping out for five minutes. Not a hope.'

'No,' said Sir Erris. 'Funny about Aldhelm.'

'Yes. He'd really had to shift to get that far, and he was extremely edgy.'

'Have you talked to your original eight?'

Bognor struck his ball through from an impossible angle, making up a little of his lost ground. 'Softly, softly catchee monkee,' he said. 'Except of course that they're friars not monks. Technical point. No I've taken your advice and gone slowly and methodically. Before long I shall interview Father John and Brother Bede. Bede made the soup and I don't even know what he looks like. John's the bee mandarin. He's got weak ankles and creeping arthritis.'

'If Bede made the soup he'd have been in the kitchen,' said Sir Erris, 'so he could have one, two and three to his credit.'

Bognor leant on his mallet and watched Sir Erris make the winning hit. 'Congratulations,' he said. 'You could be right about Bede,' he went on. 'But I just fancy I shall leave him till the morning. There are a few other people I want to talk to first. Not least Father John. His pins may be poor and his hands going, but he does look after the honey and that's where it all starts. Don't forget that.'

By the time he got back to the Friary it was getting close to Evensong and it was past the time that Inspector Pinney reckoned to knock off. The Inspector was waiting in the yard, occasionally throwing pieces of bread at the chickens and rather obviously pacing up and down. He had been hoping to stop off for a quick one on his way home but the prospect of doing so and not making his wife suspicious was growing increasingly distant.

'Ah, there you are,' he said pointedly as Bognor alighted. 'I was beginning to get worried.'

Bognor grunted. 'Nearly ran out of petrol. Nothing otherwise. Have you got that list?'

'Yes, sir.' The Inspector handed over a piece of lined foolscap. 'The following friars and associates were on the duty roster for serving and cooking of luncheon today', it said. Bognor scanned the list quickly. There were eight names in all and the only ones he recognised were those of Brother Bede and Brother Paul. He frowned. Perhaps the whole thing was a hopeless red herring. Perhaps after all the deranged Thomas had killed Collingdale on a mad whim and committed suicide. Perhaps the whole thing was a dreadful sick mistake.

But in that case why the odd business of Brother Aldhelm? And the honey labels? Or the innuendoes from Xavier and the landlord of the Boot? Why in any case had Thomas approached him that morning? Surely not to warn him of impending suicide?

'Anything else?' he asked the fidgety Inspector.

'Well they seem quite happy about the suicide. Sight too happy if you ask me.'

'You might admit that suicide wraps it all up.'

'Oh it was murder all right,' said the Inspector morosely.

'You're probably right.' He stared round at the old stone and across to the camouflaged Nissen huts, searching vaguely and vainly for inspiration.

'Anything else?'

'They seem quite sorry. Except for Brother Bede, that is. He was rambling on about heredity and that. The deceased was gentry, and our Brother Bede doesn't hold with that.'

'Oh?'

'No. Bit of a firebrand I should judge.'

'But not a murderer?'

'Wouldn't have said so, no.'

'What about Brother Paul?'

‘Seems a nice enough lad.’

‘Alibi?’

‘They all spent most of lunch going backwards and forwards between the kitchen and the dining room. Any of them might have gone for a few minutes. There aren’t any real alibis. Not what I’d call alibis.’

‘And the doctor?’

‘What you’d expect. Usual stuff about lacerations and contusions and broken this and fractured that and death most likely having been instantaneous and most probably caused by hitting his head on a sharp or rough object, possibly consistent with having bounced from side to side down a deep well shaft. You know the sort of thing.’

Bognor knew very well. ‘He didn’t say anything about murder?’

‘Didn’t give him much chance.’ Inspector Pinney allowed himself a brief smirk. ‘Like Father Anselm said, sir, “Doctor Baines,” he said, “is certainly not what you might call an original thinker”. Very true. Bloody fool, if you ask me.’

‘Good. It looks as if you’ve done a good day’s work. I’ve spoken to Sir Erris and I don’t think we’re going to have too much trouble with this suicide idea.’

‘No?’

‘What do you think?’

‘Me think?’

'Yes.'

The Inspector looked at him as if he was mad. It was bad enough to be kept hanging around answering questions which were relevant, infuriating to be detained answering one's superior's sillinesses.

'I'm sorry,' he said eventually, 'I'll do my duty, but right now that's it. As far as I'm concerned if you say "suicide", then suicide it is. And now I'll be going.'

Bognor grimaced. 'Good night,' he said and waved abstractedly to the policeman as he hurried towards his car and vanished still hoping for at least a pint before getting home to supper. Faced with a rather longer working day, he turned in the direction of the Father Minister's study/office. Father Anselm, he feared, would be pleased by the 'suicide'. If he was guilty, he would be pleased because he would believe that he had thrown his pursuers off balance. If innocent, because the whole smelly business had been resolved with the minimum of discredit to himself and his Community.

He knocked on the heavy door, entered and found his worst fears realised.

'Ah, Simon, my friend. So your visit proved unnecessary after all!' Father Anselm advanced on him, right arm extended in greeting. 'Sad perhaps to be proved right in so gruesome and violent a fashion, but a little gratifying none the less. I have always felt the simple virtues of the Old Testament were not as absurd as contemporary fashion would have us believe.'

'I'm sorry.' Bognor was quite genuinely at a loss.

Father Anselm looked surprised. 'Your admirable Inspector Pinney, wholly admirable, I thought, told me about the letter. I meant simply that in the end it was prayer rather than modern forensic science which solved our little mystery. As I had predicted in the first place. The Almighty, as the cliché has it, moves in mysterious ways. I suppose that you'll be leaving in the morning. Such a pity. You must come again soon.'

'I'd like to stay on a little if you don't mind.'

'No. Really. How flattering.' Father Anselm scarcely faltered, though the idea obviously disappointed him. Bognor sat down heavily on the faded chintz sofa, uninvited, emphasising his reluctance to leave. 'I take it that doesn't mean that you aren't satisfied at the outcome of these proceedings?' asked Anselm.

'No. I'm satisfied,' said Bognor wearily. 'Though I'd have preferred to have done without another death.'

'Now you mustn't blame yourself for what happened today,' said Anselm. 'I think it is perfectly proper to regard it in a very real sense as an act of God. A little sherry to set the seal on the matter.'

'I'd love one,' he said, wishing it were a Scotch. 'I didn't know you drank.'

'Good heavens no.' Father Anselm looked offended and it occurred to Bognor that the Abbot thought that he was being accused of alcoholism.

'I mean, I thought that alcohol wasn't allowed.'

'It isn't. But when there are guests I'm afraid I do indulge a little. It is after all a gift of God. Tell me, why do you wish to stay on? Not that I'm not delighted.'

Bognor could scarcely explain that it was because he had to make a resounding success of his first solo assignment. He looked round the room and took in the fussy water colours, self-perpetrated, the *Daily Telegraph* and a book by Beverley Nichols on the pouffe, the collection of Copenhagen China pieces scattered about the shelves. Then he had an inspiration.

'Tell me,' he asked, 'how were you able to know that Father Xavier had been to see me last night?' Father Anselm was pouring sherry from a cut-glass decanter. He spilt some.

Bognor watched him as he crossed the room with the glass in one hand. He was shaken but controlling it well.

'You may think,' he said, 'that I am badly informed about what goes on here. Like a housemaster who's got out of touch. But I do make it my business to be informed. It is a very important part of my job. Of my ministry you could say.'

'All the same . . . I mean it wasn't exactly Christian of you.'

'Come come, Simon. As you yourself would be the first to acknowledge, we are—or *were* I should say—investigating a murder.'

'But you surely didn't suspect *me*?'

'It's wrong to argue like this,' said Father Anselm, his self-control now completely restored. It was, Bognor recognised, an immaculate performance. 'Tell me instead why you want to stay on. Do you find us so fascinating?'

'I'd like to stay for the funeral,' he said, sipping his sherry which was good but too sweet for him. 'And yes I have to confess my curiosity is aroused. I'll pay of course.'

For once Father Anselm really was offended. 'That is certainly not necessary,' he said. 'You're very welcome to make a donation but there's certainly no question of paying a fee.'

Bognor was genuinely dismayed. 'I'd no idea there was a difference,' he said.

'The difference between alms and debts, between volunteering and being compelled. Rather a significant difference I think.' He finished his sherry and looked at his watch. 'Will you be joining us at Evensong? We haven't seen as much of you in chapel as I might have hoped.'

'I have been rather busy.'

'I'm delighted that it was to no avail.'

Bognor put his glass on the coffee table and smiled. 'I can't promise to stop being inquisitive,' he said. Father Anselm smiled patronisingly.

'I like nothing better than an enquiring mind,' he said.

They were quite late for chapel. It was in any case Father Anselm's privilege to enter last of all and so when Bognor took his place he discovered that the choir stalls were full and also that several of the tubular steel chairs were occupied by guests, or in some cases by completely strange faces which he took to belong to visitors. A second later Anselm entered wearing a beatific smile. He paused to genuflect and then to pray, rose and announced 'Hymn 573'. The pianist, the same, to judge from his inexpertise, as the one who had been practising earlier in the day, played a sample verse and then the Community joined together in the familiar words.

'All things bright and beautiful,
All creatures great and small,
All things wise and wonderful
The Lord God made them all.'

Anselm's own satisfaction seemed to have permeated the whole congregation. There was an apparent and pervasive relief which increased with every verse and every note.

Even the piano had a tiddly pom, tin pan alley, sort of complacency about it.

'The rich man in his castle,
The poor man at his gate,
God made them high or lowly,
And ordered their estate.'

All's right with the world, all's well that ends well, thought Bognor, watching and listening with growing alarm. Practically everyone there, he supposed, felt that a great burden had been lifted with the death of Batty Tom, that a potential slur on their very reason for being had been removed almost without pain. Only Bognor and one, perhaps two, others knew the truth: that there was still murder to be solved and to be answered for. The thought made him apprehensive, and yet excited too.

'He gave us eyes to see them
And lips that we might tell,
How great is God Almighty,
Who has made all things well.'

They sang well, wafting the clichés skywards in an orgy of simple pleasure. Bognor looked round uneasily at the starkness of the chapel itself and the symbolism of the stations of the cross. Searching for some more human contrast, some hint of non-conformity, he noticed Father Xavier. He was standing arms folded, steadfastly refusing to join in with Mrs. Alexander's words. Bognor caught his eye and got a massive wink in return. He smiled. Father Xavier reminded him of someone.

By the time he got out of Evensong he was desperate for his whisky. Father John would have to wait till later, and as for supper if it was Brother Bede's broth accompanied by readings from the life of Elizabeth Fry or William Booth then he would rather have a stale ham sandwich at the Boot. He broke a switch of hawthorn from the hedge and set off down the lane swinging it vigorously and trying to forget the hymn tune which kept hammering away at his brain. He was exhilarated. He knew he was being patronised, and he was determined to prove himself.

He made the hamlet in a shade over twenty minutes, walking fast and aggressively. The Boot itself seemed completely unchanged, which was hardly surprising as it had almost certainly been exactly the same for the last fifty years. The same smell of cow-dung and cigarettes and stale beer, the same two (or similar two) cowhands drinking morosely, and Mr. Hey himself, faintly sinister and looking as if he had been wrapped round the same pint of mild and bitter that Bognor had bought him the night before.

'Double Bell's,' said Bognor, nodding perfunctorily at the landlord and his guests. 'And whatever you fancy.' 'Fancy' was a word he disliked and seldom used. He hoped it was appropriate. It was what Collingdale would have said.

'Fine day,' said Mr. Hey when he had poured the drinks.

'As far as the weather goes, yes,' said Simon.

'Ah.' Mr. Hey's eyes, never a picture of wide-eyed credulity at the best of times, narrowed swiftly. 'I hear,' he said, putting his elbows on the bar, 'that you've had a spot more trouble. You don't seem to have blown anyone any good.'

'You hear a lot, fast,' said Bognor.

'Can't help it. Not in a place like this.' Mr. Hey was as pleased with himself and his intelligence system as Father Anselm, in a different way, was with his.

'Do you have anything to eat?'

'Sandwiches,' said Mr. Hey without pride. 'Ham, cheese, cheese and pickle, beef.' He peered into a plastic display cabinet on the bar counter and frowned. 'Sorry. Ham or cheese. Cheese and pickle's off. So's beef.'

Bognor accepted with good grace. 'A round of ham,' he said, 'and another Bell's please.' Mr. Hey opened the cabinet and using his dark grainy hands, as impregnated with cow-dung as his surroundings, he produced a sandwich, curling gently at the edges and with a filling more margarine than meat.

'Found out much?' he asked.

'Not much.' Bognor bit into the bread. It was as bad as it looked. 'I wonder,' he said. 'You obviously know everything there is to know about these parts. Do you know anyone with a Red E-Type?'

'Red E-Type . . . What, Jaguar?'

'Yes. Another pint?'

Mr. Hey poured his second pint with alacrity. 'Only one car like that round here,' he said. 'Most of them drive farm things or big saloons for going to London. Some of the week-end people have sports cars. Cheap ones mostly. Caundle's son has a Maserati, I'm told. Doesn't come down much these days.'

'But the E-Type?'

'Strudwick, that is, the Old Manor at Melbury.'

'What, Strudwick the M.P.?' Bognor had a mental image of a purple-faced backwoods M.P. who had introduced a bill for the reintroduction of capital punishment a couple of years before.

'That's right. Not that he's here much. Too busy striking attitudes round Whitehall and going on the telly.'

'Wasn't there a divorce?' Bognor had a further image of something faintly sordid: a twenty-year marriage being overthrown with the maximum publicity . . . a middle-aged, plain, discarded wife. Something new and glamorous.

'That's right,' said Mr. Hey. 'Traded the old woman in for a new model. Foreign job. Not a bad looker. Much good it did him.'

'Oh?'

'Well, you know.' Mr. Hey raised his eyebrows and would, Bognor reckoned, have dug him in the ribs but for the intervening counter. 'Let's just say she's not all the local M.P.'s wife should be. I mean her idea of a local fête isn't quite what the Women's Institute would like. If you see what I mean.'

Bognor said that he thought he saw what he meant and was about to change the subject when it was changed for him by the sudden advent of Father Xavier.

'Aha,' he said. 'Aha aha. Usual please. And the same for P.C. 49.' He unshouldered his duffel bag. 'You can take it out of my winnings on the 3.15,' he added.

'Do I take it you don't care for the more conventional Hymns Ancient and Modern?' asked Bognor, trying to look quizzical.

'Just can't sing,' said Xavier, taking a massive gulp. 'And even if I could the words are unspeakably bloody. Not to say inappropriate. I mean, say what you like, Batty Tom was our second death in three days and that can't be good.'

'Could be for some,' said Bognor with contrived ambiguity, and thinking of Humphrey Bogart.

Father Xavier gave him a very unambiguous old-fashioned look. 'Meaning?'

'Meaning nothing in particular.'

'You never mean nothing in particular.'

Bognor sipped. 'Anyway,' he said, 'when's the funeral?'

'Tomorrow,' said Xavier. 'No reason to waste time.'

'Bit quick, isn't it?' said Mr. Hey.

'Not in the circumstances,' said Xavier.

'What circumstances?' asked Mr. Hey, maliciously.

'You know bloody well what circumstances. "No muss, no fuss," like the commercial used to say. You know who his father is. You know what he did. No point in letting the yellow press make a meal of it. As our friend here will agree.'

'Up to a point,' said Bognor.

They finished their drinks. Bognor toyed with the idea of another revolting sandwich, and thought better of it when Xavier said he'd better get back for a spot of quiet meditation.

They walked back together. It was getting dark and banks of dark cloud were edged in purple.

'Feels sticky,' said Xavier, when they had

been walking for a few minutes. 'Thunder soon, I should think.'

'Yes.' Bognor was wondering if he could ever have met Xavier before. He did seem oddly familiar, but it might just be that he was overtired. Fatigue sometimes gave him that sort of hallucination. The feeling that he had been somewhere before; that an event he knew perfectly well to be brand new and totally unique was in fact a repeat of something he had witnessed years earlier.

'Have you ever been on one of these Expo-Brits?' he asked.

'Huh,' Father Xavier snorted. 'Not me. For a kick-off they wouldn't trust me. And then again I've never seen any bloody reason for going. Commercial traveller isn't a role I particularly relish.'

'Father Simon was giving me a very sympathetic picture of the free world's friars bringing spiritual relief to their oppressed brethren behind the Iron Curtain.'

'Oh balls. That's typical of Simon. He's almost as sanctimonious as Anselm, and that's saying something, as you know.' They continued in silence to the Friary. 'What amazing piece of detection are you embarking on now?' asked Xavier, as they passed through the gates.

'I was going to have a word with Father John.'

‘Ah, he’s not sanctimonious. Quite sharp too. You’ll like him.’

‘Good.’

‘See you in Compline, then.’ Father Xavier slouched away towards his room, and Bognor turned towards the old farmhouse where John lived. He walked down the passage, his feet echoing dramatically in the silence, past Father Anselm’s door, past Father Simon’s and knocked on the next. It was a great deal easier finding people’s rooms in the farmhouse, since, unlike the Nissen hut where the only identification was numbers, in the farmhouse each man had his name written on a card and displayed in a cheap brass holder on the door. Immediately below the card on Father John’s door was a heavy knocker shaped like a dolphin. Bognor used it to tap lightly three times, and entered as soon as he heard the faintly querulous invitation to do so.

Father John was sitting at his desk reading by the light of a battered reading lamp which hung only inches above his book. Alongside the desk at his feet there was a sturdy blackthorn walking stick.

‘Good evening,’ he said, pushing his glasses towards the end of his nose and looking over them at Bognor with an expression of mild amusement. ‘I was wondering when I should have the pleasure of a visit. Would you like a cup of coffee?’

'That would be nice, thank you.' Bognor felt patronised, yet again.

'In that case I'll put on the kettle.' He shuffled to his feet, picked up the stick with one hand and wandered over to a corner cupboard from which he extracted two blue-and-white half-pint mugs, a teaspoon, a tin of instant coffee, a packet of dried milk and an aluminium kettle which had lost its whistle. 'Won't be a second,' he said, going outside with the kettle. 'The gas ring's just at the end of the corridor.'

Bognor muttered something half-hearted and semi-coherent about not wishing to be any trouble and looked round the room. He hadn't realised how old Father John was. At close quarters he was much more lined and grey than he had seemed at a distance. Certainly in his mid-sixties, he thought, as he went over to the desk to see what it was that he'd been studying. He had been expecting the New Testament or at least Thomas à Kempis, but it wasn't anything so proper. It was a heavily thumbed copy of Ribbands' *The Behaviour and Social Life of Honeybees*. He turned to the small walnut bookshelf which hung on the wall and read through the titles.

There were a few predictables: a book of Offices, Bishop Bell on *Christianity and World Order*, Lebreton and Zeiller, de Chardin's *Phenomenon of Man*, but these were greatly outnumbered by other more secular works.

He was no apiarist and the titles were unfamiliar: Fraser, *Beekeeping in Antiquity*, Grout, *The Hive and the Honey Bee*, Root, *The ABC and XYZ of Bee Culture* and Von Frisch, *Bees: their vision, chemical senses and language*. On a table below the bookshelf there were stacked a sieve-like mask and a pair of leather gauntlets together with bound volumes of the *American Bee Journal* and *Gleanings in Bee Culture*. He had selected a hefty gleaning of Bee culture and was reading with increasing disbelief about something called Isle of Wight disease when Father John returned with a boiling kettle.

'I understood from your namesake that you had displayed an interest in the manufacture of honey,' he said drily as he made the coffee. 'It seems rather unlikely, somehow, but there's no accounting for taste.'

'I've always been interested in bees,' said Bognor.

Father John looked profoundly sceptical. 'I must say,' he said, 'that I find your credulity concerning today's little incident surprising.'

'Well, I do have the benefit of having seen the letter he wrote.'

'So I believe.' They sipped at their coffee. 'Anyway, since you pretend to an interest in my obsession I shall tell you about it,' said the older man, smiling swiftly. 'I take it that we shall have to start at the beginning.'

Bognor nodded wearily and remained silent for the next fifteen minutes while Father John rambled tediously on about fructose and glucose and sucrose, the relative merits of different kinds of clover, the brilliant thinking behind the Langstroth hive, the exact shape and size of the hive tool, the excellence of research findings from Baton Rouge, Louisiana, and Logan, Utah, the disastrous results of mite infestation of the adult breathing tract, and the predatory habits of mice.

'Well,' he said finally, pulling a pocket watch from the folds of his habit, 'perhaps you'd like to come and see for yourself. We've just about got time before Compline.'

It was really too dark to see the hives properly. Father John brought a torch, and shone it around them, pointing to the various features which he felt should interest Bognor. The atmosphere was even more oppressive than it had been on his return from the Boot, almost as if the clouds had physical weight. After a few rather ineffectual minutes standing in the corner of the field where the bees lived, he asked if he could see the honey store.

'It's not in the least interesting,' said Father John.

'I'd like to see it, all the same,' he said.

He half saw, half felt Father John shrug in the gloom, before he led the way back to the buildings a hundred yards away. Just inside the courtyard he produced a key and opened a door on the left, the first in a range of what had once been stalls or loose-boxes. The light snapped on and Bognor saw that year's consignment of the famous Beaubridge honey.

'Not very much of it,' he said, looking round the wooden trestles stacked with jars, still unlabelled owing to the peculiar muddle which had so upset Father Simon.

'We only manage twenty pounds a hive maximum,' said Father John.

'Even so,' said Bognor. He picked a jar up and held it to the light. It was strangely pale, almost like a very old vintage brandy. He had vaguely assumed that it might be like supermarket honey, solid and opaque. That therefore it might have been possible to conceal some object, message, piece of film in the honey itself. Obviously that would have been out of the question. Father John was saying something about the weather having been particularly difficult that year. Bognor put the jar down with a feeling of disappointment.

He looked round the room once more. It told him nothing. There were just the trestles, the honey, stone floors, whitewashed cobwebbed walls, a second door in a far corner. But he was certain the answer lay in this room. It had to.

'And what goes on through there?'

'It's just a cupboard.'

Bognor checked himself. The nonchalance of

the remark was a shade too studied, there was a tension about it. He moved over to the door, and put his hand to the handle.

'It's only a cupboard,' said Father John. And this time there was no mistaking the tension in his voice. Not quite fright but definitely anxiety. 'Anyway,' he continued, 'it's locked.'

'Do you have the key?'

'Good Lord no. It hasn't been opened for years.'

Bognor looked swiftly along the crack between the door and the wall. It was clear of cobwebs; nor were there any round the hinges.

Mentally and metaphorically he patted himself on the back. Practice was, he told himself, making him increasingly astute.

'Could you find a key for me?'

Father John was still agitated. 'I think it really is time to be moving towards Compline,' he said. 'No, I'd have no idea where to start looking for a key. It hasn't been open for as long as I can remember.'

'Then how do you know it's only a cupboard?'

Father John looked at him with exasperation and something very near fright. 'Your curiosity,' he said, 'sounds almost professional. If you *are* still investigating some crime, then I think you ought to tell us what it is. In which case perhaps we could arrange for this lock to be forced, though what good it would do I can't imagine. If, on the other hand, you're simply being inquisitive for the sake of it, then I have to tell you that you're wasting everyone's time. That cupboard is simply a cupboard. It has always been a cupboard. It always will be a cupboard. It has not been open for years. It is not open now and it is not going to be opened again. Not by me, anyway.'

Bognor stood watching this outburst with interest.

'I'm sorry,' he said, when the honeymaker had finished. 'I didn't wish to interfere with your routines. I'm sure it's not important.'

They stood staring at each other in the naked light of the single bulb in its wire cage and then the warning bell for Compline chimed in on the confrontation.

Father John smiled with evident relief. 'I don't know about you,' he said, 'but I'm afraid I have a duty to attend this office. Will you join me?'

Bognor suddenly felt rather sheepish. 'Of course,' he replied. 'I feel this is a particular service I might grow to like.'

* * *

It was true too. There was more ritual and more mystery about Compline than about the other offices. It was dark outside, which helped, and the lighting in the chapel cast shadows. Some were inanimate black shapes of beams and rafters thrown in black relief against the white walls; others were those of the friars themselves, constantly moving, changing in an almost musical pattern. That night it was more theatrical than before because the storm broke with almost absurd symbolism just as Brother Aldhelm, whose singing voice was more competent than most, was calling upon his brethren to be sober and vigilant. As he did there was a great shimmer of light from outside, and he started slightly, just as Bognor did. Then he continued intoning: 'Because your adversary the devil, as a roaring lion, walketh about, seeking whom he may devour,' and, just as he finished, a treble thunderclap blasted them, as if from immediately overhead, and then bounced back off the hillside, echoing away for several seconds and merging into the mounting drum of the rain.

He found it impossible to order his suspicions against this melodramatic background. It had been a tough and frustrating day and he was tired. The death of Batty Thomas already seemed years old, the strange business of Brother Aldhelm could have happened at any time in the last few weeks. Already, he realised, as he tried to focus on the dim brown shapes in front of him and tried to make out the words of the precise chant, he had become part of this place. Whereas twenty-four hours before the idea of crime and intrigue, let alone murder, had seemed absurd in the context of the Friary, now anything seemed possible. It was the Community which was real now; Sir Erris and the Land-Rover and Whitehall and his department which had become illusory. He shook himself from drowsiness as another thunderclap cracked overhead, and remembered the cupboard door.

From where he sat, on the cross-benches, as it were, he could see Father John kneeling, muttering prayer. The top of his walking stick protruded just above the level of the pew and the friar's arthritic hands clasped in front of his face with a tortured clumsiness reminded him that Brother Luke had been murdered by strangling. Father John's face, raised to the rafters, eyes tightly shut, seemed almost rapturous. He looked saintly. And yet he was hiding something behind that cupboard door. Bognor decided to concentrate on that particular little mystery. It was easy and straightforward, a proper and manageable concern for a man as tired as he was.

The thunder seemed to be moving away, north towards Banbury, as they rose to sing a final hymn. It was that haunting song of thanks for 'the day thou gavest'.

To his surprise Bognor found that he knew the words, and that they came creaking out of some corner of his memory with total accuracy.

'We thank thee that thy Church
  unsleeping,
While earth rolls onward into light
Through all the world her watch is
  keeping
And rests not now by day or night.'

The words made him sleepier still, though the suggestion of the Church's permanent watchfulness and insomniac tendencies made him unhappy. He let the few remaining prayers pass him by until he was jolted out of his lethargy once more—this time by the departure of the friars. The raising of their cowls, which had seemed menacing the night before, was even more chilling tonight. The storm and the tiredness heightened his imagination and he had a sudden vision of pulling the covering off one of those heads and having a skull revealed. He shivered.

Outside, the storm rumbled in the distance on the other side of Oxfordshire, but the rain came down with an ever-increasing strength. There was little wind, but the rain was so thick that it bounced back off the ground, as if someone was throwing it from above. The friars gathered up their habits and ran, looking absurd in the gloom. Bognor hesitated in the doorway for an instant and sprinted off like the others. He reached his cell sopping, his hair flattened against his scalp, splashes of mud up to his knees, and water seeping extravagantly from his left shoe. He took it off and saw to his irritation that there was a hole in the bottom. He cursed and looked at his watch.

If he was to make an outing to Father John's cupboard it would be best to wait. Even if the Friary followed the verse of the hymn and stayed awake, no one was likely to be wandering round in this rain.

However, to be safe he decided to leave it for an hour. He took off the other shoe, thought for a moment and took off both socks as well. Then he picked up *Wisden* and lay down on the bed. An hour's wait should be enough to make it safe to go snooping, he reckoned, and he started to read the Somerset batting averages.

An hour and a half later he woke. He had been dreaming about sex in the pavilion at Glastonbury, and the first thing he saw as he opened his eyes was the Holman Hunt staring at him. He looked at his watch and swore when he saw that it was almost eleven. The dampness had soaked in and he felt very stiff and even more tired. With a sigh he sat up, threw the still-open *Wisden* back on to the chest, felt in his pocket and with a little smile of satisfaction withdrew a six-inch metal rule. It was a standard piece of equipment for operatives and although he had a very imprecise idea of what to do with it its presence reassured him.

He put on another pair of socks and tiptoed outside and down the passage to wash the sleep from his eyes. There wasn't a light to be seen anywhere and the only noise was snoring from behind one of the flimsy doors. That and the thudding drum of the rain which was still coming down as hard as before. Outside it was blacker than black, the rain making it impossible to see further than a few yards. He stood at the corner of the new building for a moment, pressed against the wall while the rain poured all over him and dripped down his neck from the guttering. No sign of anyone. He ran as lightly as possible with holes in his shoes, up the path towards the courtyard and stopped again at the entrance where he repeated the quick look out. Still no movement and no light. He was absolutely wet through.

Peering round the corner and into the yard he tried to gauge the exact position of the honey store. It was the third door on the left, but in the dark and the rain it was impossible to see any doors at all. He took a deep breath and ran across to the other side of the yard. When he reached the wall he started to feel his way up it in the direction of the old farmhouse. He passed one door, stepped in a large puddle and said 'Shit' loudly, passed another door, edged on with the rain in his eyes so heavy that he could hardly keep them open, then came to the third door.

Freezing for a second, he felt for the metal rule and pulled it out at the second attempt. He wished he had brought a torch. It would be risky to turn the light on. He felt in the other pocket and hoped the matches hadn't got too wet to strike. Then he turned his attentions to the door, found the handle and was about to force the lock when he had a thought. He turned the handle and pushed slightly. To his surprise the door gave. That was odd. Father John had used a key to enter the store-room and he had ushered Bognor out before leaving. Bognor was certain he had locked it. He paused and tried to think; decided to listen. It was pointless. The noise of the rain and his own shattered physique would have made it impossible to hear anything less obtrusive than a rifle-shot. He put the rule back in his pocket and opened the door very gently, then stepped quickly inside and closed it behind him.

Inside he tensed immediately. He could make out the trestles and the honey very dimly. Nothing had changed in the room, since his pre-Compline inspection with Father John. But it wasn't anything *in* the room which interested him. It was the cupboard.

The door itself was shut as it had been that evening, but it was an ill-fitting door and from all round it came light. There was no sound above the rain, but there was a light on in the cupboard. Bognor put the matches away again, and crept as noiselessly as his soaked condition would allow to the other side of the room. Once there, he positioned himself at the hinge end and stretched out towards the handle. Then he put his ear to the crack and listened. He could hear nothing. He tried to peer through the crack, but it was too narrow for that. He could see nothing.

His preoccupation with the cupboard was total. So much so that he failed to hear the door behind him. The man was threequarters of the way across the room before Bognor realised it. He swung round sharply, saw a dark shape, tried desperately to raise a hand to parry the blow, was too tired, failed, felt a heavy horrible pain, and had a sudden brief shocked impression of vivid colour, before there was another movement, another pain, and an all-embracing black.

## CHAPTER FOUR

'It's a fine morning,' said Brother Barnabas. 'It would be a pity for you to miss it. I brought you a cup of tea. I mean, seeing as you weren't in Matins or Prime or Communion, I thought you might have overslept. And I always say there's nothing like a good hot cup of tea to wake a man on a beautiful summer morning like this.

Breakfast's in half an hour. Did you sleep well?'

Brother Barnabas was skipping from foot to foot as he had done the first time Bognor had seen him. In his present condition Bognor was in no mood to decide whether this was natural embarrassment or concern. He had only just woken. He put a hand to his head.

'Oh God,' he said with feeling, and didn't bother to apologise. He reached out for the cup and took a swig. It was hot and very sweet. 'Thank you,' he said. 'That's very nice.'

Brother Barnabas was still hovering. 'Good,' he said. 'You'll be coming to breakfast. It's kippers. Being Friday. I can fix two for you if you like. If you're keen on kippers. Some people don't like them. It's the bones, of course. Very awkward, kipper bones, and so many of them. Father Xavier always says that if God had meant man to eat kippers he wouldn't have made them with so many bones. Personally I think that's sacrilegious. But Father Xavier will have his little joke.'

All this time Barnabas was continuing to fidget, his North Country accents becoming squeaky as he talked faster and faster, and shuffled his feet.

'No kippers,' said Bognor, almost shouting the words. 'I'm sorry,' he added. 'I'm afraid I've got rather a headache. If you want to stay, please could you stand still. You're making it worse.'

'All right.' Barnabas seemed more relieved than offended. 'But we'll see you in breakfast?'

'Yes.' He took another draught of the tea and looked at Barnabas with pleading. 'Now, please?' Brother Barnabas went.

Left on his own, Bognor tried to think. His mind was a jumble of random disconnections: Harold Gimblett, the Unsleeping Church resting neither by day nor night, a very sunburned girl talking to him in Spanish and feeding him spoonfuls of honey, a disembodied voice saying over and over again, 'There's no such thing as idle curiosity,' croquet mallets, stations of the cross, the *American Bee Journal*, Holman Hunt. All muddling round his mind in a mess of pain like dried fruit in a cake dough. He focussed very hard on the text on the wall, treating it like the testing board in an optician's. It was a struggle.

'Verily, Verily, I say unto you, except a corn of wheat fall into the ground and die . . . fall into the ground and die.' He managed a half-smile, and winced, leant over to the chest of drawers and picked up his file and a pencil.

'Notes,' he thought to himself. 'Must make some notes.'

He started to write. 'Visited honey store with Father John . . . went to Compline . . . returned to room . . . decided to investigate mystery cupboard . . . went to sleep.' He remembered Somerset batting averages. 'Went out in rain . . . light on in cupboard . . . hit on head . . . wake up in room.'

'Oh God,' he said again. He reached tentatively to his head and put a couple of fingers on the spot where the pain was coming from. It was agony. Whoever had done it had the luck or the foresight to hit him above the hairline. Nothing would show. He ran his finger round the damage, biting his lip as he did. There had been blood, but it had dried in the night. He sat up and looked at the pillow. There was a slight rust-coloured patch where his head had been.

Around the area of dried blood, a lot of which had matted the hair, there were two distinct and separate lumps. Two blows. He remembered the arm rising and falling. It was all embarrassingly unprofessional. Then he remembered the rain and the fatigue. The tea was helping him.

After another gulp which almost finished it he got out of bed and tried standing. To his surprise it seemed to work. He tried a few steps. It was like having a terrible hangover. He felt frail, slightly dizzy, had a ghastly headache and was on the verge of being physically sick, but he'd live. There was a packet of aspirin in his suitcase and he opened it up and took four. He washed it down with the last of the tea.

Suddenly he realised that he was wearing his pyjamas. That was odd. Then he looked at the chair. His corduroys and the blue sweater were draped over the back, his underpants and socks were on the seat. He walked over and felt them. They were dry. Warm too. Someone had had them over hot pipes. Who? Brother Barnabas? Had Brother Barnabas hit him? No. Whoever had done it had been stronger than Barnabas had appeared and bigger. Bognor was certain he remembered someone taller than himself. He went to the mirror and bent to inspect his wounds. Leaning forward, he held the hair apart with his finger-tips and stared at his scalp. The bruising looked terrible, but the cut was nothing too serious. It looked as if it had been cleaned up. Bognor judged that he must have lost more blood than what was caked on his head and stained on the pillow. So. He picked the file up again.

'Three attacks,' he wrote. 'Two deaths. One injured. Considerable efforts to ensure survival and well-being of injured party.'

He chewed the pencil. It could mean two things. Either the attack had been a mistake perpetrated by someone who had nothing to do with the murders. No, surely not. All right. He started writing again.

'Theory One. I was hit on head by murderer of Collingdale and Thomas. If so, why not kill me too? Theory Two. I was hit on the head by someone unconnected with murder.' He threw the pencil down in exasperation and decided to face breakfast. There was no point in giving his assailant the satisfaction of seeing him staggering about like a man on the point of death. On the other hand, if the assailant had taken the trouble to bathe his wound and put him to bed in his pyjamas and dry his clothes he would presumably want to see him fit and well. He decided to compromise in the way he had originally suggested. Breakfast yes. Kippers no.

He slipped on the blue sweater and looked at himself again in the glass. He looked terrible. The dark blue accentuated his pallor more than the brown pyjamas had done. It was conceivable, he supposed, that he could have made his own way back to his room without remembering anything about it. He had done that a couple of times about ten years ago, when very drunk. No, it wasn't credible. He would have remembered. He was sure he couldn't have managed it. In any case he wouldn't have bothered with pyjamas, couldn't have cleaned the wound, and didn't know where to get clothes dried even if he had had the energy. He had been put to bed by someone and that someone was a strong man to have carried him or even dragged him the hundred or so yards from the store-room. Certainly not Father John. Nor Barnabas. Nor even the two between them.

Then again, perhaps the man—or men—who had put him to bed had nothing to do with the attack. Perhaps he had been slugged by someone, left there, and been found by someone else quite different. His shoes were still damp, though he noticed that someone had attempted to dry them by putting rolled-up balls of newspaper in them. He put them on and went outside.

Brother Barnabas had been right about the quality of the morning. The storm had cleared the atmosphere, and the sun, shining on the overnight rain, had brought out an indefinable smell of fertility, of things growing very fast. Bognor paused and sniffed. It made him feel better. Some birds—he wished he was able to recognise individual birdsongs—were singing slightly hysterically and from somewhere up the hill came the sharp rat-tat-tat of an industrious woodpecker. There were human noises too. The whine of electric saw, chug of tractor, chime of breakfast bell. People start early in the country. Bognor began to walk gingerly in the direction of the refectory, looking aimlessly for any sign of the previous night's adventure and still trying to explain it.

There could now be no question that the cupboard held some secret, and that Father John was party to it. It seemed probable too that Brother Barnabas knew at least something about his injuries. Yet neither could have contributed anything very physical to the affair. It began to look like conspiracy. He wished he knew if there had been someone in the cupboard when he was hit. Was his attacker the man who had turned on the light? Was he just returning? Or was it someone arriving to join the man in the cupboard?

He kicked a pebble fiercely off the path and swore loudly. His head hurt and the whole situation was becoming more and more confused. He hated it. They were all in it together, trying to make a fool of him. He followed the pebble up the path and kicked it again. It took off and hit the side of a wheelbarrow with a satisfying ping.

'Shot!' said a voice behind him. It was Xavier.

Bognor waited for him to draw level.

'Lovely morning,' said Xavier, 'although I must say the prospect of kippers doesn't appeal.'

Bognor might normally have made a joke out of it. His head throbbed, and he didn't. Instead Xavier looked suddenly and genuinely shocked. 'Good heavens,' he said. 'You look terrible. What in God's name have you been doing? Have you been on the sleuth all night? You look like death.'

'It's nothing,' said Bognor. 'I'm just tired.'

'You look worse than tired,' said Xavier. 'Are you sure?'

'Sure.'

'Oh well,' Xavier sighed. 'It's none of my business, I suppose. Anyway. Did you hear the wireless? Anselm must be wetting his knickers by now.'

'He what?' Bognor was disturbed by the vulgarity of the phrase, then he had a worrying thought. He hoped nothing had leaked out to the B.B.C. That would make life difficult. 'Why?' he asked. 'What's happened now?'

'It's Brother Bede. He's done over the Bishop.'

'What Bishop? Why?'

'That pompous old bugger Woodstock. He's really massacred him by the sound of it.'

The aspirin hadn't worked yet.

'I'm sorry,' said Bognor, 'could you go a bit slower, please?' They had almost reached the door of the farmhouse. Xavier put a hand on Bognor's elbow.

'We're late,' he said. 'If I tell you now you'll miss your kippers. Do you like kippers?'

'No.'

'Nor do I.' Xavier looked reflective and added: 'I always say . . .' but Bognor, almost involuntarily, cut him short.

'I know what you always say,' he said.

'Oh, what?'

'That God didn't mean kippers to be eaten because of the bones.'

'Ah.' Father Xavier was amused. 'I suppose Barnabas told you that.'

'Yes.'

'He would. Anyway, are you prepared to take

a risk of missing some breakfast?'

'Yes.' Bognor was suddenly impatient. 'I'd like to know precisely and in some detail what you're on about and if necessary I'm prepared to miss the beginning of breakfast.'

'O.K.,' said Xavier. 'You know Woodstock, Bishop of.'

Bognor had an uncertain image of an elderly person of reactionary sentiments. 'Sort of,' he said.

'O.K. Well, the other day old Woodstock, who is a genuine cast-iron horror, a hanger and flogger of the old school, wrote a letter to *The Times* about church involvement in politics. Exceptionally silly letter even for Woodstock. He kept rambling on about the Lords spiritual and the Lords temporal. Even invoked the spirit of Thomas à Becket, which struck me as singularly ill-advised. All very confused.'

'The gist of it being,' said Bognor, 'that the Church should stick to religion and leave everything else to the experts?'

'Yes. In so far as there was gist. He's a complete moron, Woodstock. I don't know why *The Times* printed it. Basically he was laying in to leftie clerics whether they were in Brazil or Spain or here or anywhere else.'

'And Bede?'

'Well, Bede is by way of being rather a free thinker. You've met him, presumably?'

'Not yet. I thought he was just an indifferent

cook.'

'That's true. But he's also our tame revolutionary. He's currently sold on a rather complex mixture of Basque nationalism and Jung. Between you and me he's not much brighter than Woodstock. He's a sort of champagne navvy. Oh and he won't eat meat. Though I think that's more biological than metaphysical if you follow.'

'So he wrote to *The Times*.'

'I thought I said that.' Xavier was irritated. 'I must say you really aren't your incisive self today, are you?'

'I'm sorry.' Bognor wondered if he should be flattered by Xavier's reference to his incisiveness.

'That's all right. Yes. It was on the seven o'clock news. Not very prominent, but prominent enough. He seems to have delivered himself of as all-embracing a message as Woodstock but there were some rather choice phrases if the B.B.C. is quoting accurately. "The sort of thinking—or lack of it—which has characterised the Church of England for too long", "calculated to do immense harm", "positively unchristian" and "mindless bigotry". Those are the ones that stick in the mind.'

'They seem to have stuck in yours.' Bognor was feeling a bit better. He wondered whether it was aspirin or adrenalin.

'Well, considering he's not frightfully well educated they do have a certain ring to them.'

Bognor looked at him, with a suspicion of intuition. It was a face full of humour certainly, but it was by no means lacking in malice.

'Almost as if he'd had some help with it.'

'Dear boy,' said Xavier, chuckling a little, 'I do believe your critical faculty is returning. But what a very unworthy suspicion.' He looked up at the sky, which was clear and blue and almost perfect. 'It really seems a pity,' he said after a moment, 'to waste any of a morning like this in the company of kippers, but I think you ought to eat something. It will set you up.' They went on in.

It was a silent meal. Only the noise of eating, which was considerable, interfered with the tedium of Father Simon reading from a Victorian life of St. Augustine. It was poor stuff, monotonously read. The combination of sounds made Bognor irritable and the fact that the coffee was stewed and the porridge burnt made him feel still worse. He wondered if Brother Bede was in the kitchen again.

There was no mistaking the atmosphere. Although everything superficially appeared normal, there was an air of tension and expectancy which was greater even than after either of the deaths. Someone dropped a plate, which smashed on the stone floor, and it was as if the Abbot had been shot. When Xavier and

Bognor entered late the air of corporate inquisitiveness was almost tangible. The main object of attention was Father Anselm.

He sat at his place, his face a dull grey, not eating at all and barely touching the bitter coffee. Every time he looked up at least thirty faces had to turn away for fear of being caught staring. At length the apology for a meal, and with it Father Simon's half-hearted recital, came to an end, and Father Anselm rose to speak.

'Save me, O God,' he said, 'for the waters are come in, even unto my soul. I stick fast in the deep mire, where no ground is: I am come into deep waters so that the floods run over me. I am weary of crying; my throat is dry; my sight faileth me for waiting so long upon my God. They that hate me without a cause are more than the hairs of my head: they that are mine enemies and would destroy me guiltless are mighty.' He paused for what seemed a very long time and continued very precisely. 'A short time ago the B.B.C. Home Service news announced that one of our number had gravely insulted our Beloved Visitor in a letter to one of the national newspapers. It is no business of mine to enter into political dispute with any of my brothers. However, I cannot countenance vicious and unprovoked personal attacks on our Father in God, Ernest Bishop of Woodstock. I have to tell you that on hearing the news I summoned the brother concerned, heard his words of mitigation and dismissed him from the order. His name will not be mentioned here again. It must be as if he has never been.'

Bognor, whose headache had fully returned, found his irritation worse than ever. The man was making an absurd fuss over a rather adolescent letter in *The Times*, but, much worse, he'd expelled one of his few remaining suspects. It was too much.

The effect on the Community was extraordinary. This was real drama. You could read it on their faces. They were enjoying it, each one of them. Bognor was reminded of school again, and of expulsions. But Father Anselm was not finished.

'This,' he continued, 'is without doubt the worst few days in the history of the Community. Today we have the funeral service for Thomas who was our friend. Just as, so lately, we witnessed the passing of Luke who was our brother. These are tragedies. I feel as the great majority of you do that these things are sent to try us. That we must not succumb.

'I had thought that in this time of adversity we might be compelled to cancel our retreat scheduled for this week-end, at least to visitors. But I am convinced that it would be proper to go forward and not to look back. We must be courageous. We must be hopeful. Above all, we must not lose our faith in the Lord God

Almighty.'

As they all rose to go, Bognor noticed Xavier. He was looking almost shocked and deeply angry.

'The sod,' he said softly to Bognor as he left.

In the yard Anselm was standing, the big black bible clasped to his chest and an expression of sorrowing martyrdom on his face. He said good morning to Bognor, and added a remark about his sorrow at exposing him to the embarrassment of family feuds and difficulties.

'Don't worry,' said Bognor, 'I'm only sorry that I don't really appreciate the significance of this disagreement. From what I've heard he was quite justified in most of what he wrote.'

Father Anselm smiled patronisingly. 'You are an outsider and a layman. I understand that it is difficult for you to see that this was a betrayal of every vow in our life.'

'Oh balls,' said Bognor and regretted it almost immediately. However, by the time he did he was walking away across the yard, having turned his back on Father Anselm, who was still standing in the same position smiling vacantly and shaking his head from side to side with an expression of great melancholy and world weariness.

There were a number of aspects of the business which upset him. Of course the retribution of the Community was one but more selfishly he was desperate because one of his suspects had probably left already and he was the one suspect who was a real possibility for every crime. Moreover, this morning's letter had revealed a sort of motive for espionage which while woolly was still better than anything else he'd managed to find. It was after eight now and the Community had filed into the chapel for Terce. No doubt they would be offering up some frightful comminations, wishing no good for Brother Bede.

He ran his hand through his hair and was reminded painfully of his earlier experience. Everything was moving too fast for his liking. He walked out of the yard and into the lane to wait for the friars to come out of chapel, and for Inspector Pinney to arrive for his day's work. Already the day was becoming hot. It was only a short drive to Oxford with its beckoning profusion of punts and Pimms. It was a genuine temptation, as genuine as Pinney's pint of beer, and he actually toyed with it for a moment.

It was half past eight before Pinney arrived. By that time Bognor had chewed through a great many stems of grass grabbed from the edge of the lane and had discovered from Barnabas that Brother Bede had been driven off in the Community van by Brother Vivian in the hope of catching the eight o'clock train from Woodstock. Such belongings as he had not been able to bundle together in twenty minutes flat were to be sent on to his elder brother, a G.P.

with a practice in South London. He had been given the price of a rail ticket and five pounds.

During his perambulations up and down the lane he had also seen Paul. The youth had been in the kitchen with Bede and a couple of others at the time of Thomas's death. Bognor asked him more or less idly whether he had heard anything and he replied that there'd been a lot of noise and he'd been busy so he hadn't. There was something strangely familiar about the boy. He almost felt he'd met him before but it was scarcely likely. It was probably just that he was feeling tired.

So even though Inspector Pinney was late he got a distinctly less hostile reception from his superior than if he had arrived half an hour before. Bognor's temper had cooled, and his head just ached dully so that it was bearable if not pleasant.

'More trouble, Inspector Pinney,' he said. 'Would you mind frightfully if I went down to the village to make a phone call while you keep an end up. I'll be back in time for the funeral.'

Inspector Pinney nodded with more than a touch of surliness. He had no idea why, if it were suicide, his presence should be required. Nor could he see, if it were not suicide, why he shouldn't be told. Besides, he had a hangover and had come fresh from a row with his wife.

Bognor thought of taking the Land-Rover, but decided that he needed the walk. There was nothing much he could do for the moment up at the Friary. As he walked to the phone box by the Boot he arranged his programme. There were two outstanding mysteries either of which could be crucial. The first was Brother Aldhelm's afternoon walk and the second was the light in the cupboard. Even if Aldhelm took a walk every day he certainly couldn't get away for long before afternoon, so he would have to wait till after lunch. As for the honey store cupboard he had a hunch that that particular secret would be yielded after dark. In any case, suspicions might be aroused if he tried to sneak in during the day. He was also hoping that a chat with Lord Camberley might produce something, and he had great hopes for the week-end retreat. By the time he got to the kiosk he had it decided. To stay beyond the week-end would make them realise he was still dissatisfied. He must solve as much as he could by Sunday night. If he had no spy and no murderer by then he would have to take the easy way out. Wait for the next Expo-Brit and have the Beaubridge representative or representatives thoroughly searched. He made a mental note to find out who was going this year. It was halfway through September that the Expo-Britons left for Eastern Europe. Less than a month away. That wasn't a long wait. In some ways he should have decided on that the minute Collingdale had been found in the potato patch.

It would have made life a lot less painful.

He dialled a Whitehall number and asked for Parkinson, who seemed unduly abrupt. Eventually he agreed that the eight o'clock from Woodstock to Paddington was to be met and a passenger (he gave a brief description of Brother Bede, emphasising the distinctive brown rucksack with C.N.D. badge which Barnabas had mentioned) to be followed. No move would be made unless the man tried to leave the country. Finally Parkinson said tersely: 'You're on your own, Bognor. Don't bother me again, just liaise with Erris Beg.' Bognor put the phone down with a heartfelt grimace and a deep sense of wrong.

Meanwhile, back at the Friary, Inspector Pinney was pursuing his inquiries.

'Did the deceased at any time give evidence of a melancholic disposition?' he asked Anselm. 'Were you at any time aware of any circumstances of a suspicious nature?' he asked Father John. Unhappily the Inspector's heart was not in it. He failed to see what all the fuss was about. Some nutter had done in a friar and then chucked himself down a well. At least that was the half-baked theory of the other nutter from London.

The routine of the Friary was in full swing and its essential homeliness increased the Inspector's feeling of being superfluous. Blokes cleaning out drains. Old bloke with a mask on looking at bees. Blokes making soup and washing up after breakfast. Blokes cataloguing library books, feeding hens, chopping down trees, shifting manure. Inspector Pinney would rather have been in Bicester on the drug ring investigation or working at the horse doping up at Chipping Norton. This was like putting in time on a garden fête.

He was sitting on a wall having a cup of tea with the solicitous Brother Barnabas, wondering what possible further routine enquiry he could carry out and also what was holding up the absurd Londoner, when there was a fruity hoot from the lane outside, followed by a rasping gear change and an elderly and very upright maroon Rolls-Royce turned into the courtyard.

'Lord Camberley,' said Brother Barnabas in explanation, and got to his feet.

Inspector Pinney watched with something that was almost interest as the car crunched to a halt. The chauffeur, who wore a stiff cap and leather gloves, dismounted and opened the rear door. There was a moment of delay as a travelling rug was thrust aside and then a tall spare figure in striped trousers and black tail-coat emerged and blinked into the morning sun. He held a black top-hat in his left hand and a silver-topped cane in his right. Inspector Pinney judged him to be in his early seventies. After a moment's blinking and minor adjustments to his dress Lord Camberley turned languidly to Brother Barnabas, who genuflected. Lord Camberley smiled, Brother Barnabas smiled and the two of them went off to the farmhouse.

Inspector Pinney lit a cigarette and walked over to the chauffeur, who had taken his cap off and was standing with one foot on the running board, looking lost.

'Cigarette?' asked Pinney.

'Thanks.' The chauffeur accepted and inhaled deeply. 'It's a long drive from London,' he volunteered. 'Specially this time of the morning. And with his Lordship in this kind of mood.'

'Oh?'

'Well, you can't expect him to be exactly happy.'

'I suppose not.'

'Anyway, who are you? You don't look much like one of yer actual brothers.'

'Pinney. C.I.D.'

The chauffeur's eyes narrowed and he inhaled again very deeply.

'That's funny.'

'Why?'

'I thought Master Tom killed himself?'

'Yes.'

'Well then, what are you doing here?'

'Just a few routine enquiries.'

The chauffeur looked at him sharply. 'Pull

the other one,' he said.

'Why?' asked Pinney.

'Because if you're just here for routine enquiries, why did his Lordship go mad last night after he had a telephone call, and why did I have to take him to some office in Whitehall before seven o'clock this morning? I'm not stupid.'

It was Pinney's turn to be puzzled. He threw away his cigarette and made a long job of grinding it into the ground with his heel.

'Don't ask me,' he said eventually. 'Nobody ever tells me anything round here.'

The Inspector was saved further embarrassment by the return of Simon Bognor. The reason for his delay was that after making his phone call he had gone to the post office to look up the exact whereabouts and telephone number of the Old Manor at Melbury. He had also taken some more aspirin and was feeling rather faint.

The chauffeur got back into the Rolls, tilted his cap over his forehead and prepared for a rest.

'Camberley, I take it?'

'Yes.'

'Well?' The Inspector was very obviously pleased with himself and Bognor had no alternative but to humour him.

'Well, I'm afraid Lord Camberley's on to something or other. I understand he had an interview in Whitehall early this morning. Seems he's most unhappy, sir.' The Inspector was enjoying himself. 'Went quite mad, his chauffeur said.'

Bognor feigned indifference, since he could think of nothing more constructive to do.

'That's very natural, don't you think? After all, his son is just dead.' Inwardly he was perplexed by Sir Erris. It surely hadn't been necessary for him to tip off Camberley and that was obviously what he'd done. On the other hand, Sir Erris wasn't that much of a fool. Perhaps it would be better for Camberley to be aware of the situation now; better, at least, than for him to harbour doubts and ask difficult questions. The damage was done now. He wondered who he had seen that morning. Not the Minister anyway. The Minister wouldn't have dragged himself out of bed at that hour of the morning. Not even for Camberley. More likely to have been Parkinson. Parkinson wouldn't have let him down, surely.

To Inspector Pinney he said, 'I'm afraid I had rather a bad night. If you'll forgive me I'm going to get an hour's sleep before the funeral. I'll see you then.' He was still feeling terrible, but it was more and more important to stay alert. He would have to ask Camberley to give him time, but it wasn't just Camberley's interference that worried him. Anselm's sacking of Brother Bede was almost certain to get to the press. Anselm had probably issued a statement already, and if he hadn't the frightful Bishop would have. That would mean journalists nosing around. Worse still, it was the end of the week. That would mean journalists from Sunday papers. Red-nosed men in hats. That was all he needed.

Inspector Pinney watched him walk rather unsteadily towards the Nissen hut.

'Ungrateful ponce,' he said.

The cortège formed in the courtyard. It was true that a combination of bleach, carbolic and honest industry had removed the unpleasant stain from the well side, but the proximity of the death place, and the corpse securely nailed into its freshly smoothed oak, was macabre. Bognor who was among the last to arrive was just in time to see the coffin borne from the chapel by eight of the younger stronger friars. It was a sturdy sensible coffin, a source of some pride to its maker, Brother Eric, a joiner by trade, who had stayed up all night planing and polishing and screwing. If it was not quite grand enough for the elder son of an earl it was entirely proper for the funeral of a friars' friend.

The whole Community was there, together with the guests in their Sunday best and Lord Camberley, Inspector Pinney, and Bognor himself. Bognor had no black tie but wore his dark blue sweater under the shepherd's plaid. He felt rather shamed in the presence of the immaculately clad father, but it was the nearest he could get to a mark of respect.

A gentle eddy of wind flicked teasingly at the skirts of the habits, as the coffin and its bearers stood facing south while the procession formed. Father Anselm in silk vestments took up a position immediately in front of the coffin, Lord Camberley immediately behind. He looked bleakly incongruous, a gaunt Victorian figure, made even more imposing by the shining black top-hat, worn absolutely straight. Bognor and Pinney took up a station at the very rear, behind the friars and their guests who arranged themselves in a procession, two by two behind the mourning earl. The sun was now high in the sky, which was cloudless, and the bearers in their prickly, heavy habits dripped sweat.

It was half a mile to the Community's burial ground and they would be exhausted by the time they arrived. Bognor noticed that the Rolls-Royce had disappeared and wondered if the chauffeur was propping up the bar of the Boot. He felt he should have shown a little more respect and wondered if it worried Lord Camberley.

Up at the front Anselm was peering about like a pernickety sergeant-major making sure that the dressing was right and there was no talking in the ranks. After a minute or two he was apparently satisfied, because he turned and moved off, singing as he did the first verse of the Benedicite: 'O All ye Works of the Lord, bless ye the Lord: praise him and magnify him for ever.' The friars behind him took up the chant and followed, walking slowly out of the yard and out on to the path past the Nissen Hut. Canticle followed canticle and psalm followed psalm as they made their way past the hut and out into the open fields beyond. It was a bizarre but moving scene. Earthy brown habits, the striking black contrast of the Earl of Camberley, lush green all around them, and the neat deep rhythms of King James's Bible floating into the soft Oxfordshire air.

'O all ye Green Things upon the Earth, bless ye the Lord: praise him and magnify him for ever.' Cows in the neighbouring field looked up and gazed at them for a moment before lowering their heads and returning to chew. Bognor dropped back a few yards to get a better view of the procession. He wished he had a camera.

It was a full twenty minutes before they reached the graveyard: a small triangular field with a horse chestnut in the middle and a handful of headstones clustered beneath.

Just to the east of them, at the point where the shade of the tree gave way to the pure sunlight, was the fresh raw trench which was to receive Batty Thomas. Bognor always disliked the sight of new graves. They made him think of worms and decay.

'I know that my Redeemer liveth,' sang the friars as they neared the graveside, 'and that he shall stand at the latter day upon the earth. And though after my skin worms destroy this body, yet in my flesh shall I see God.' Then they broke ranks and formed a half-circle in the shade. Bognor and Pinney stood a little apart, partly because they felt outside this experience and, in Bognor's case at least, partly because he felt a little ashamed.

And so they buried him. The old phrases struck Bognor as forcibly as always. He had been to too many colleagues' funerals for a man who was only on the verge of middle age, and he had still not got used to them. Rather the reverse.

'Man that is born of a woman hath but a short time to live,' intoned Father Anselm. '. . . he cometh up and is cut down like a flower.' The coffin was obscured from Bognor by the wall of brown habits which grouped round it, but he saw that it was being lowered into the grave, and watched each man fling a handful of earth . . . 'earth to earth, ashes to ashes, dust to dust, in sure and certain hope of the Resurrection to eternal life'.

It was all over, as usual, almost too quickly. Brother Eric's handiwork was under ground. Two men had stayed behind to finish the job and the rest of them returned in silence to resume their interrupted routine. Except that for Bognor there was no routine. Every hour brought new trials. His next task was a confrontation with Lord Camberley and an apology to Father Anselm. He didn't relish either.

Neither death nor dismissal could alter the strict calendar of offices and the instant the friars returned they went straight to the chapel for Sext. Bognor allowed Inspector Pinney to go to the Boot for an early lunch and looked round for Camberley. He found him peering gloomily down the well shaft.

Bognor introduced himself, and Camberley surveyed him searchingly. He was an old man, but there was no lack of intelligence in the grey eyes, nor of compassion.

'Erris says you're all right,' he said at length, 'though from the way you've handled this I'm inclined to doubt it.'

'I'm sorry, sir,' began Bognor.

'Bit late for that.'

'That wasn't what I was going to say. I was going to say that I was sorry Sir Erris had told you anything. I'm afraid it does represent a breach of security.'

Lord Camberley looked at him with contempt and said nothing. Bognor tried again. 'I have to conduct this investigation my way, sir. Really.' He shuffled his feet and stared at them.

Lord Camberley was very obviously

unimpressed. Eventually he said, 'I know probably as much as you do about all this. I found out this morning. I don't propose to interfere more than necessary. However, I am going to give you some help. If, of course, you'll accept help.' The last remark was infinitely patronising.

'Of course, sir.' Bognor at that moment would have accepted help from anyone.

'Very well, then. For a start you must appreciate that there is absolutely no question, no question whatever, of my son having killed himself or anybody else. None at all. Do I make myself clear?'

'I agree with you, sir.'

'Mmm.'

Lord Camberley had difficulty with the next bit. 'I know,' he said, 'that my son was, to put it kindly, eccentric, but that didn't prevent him from having some remarkable insights, and from being perfectly normal a great deal of the time. You had a conversation with him the morning of the day he died. What did he say to you?'

'That he had seen Brother Luke's murderer.'

'Anything else?'

'Something about his not having been supposed to have been there.'

'Who?'

'The murderer, I suppose. It wasn't easy to understand what he was getting at.'

'I should try to think about that if I were you.' Lord Camberley was crisp. The remark had been unfortunate. 'May I see the supposed confession?'

Bognor withdrew the note from his wallet and Camberley read it quickly and without expression, then returned it.

'Crude,' he said. 'Not totally unlike Tom's writing. But not very good.' He tapped his cane against his shoes. 'There's one other important thing,' he went on. 'You've been grossly unfair to Anselm.'

'About dismissing Bede? I can't agree, I'm afraid.'

Lord Camberley looked puzzled, then dismissed the remark.

'I have told him everything,' he said.

'You what, sir?' Bognor was flabbergasted.

'I told him who you were. I told him that Luke was one of your agents. I told him that Tom was killed by someone in the Friary. I told him that important secrets were being smuggled out with the honey every year.'

'Good heavens.' Bognor was dumbfounded.

Camberley looked at him with scorn. 'I can't conceive why you didn't tell him yourself. This elaborate charade of yours has confused everyone. It's pointless and childish.'

'With respect, sir,' Bognor was quite angry, 'I didn't tell him because he is an obvious suspect. He could easily have killed Luke. He had permanent access to the honey.'

'Father Anselm is an honest man. He is not a spy and he is certainly not a murderer.' Camberley was adamant.

'Are you certain?' he asked.

His head throbbed.

'I have known Anselm practically all his life. I trust him totally. He is almost wholly good. Why else to you think I sent my poor son down here to live?'

Bognor tried to sound reasonable. 'People said that sort of thing about Burgess and Maclean and Philby, sir.'

Camberley sighed. 'You young men,' he said. 'At all events, it's done. Anselm, thank God, knows your job and your suspicions. From now on you will just have to be frank with him. Then perhaps we'll get somewhere.'

'I'm sorry, sir,' he said. 'Maybe I have been a little over-suspicious. At any rate, as you say, I have no choice now.' He made a silent vow to tell Anselm nothing that he didn't have to.

Luckily the Brothers emerged from Sext before this fragile truce could be broken. Anselm came over to them and smiled ingratiatingly. Bognor started to apologise, but the Abbot stopped him.

'Simon, Simon,' he said taking him by the elbow. 'We can all make mistakes. I'm distressed, of course, but what is done is done. As I said to you all this morning these things are sent to try us. We must look rather to the future.'

Lord Camberley was to return to London immediately after lunch and he made it quite plain that he was going to watch Bognor brief Anselm. Any backsliding on that score was going to be brutally and forcefully stopped. The three men therefore took lunch in Anselm's study. It was a painful affair, and not redeemed by the food. Lord Camberley claimed travel sickness and made do with an apple and a couple of glasses of Anselm's sherry, but Bognor had no such excuse.

He repeated, at length and in more detail, what he had already discussed with Sir Erris. Which, of course, was what Sir Erris had told Lord Camberley and what Lord Camberley had passed on to Anselm. It was no news to any of them, therefore, but the detailed recitation was accepted by all three as a necessary promise of good faith. He was careful to make no mention of Brother Aldhelm's walk, the honey cupboard or even the delay over the labels. He did, however, point a finger in the vague direction of Brother Bede.

'Good heavens,' said Anselm when he did. 'That seems all too likely. If only I had known then what I know now I should never have dismissed him. As it is, alas, our bird has flown. Regretfully I really can not accept much blame.'

'We won't lose him,' said Bognor, with

ill-assumed authority, 'though I admit it would have been easier if he were still here.'

Lord Camberley gave him an admonitory stare.

'Well then,' said Anselm, pretending to ignore this friction. 'What is the best way out of this distressing situation? What do you propose, Simon?'

Simon thought for a moment. 'I can't stay beyond the week-end,' he said. 'If I do our murderer or spy or whatever will realise that I'm not happy with the solution they've fed me. Therefore I have this afternoon and the whole of Saturday and Sunday.'

'And how do you propose to use this time, Simon?' Father Anselm smiled.

'I'm sorry,' he said. 'I really can't . . .'

'I think you should, Mr. Bognor,' Lord Camberley frowned. 'It would be unfortunate if I were to mention certain aspects of this case to certain people.'

Father Anselm continued to smile as if he had not heard the threat at all. If it hadn't been Camberley's own son who was dead Bognor would almost have believed that the two men were organising the conspiracy themselves.

'I should like to observe as much of the retreat as possible,' he said. 'I understand that people from all walks of life will be attending and do attend regularly. I believe that this is how the information is handed over.'

Camberley nodded. 'It's plausible,' he said.

Anselm appeared shocked.

'Dear me,' he said. 'To suggest that any one of us should use such an occasion as a cover—that is the word, isn't it?—for espionage . . .'

'So I just want to see who comes and who talks to whom,' continued Bognor. 'I'm right in thinking this is the last retreat before the Expo-Brit?'

'You are.'

'And so,' said Bognor, 'it seems probable that this will be the last opportunity our courier will have of handing over detailed information.'

The two others nodded agreement. Bognor began to feel almost important.

'Who is going this year?'

Anselm coloured and laughed artificially.

'In view,' he said 'of your earlier suspicions it is rather embarrassing. Lord Wharfedale has been more than usually generous this year and he is allowing us to send two representatives. One is myself. The other is Father Simon.'

'How unfortunate,' said Bognor, his confidence suddenly getting too much for him. 'If I don't discover anything conclusive by Sunday night I have only one way left. We shall wait until you and Father Simon are sitting in the departure lounge at Heathrow, and we shall then detain you and search you until we find what we're looking for. If necessary we shall empty every jar of honey in the process.' He blushed. Perhaps he had overdone it.

Lord Camberley finished his second sherry and puckered his mouth.

'In the circumstances I should have thought there was a better than evens chance that our spy won't be operating this year,' he said. 'He must realise that you're on his tail. Even . . .' he added softly, 'if you've still got a long way to catch up.'

'He hasn't missed a year yet,' said Bognor. 'And my personal feeling is that he is an extremely confident operator.'

'One other question,' said Anselm. 'I don't understand how you think these secrets are getting through. You do realise that the same person is never sent on an Expo-Brit two years running?'

'I must admit,' he said slowly, 'that when Father Simon became so anxious about the missing labels I wondered if that might not be the method.'

'Ah. Ingenious.' Father Anselm didn't seem in the least alarmed.

Lord Camberley moved to get up. Bognor turned the other way as he put an arm across Anselm's shoulder. He only heard snatches.

'Horrid business . . . very well done . . . not to worry.' A sequence of platitudes. Then they turned back to him.

'I must get back to London,' said Camberley,

extending a hand. 'Glad to have met you. I hope I've been of some assistance.'

The three went out to the yard where the Rolls had returned. The chauffeur, slightly flushed, jumped out and opened the back door. Camberley and Anselm exchanged muffled words, then Camberley turned to Bognor once again.

'Just in case I think of anything else,' he said, 'could I have your home address? Just in case.' Bognor scribbled on the back of an envelope and Camberley gave him a card with a terse 'You'd better have mine as well. You never know.' Then he embarked. The chauffeur shut the door with an expensive thud, climbed in, started the engine first time, and the old machine purred away with its aristocratic cargo sprawled in the back, not bothering to wave or make any other gesture of farewell. Bognor delivered a mental 'V' sign at his parting rear bumper.

'The most delightful man,' said Anselm. 'Such a tower of strength to we lesser breeds.'

* * *

It would have been a perfect day for a swim. Only a very occasional breeze disturbed the stillness. Some of the friars and their guests had stripped down to an inelegant variety of shorts and bathing trunks which looked like a job lot from a jumble sale. They were lying, most of them, on the lawn. A couple were playing lazy and inefficient badminton without a net. Father Xavier sat in a canvas chair under an immense black 'Cordobes' hat, sketching. Even if a swim wasn't possible Bognor would have enjoyed a quiet siesta.

Instead he hurried to his room, took another handful of aspirin and ran back to the Land-Rover. If he didn't hurry he would be late for Brother Aldhelm's afternoon walk. He hoped he wouldn't pass him on the road, but if his instincts were correct Brother Aldhelm would walk across the fields and through the woods. Again, if he was right, he wouldn't be stopping to pick daisies or wild garlic. Nevertheless it was always possible that yesterday had been a fluke, a coincidence, insignificant.

As he forced the protesting machine up the hill he rehearsed the alternatives. If Aldhelm had been telling the truth he simply went for a walk and exhausted himself. It might not have been him who raced through Great Ogridge in the passenger seat of a red 'E'-Type Jaguar. But if it was, why had he preferred that to the passenger seat of a perfectly adequate Land-Rover? If, as seemed obvious, he had had an appointment, when had it been arranged? Why had he had to get away so soon after Thomas's death? Was it Mrs. Strudwick's car?

Was it Mrs. Strudwick driving? Did Aldhelm have regular assignments on the hill-top? Or just the day Thomas died?

He accelerated erratically to seventy on the straight at the top of the hill and was greatly relieved, after a couple of minutes, to arrive at the staddlestone under the chestnut tree and find it empty. Brother Aldhelm had not arrived. Or perhaps he wasn't coming.

He drove on for about a hundred yards and found a flaking five-bar gate which led into a hayfield. He backed the Land-Rover into the entrance and got out. No one would give it a second thought because every local farmer would have one. He climbed the gate, paused astride it and gazed across the downland in the direction of the Friary. He stood like that for a full minute until suddenly he saw what he'd hoped for. With a little grunt of satisfaction he jumped down from the gate and using the hedgerow as cover slipped clumsily back in the direction of the staddlestone. Some ten yards short he stopped and crouched. From the other side of the stone came the noise of footsteps and heavy breathing. Bognor lay flat and elbowed himself virtually into the hedge, scratching his face on some brambles as he did. A few seconds of squirming and he was in position. From where he lay, securely if uncomfortably camouflaged, he could see a hundred-yard stretch of roadway and in the middle of that expanse was the staddlestone under the chestnut tree. Just as he had arranged himself, scraped a couple of burrs from his hair, and dug a sharp flint-like stone from under his right elbow, he saw Brother Aldhelm. He was not as puffed as the day before but he was still sweating.

His breath came in staccato gulps and as he got to the stone he flung himself down on it and sank his head between his knees, a picture of exhaustion. Eventually he regained some composure and raised his head to look down the road. Bognor smiled smugly at a couple of cabbage whites which flickered in some intricate sexual dance a few feet from where he lay. Everything so far was as suspected. They waited like this for a while until Aldhelm started to display signs of unease. He looked at his watch, stood up, sat down again, looked at his watch again, stood up and walked a few paces in Bognor's direction. He stopped only a few feet short. If Bognor had had Father John's blackthorn or even Camberley's silver-headed stick he could have fetched him a blow across the shins without moving. He stood there thinking, put a hand inside his habit and massaged his chest for a second, then stopped to listen.

Bognor heard it at the same time. He watched as all the tension left Aldhelm's body, and heard the distant sound of a noisy gear change on the empty road, still some miles away to the west. He looked at Aldhelm remembering the pain in his head. The friar was quite big enough and quite strong enough to have inflicted it. He could have killed Collingdale but not Thomas and he could have spied. If Mrs. Strudwick was a crucial contact—if indeed this was her—could he have known her for the necessary eleven years? Not that that mattered. Contacts could, indeed should, be changed to avoid danger. Like codes.

The car was being driven in the same distinctive fashion as on the road through Great Ogridge. It was Italian driving. Gear, brake, squeal, rev, gear, brake, squeal, rev. Everything being worked to excess.

He edged nearer the road to get a better view and caught his head on a branch of May. He only half stifled his cry of pain. Aldhelm gave a little jump and turned round. He seemed to be staring straight at Bognor, but the car was almost on them. The friar turned back slowly and walked into the road. There was a final burst of acceleration, then a sudden rip down through the gears until the car slowed to walking pace alongside the staddlestone. The nearside door was flung open and Aldhelm leapt in. Without even stopping the 'E'-Type jerked forward like a jet approaching take-off and shot down the road and out of Bognor's vision.

There was another virtuoso sequence of gear changing and the noise subsided into the distance. The whole episode was finished without Bognor being able to distinguish anything about the driver except for the long blonde hair. He would swear to that. Also that the car was red and almost certainly an 'E'-Type, well, some sort of sports car.

He would like to have given chase, but Sir Erris's Land-Rover shook horribly at speeds over eighty and was certainly no match for a fast car driven with that sort of élan. Instead he extricated himself in a series of almost stealthy movements, brushed himself down, and ambled back through the waist-high grass to the waiting Land-Rover. He got in and sat staring down the high khaki bonnet across the road through the heat haze to the shimmering hills beyond.

'Sing Heigh for the Old Manor at Melbury,' he said idiotically. 'And a nasty surprise for Brother Aldhelm.' A nasty surprise too for that pillar of the 1922 committee, the Rt. Hon. Basil Strudwick. He pictured the headlines: 'Tory Member's wife in Secrets Case.' 'L'affaire Strudwick.' He steered the vehicle back on the road and pointed her in the direction of Great Ogridge.

It was only ten miles to Melbury, but he was in no hurry. By the time he had taken two wrong turnings and ended up once in a farmyard and once in the middle of a field of cattle threequarters of an hour had elapsed. The village itself was pretty and unspoilt by the demands of tourism; no antique shops, no cream teas, but a distinguished Norman church, a listed tithe barn and seventeenth-century cottages bowed under the weight of roses and clematis and honeysuckle. It was bisected by the River Cherwell, which ran under a narrow hump-backed bridge near the post office. The Old Manor itself was two miles downstream.

An old man sitting on a bench staring blankly into the road gave him directions and said elliptically, 'She'm there. He'm not.' Bognor found the dialect as confusing as the directions. Eventually he came on it quite by chance: an open gateway and a tiny Cotswold stone lodge with a thatched roof. He drove slowly past and saw that the drive curved away up a gentle incline and through a copse of lime trees. The house was invisible. For a moment he pondered on whether to walk up or drive, then reversed and turned up the well-maintained gravel. After half a mile the drive swung sharply to the right and dropped away to a shallow hollow which contained the Old Manor. It was small as manors go—more like an Old Rectory—but exquisite. Bognor guessed William and Mary. Everything about it was immaculate. The red brick had been recently re-pointed, the heavy white front door shone with new paint and the lawn which sloped away towards an Indian file of weeping willows had been recently mown. There was a smell of new cuttings and instead of green parallel lines there were squares like Battenburg cake. It was an effect he had only seen in pictures.

He had parked the Land-Rover at the top of the incline so that he could take stock.

Again he paused, wondering whether to leave it concealed or to adopt the overt full-frontal approach. He decided on the latter—he had nothing to hide—and nosed the Land-Rover downhill, bringing it to an abrupt halt immediately behind the red 'E'-Type, which sat, still steaming, on the wide turning area immediately in front of the door. He glanced casually in. That was curious. On the passenger seat was a heavy brown bundle, like sacking. He leant down and examined it briefly. It was coarse and damp to the touch and when he lifted the corner he saw the white dressing-gown cord. Bognor raised his eyebrows.

He turned to the front door. There was a wrought-iron handle on the right-hand side and he pulled it firmly. From a long way away there came an answering clang. Rather old-fashioned. He turned back to the lawn and shaded his eyes to take in the view. The line of willows, he reasoned, must be the river bank. They needed pollarding, which was unusual, since everything else was so well maintained. It was a pity. Not only would the willows be lucky to survive if they were left like that many more years, it meant that the river itself and the bank beyond were obscured from the house. He rang the bell again and wandered to the first tall window on the left . . . Looking through, he saw panelling and chintz and portraits of ancestors. They looked unreal; even, though Bognor baulked at the thought, fake. Strudwick's ancestors were small shopkeepers. Strudwick had pulled himself up by the boot-straps. Hence the affected mannerisms and fruity accents, and, of course, the reactionary politics.

There was still no reply. Either they were not going to answer, which was unlikely, or they were somewhere in the grounds. If they were inside it would be a problem. He couldn't very well break in. There would be questions; Camberley, for one, would have a fit.

He tried the door. People rarely locked doors in the country, unless, he reflected sadly, they were keeping honey safe. It didn't budge. He shrugged. There were two alternatives. He could sit in the Land-Rover and wait for something to happen. If he did he might wait for ever. There were back doors, and almost certainly at least one other car in the garage. Better to be positive and make a search. He decided to leave the formal rose garden, and whatever lay behind the high brick wall (vegetables probably), till later and start with the river. His feet walking across the forecourt made a noise like a man eating toast. It was still very hot and the small of his back was wet.

He had only gone half a dozen paces when he noticed something lying on the grass just in front of him. It was grey and brown and he judged, on closer inspection, a size nine. He picked it up and put it down hastily. Brother Aldhelm had very sweaty feet. He looked round for its mate and saw it five yards away.

'One habit, brown, in seat of car. One pair sandals on lawn,' he said out loud, and walked on. A few yards further on he found another pair of sandals. They had rope soles. He judged a size four: the grass was extraordinary, almost entirely devoid of divots or daisies, almost artificial it was so perfectly green. It was easy to pick out any alien object against its velvet surface. The next one was a man's shirt about thirty yards further on. He squatted on his haunches and looked inside the collar.

'Size fifteen and a half. Marks and Spencer.' He wrinkled his nose and wondered which friar was in charge of laundering.

The line of willows was quite close now and he noticed that the lawn merged into a rough shrubbery of azaleas and rhododendrons as it dipped away towards the river bank.

About fifty yards beyond the Marks and Spencer shirt was another: a flimsy filmy cream one with an Yves St. Laurent label. The smell was just as strong as on the other and as familiar to Bognor, but it was some compound of jasmine rather than B.O. Could it be one of the Floris scents? he wondered, inhaling and trying to remember where he'd last smelt it. Somewhere expensive. Just short of the first of the rhododendrons he found a pair of fawn cotton slacks.

'So that's what they wear under their habits,' he thought with a genuine sense of discovery.

Now he was almost certain what he was going to see and he stopped, embarrassed. He had no wish to play the voyeur, but he could be wrong and he had to be sure. He brushed between a couple of Japanese shrubs and dropped hurriedly to the ground, hiding himself behind the trunk of the nearest willow. Farther down the bank and slightly to the right was a pile of clothing: something lilac which he judged to be women's trousers, a grubby pair of aertex pants and something very small and black and frilly.

His embarrassment, by now most acute, made him redden dramatically.

The River Cherwell is not really a river at all, indeed at most points it is scarcely a stream, but a hundred yards downstream from Bognor's hiding place there was a narrow weir which served as a dam. The area from the weir to Bognor's willow was therefore almost an artificial lake, certainly a more than adequate swimming pool. His gaze moved across the river from the pile of clothes to a man standing in midstream. It was deep there and the water lapped round his shoulders occasionally coming close to the bottom of his jet black hair. As he watched, the man threw himself forward and started to crawl, powerfully and elegantly, to the far bank.

Watching him from a sun trap on the other side of the Cherwell was the woman Bognor assumed to be the wife of Basil Strudwick. She was a swimming bath's length away but he could still see that, despite being very slightly hidden by some giant buttercups, she was very lovely, extremely brown and quite naked. He watched for a moment longer as the man reached the shore, clambered out, stood up, shook himself like a dog, then turned for a second to look back at the water. Bognor had no doubt about the handsome face and the glistening black hair swept back from its widow's peak. Pulling himself together with a sudden sense of shame, he scrambled backwards until he was out of range, then rose and walked back to the Land-Rover. Questions would have to be put to Brother Aldhelm and his mistress, but it would be hardly proper to do so at a time like this. It would have been possible for him to have stripped off, swum across, and caught them *in flagrante*. Possible but hardly delicate. The role of *People* investigator was not one which greatly appealed to him, and if Brother Aldhelm wished to spend his afternoon making love to married ladies he supposed that that was his affair. If the married lady was feeding him secret information that was different. He wondered if it were possible.

It was tempting to threaten Aldhelm with giving the story to Anselm. He smiled at the thought of Anselm's reaction, arrived back at the Land-Rover and sat down to await the return of the loving couple.

He had forgotten his head in the vicarious excitement of the afternoon's experience, and also the tablets he had taken to stop the pain. So once more he had dozed off without meaning to. He woke to the sound of laughter.

Jerking alert he hit his hand on the metal of the door. It hurt. The sun had made it hot. Brother Aldhelm and Mrs. Strudwick had emerged from the rhododendrons and were playing some esoteric lovers' game. From this distance it looked like leapfrog. Bognor had a distinct feeling of recent familiarity and remembered the cabbage whites frolicking on the hill above the Friary. Mrs. Strudwick was wearing the lilac trousers, Brother Aldhelm his cotton trousers. Mrs. Strudwick leapt over Brother Aldhelm and somersaulted. Brother Aldhelm collapsed in a heap. Mrs. Strudwick pulled him up and the two kissed passionately. Bognor wondered when they would notice the

Land-Rover, and also if it would be before Mrs. Strudwick had retrieved her blouse. He had no wish to embarrass anyone. Not unduly.

The two continued their playful progress, apparently totally oblivious to anything beyond their relationship. Mrs. Strudwick put on her blouse and Bognor watched half regretfully as she did. She had an astonishingly good figure. They kissed yet again. Bognor was feeling progressively more embarrassed. Their relationship appeared to be totally carnal and if they were actually passing on secrets they did not appear, on the face of it, to have a great deal to do with agricultural plant. They were so close to him now that it was ridiculous. He noticed Aldhelm's crucifix swinging as they played a quick round of tag and decided that it was time this merriment came to an end. After all, he was investigating a couple of peculiarly brutal murders, and his personal embarrassment mustn't interfere with that.

He jumped down, landing with a crackling thud on the gravel and slamming the door behind him at the same time. It worked. His twin suspects were about to embark on some gay skipping cavort when they heard the sudden sound. They stopped immediately, almost in mid-flight, and looked briefly like a modern realist sculpture.

Mrs. Strudwick was the first to recover. She came striding across the grass wearing an outraged expression. Bognor noticed with guilty pleasure that it really made little difference whether she wore the blouse or not. It was totally transparent. The anger, assumed or otherwise, suited her. She was strikingly, if conventionally, attractive, with very long natural blonde hair and a few freckles across the bridge of her nose, and she moved well.

'This is private property,' she said. There was a hint of foreign accent there, though it was somehow contrived. A bit like an English waitress in a French restaurant.

Bognor was excited by angry ladies. She had not put her sandals on in her excitement and she didn't realise until halfway across the gravel. She yelped and started to hobble. It ruined the effect. Brother Aldhelm, who, despite his anxiety, had had the intelligence to put on his own sandals and pick up hers, came running after her. She leant on his back as he helped her on with them.

'Leave this to me, Lena,' he said, and addressed himself to Bognor.

'What in God's name are you doing here?' he shouted.

'I'm sorry,' said Bognor, 'but I'm here for a very serious reason.'

'Don't threaten me.' He was half an inch taller than Bognor, a year or two younger and in much better condition.

'I wouldn't dream of it; anyway I wasn't.'

'Then what are you doing?'

'Making some enquiries.'

'You must be bloody joking.'

Lena Strudwick was looking with perplexity from one to the other.

'Would someone please tell me what the hell's going on?' she asked. The trace of foreign accent was less noticeable, and superseded by something less glamorous. Bognor placed it tentatively as Battersea or Clapham. 'Do you two know each other?'

'We have met,' said Bognor.

'No,' said Aldhelm.

'Look, mister.' She walked across to Bognor and came to a halt about a foot short of him. 'If you're trying anything, if you're trying to fix something with my husband, then you'd better forget it. 'Cos he's not going to believe a bloody word you tell him, and if you so much as try anything like that, then I tell you, mate, it's curtains.' She emphasised the last remark by moving her right hand swiftly across her throat, as if to cut it.

'Honestly,' said Bognor, 'I have absolutely no intention of embarrassing either you or Mr. Strudwick. Not unless it turns out to be necessary.'

'And what exactly is that supposed to mean?'

'Darling. Please leave it to me.' Aldhelm seemed to have taken on a new lease of feebleness. He was plaintive.

'Don't you "darling" me,' she said with feeling. 'You got me into this bloody mess and I'm not trusting you to get me out of it. Who is he?'

'He's a policeman. From London. I wish you'd listen.'

The information silenced her, if only momentarily.

'Why didn't you say so?' she asked a moment later. 'Have you got any identification? No, skip it.' She looked at Bognor as if she hadn't noticed him before. 'Yes. So you are. I should have recognised you. Well, what do you want? There's no law against it, you know.'

'I know that.' Bognor was flattered at being taken for a policeman.

'Well, what do you want then?'

He suddenly felt agonisingly tired. His last doze had been hours ago, immediately after lunch. He blinked heavily.

'A drink, if at all possible.'

'A what?'

'A drink.'

'You have the bloody nerve to come barging in here, poking your bloody nose in where you don't belong and then you have the fucking cheek to turn round and ask for a drink.' She stopped and examined him even more closely. Then her mood changed. She smiled, showing a couple of dimples and fine, even teeth. 'You look knackered,' she said. 'All right, let's all have a drink.' She turned to Brother Aldhelm, who was looking progressively less happy. 'Come on, sexy!' she said. 'Plenty of time before prayers, and your friend here will drive you back.'

There were no servants, since for obvious reasons they tended to be given the afternoon off. However, within moments Mrs. Strudwick came into the drawing room with three silver goblets and a bottle of vintage Bollinger.

'One of the great joys of being stinking rich,' she said in mock simpering aristocratic tones, 'is that there is always, but always, champagne in the fridge.'

Bognor explained slowly, leaving practically everything out. All he revealed was that he was not convinced of Batty Thomas's suicide and that he therefore had to follow up anything which seemed remotely suspicious. He said nothing about secrets.

'You creep,' said Mrs. Strudwick, when he retailed their meeting after Thomas's death. 'Why didn't you tell me?' Aldhelm said nothing.

'So,' said Bognor when he had finished, 'I for my part undertake not to say anything about this either to Mr. Strudwick or to Father Anselm. Not unless or until I charge one or other of you with murder . . . in return for which I'd be grateful if you'd answer a few questions.'

'Fair enough,' sad Mrs. Strudwick, who seemed infinitely more relaxed, almost indeed to be enjoying herself. She lay back on the sofa and watched globules of icy moisture beginning to trickle down the side of her goblet. 'Only I don't see what makes you suspect either of us.'

'Simply,' said Bognor, 'that within minutes of our second death I come across your . . . er Brother Aldhelm, our friend here, in a state of considerable excitement. On the point of making a secret rendezvous. You have to admit that's suspicious.'

'He's always excited after lunch,' said Mrs. Strudwick, looking at Brother Aldhelm, sceptically. 'You might not think it to look at him, but he's not a bad performer.' Brother Aldhelm stared angrily into his Bollinger.

'How long has this been going on?' asked Bognor, primly.

Mrs. Strudwick thought. 'We met at the church fête,' she said. 'They had a stall, and I rather fancied him. I've always wanted a priest and I've never had the chance before. So I asked him out to tea. That would be about three months ago.'

'And you meet every afternoon?'

'More or less. Unless Basil's here.'

'I see.'

'You don't.' Mrs. Strudwick stretched out a leg and wiggled her toes, which were painted. 'But it doesn't matter. I've never had a policeman either. Still, I'm not sure I really fancy the idea. As for murder, well, Aldo here's not exactly a model brother of St. Francis but I don't think he'd kill anyone. Would you, Aldo?'

Brother Aldhelm looked up petulantly. 'I wish you'd stop treating me as if I were your pet dog,' he said.

'You said it, dear,' she said. 'You said it.'

Brother Aldhelm shrugged. 'I don't see why you can't accept that Thomas killed Brother Luke and committed suicide,' he said.

'Reasons,' said Bognor, with an air of importance.

'In any case,' added Aldhelm, 'you know I couldn't have killed Thomas if it was done during lunch. I was sitting next to you all through.'

'You were in an awful hurry to get away afterwards.'

'I should have thought the reason for that was fairly obvious.'

Bognor gave Mrs. Strudwick a stare. 'Yes,' he said. She raised her eyebrows and inclined her head. 'You're too kind,' she said.

They finished the champagne in silence, then Mrs. Strudwick said she had to change, and observed frostily that they were going to be late for Evensong if they didn't hurry.

'You can find your own way out,' she said. 'Same time Monday, Aldo?' He looked at her reproachfully and nodded.

'Same time.' She turned to Bognor and held out a hand.

'I enjoyed meeting you, Inspector,' she smiled. 'Any time you happen to be passing, do drop in. Only try to give us a little warning next time.'

The drive home was not a success. Brother Aldhelm was most unhappy. His clandestine afternoon behaviour had been discovered and he was under suspicion of murder. It was a sharp double blow for a man who that morning had been a normal, unremarkable member of a respectable religious community.

'You won't tell Father Anselm?' he said as they whined through Melbury.

'Not if you don't want me to.'

'I'd get the sack if he found out. Straight away. Like Bede.'

'Quite right too.'

It was a red berring. Bognor was almost sure of it. The woman, albeit stunningly sexy, was a standard case of bored nymphomania and the seduction of Brother Aldhelm was dreadfully crude but quite in character. Nothing in the behaviour of either of them suggested espionage. And yet . . .

'You could have killed Luke,' he said.

'I was weeding,' said Aldhelm.

'Not much of an excuse. It wouldn't have taken you ten seconds to whip across to the potato patch, pull the chain, and back to the dandelions and the daisies.'

'Why?'

'Maybe he'd found out about your affair.'

Brother Aldhelm gazed out of the window. At length he said: 'I didn't do it.'

'You can hardly expect me to take your word for it.'

'No.'

'If it's any consolation,' said Bognor, feeling some sympathy for the man's considerable unhappiness, 'I don't, on balance, think you did kill him. But if you have any idea of who might have done it would be a help if you let me know.'

Aldhelm looked at him scornfully. 'That's a pretty old trick,' he said. 'It's the sort of thing Luke used to try. He was a snooper, like you.'

Bognor's foot slipped and he accelerated into a corner and skidded, then looked across to see if the Friar was shaken. Not in the least. He remembered the maniacal driving of La Strudwick.

'Have it your own way,' he said. 'Just remember that I know your secret. That's all.'

Neither man spoke again until after they had driven past the trysting staddlestone. Bognor was depressed by the further evidence of Collingdale's carelessness, Aldhelm rapt in his self-pity. As he slowed the Land-Rover almost to a standstill before negotiating the descent to the Friary, Bognor said suddenly, and for no particular reason, 'What did you do before you came here?'

Aldhelm's reply was equally spontaneous. 'Civil service,' he said. 'I was a clerk at the Admiralty.' Bognor's brows furrowed. *That* sounded suspicious.

## CHAPTER FIVE

They were almost late for Evensong, but Bognor was in no mood for church. He left Aldhelm to wrestle with his conscience and instead walked down to the Boot, smiling to himself as he heard the increasingly familiar drone of plainsong drifting down the lane from the chapel. There was a hint of autumn chill in the air and more than a hint in the interior of the Boot. No doubt about it, Mr. Hey had got a problem with his damp course. He didn't suppose that the pub ran to champagne of any sort, let alone Bollinger, so he ordered himself the conventional whisky and bought Mr. Hey a mild-and-bitter.

'Been to see Mr. Strudwick, have you, then?' Mr. Hey leered across the bar.

Bognor was disconcerted. 'Why? Should I have?'

Mr. Hey looked knowing. 'Surprising what

you find out just sitting behind a bar and minding your own business,' he said. 'Now I don't say I've had your professional training, but I'm not above putting two and two together.'

'No.'

'Well, you were asking about Mrs. Strudwick's car yesterday?'

'True.'

'Well, I mention it to Father Xavier, see, before lunch. And he tells me what I know already. That one of they brothers spends a lot of his time over at the Old Manor. And so between us we reckon you'll be going over to have a look-see.'

'Oh.'

'Reckon we were right.'

'I'm sorry I couldn't tell you if you were.' Yet again Bognor felt unnecessarily patronised.

'That's all right.' Mr. Hey was unspeakably arch. 'I tell you, though. Nothing new in that. Nor dangerous. That lot, like I was telling you the first night you came in. That lot up there they don't know the meaning of words like poverty and chastity and obedience. I reckon I'm more chaste than most of them, the wife being what she is, if you'll pardon the expression. Only I'll say one thing, it's not usually women they go for, and that's a fact.' Mr. Hey swilled mild-and-bitter round his mouth and continued. 'Then I heard the news.

They've sacked another for writing to the papers. We had a young lad in here today from one of the Sunday papers. Didn't tell him nothing, though. Said Father Anselm sent him away with a flea in his ear.'

The combination of champagne, whisky, aspirin not to mention the effects of his injuries themselves were making Bognor distinctly euphoric.

'That will be a good story for the Sundays,' he said.

'I don't know,' said Mr. Hey. 'There's a lot else going on. They've smashed a big drug ring down Bicester way. Then there's an air crash near Manchester and this sodding Summit conference. Can't see anyone bothering much about friars, even if they are like this lot here.'

Mr. Hey, elated by his percipience, bought Bognor another Scotch. 'Father Xavier, though,' he said. 'He may not be a very holy man, but he's a real gentleman. My best customer.'

'Is he the only one who comes in here?'

'Well, that would be telling, wouldn't it, sir?'

'I suppose so.'

'I think,' Mr. Hey was clearly not averse to telling if he felt like it, and he was enjoying the role of informer, 'he's the only one. Though of course, you can't be sure. Sometimes he comes in with one of the younger fellows. Not often, though.'

'Oh, which one?'

'Don't know his name, sir. Father Xavier always makes a joke of it when he does. Talks about "corrupting the innocents".'

Bognor had a dog-eared ham sandwich and ate it while Mr. Hey served the cowhands with pints and exchanged some esoteric information about silage. It sounded careless of Xavier to share his secret drinking with another member of the Community. He wondered who it was. Mr. Hey continued talking to the farmhands for a few minutes while Bognor considered the drink and the drugs and his curious body of evidence. In the course of his short stay he felt that he had learnt enough to get the Friary dissolved, but little that was of much use in solving his own problems. It was one thing to find that a supposedly austere and proper institution was in fact an establishment which exhibited a degeneracy of medieval proportions, though that was an exaggeration, quite another to pin a murder on one of its number. He was wondering whether another drink would make him fall over when Father Xavier came in. He had another drink.

'One guess,' said Xavier, when he'd taken the first gulp. 'You've discovered Aldhelm's guilty secret.'

'What do you mean?'

Father Xavier gave an exaggerated sigh. 'Oh, all right,' he said. 'You're not a policeman, no one's dead, God's in his heaven and I'm the Virgin Mary.' He ordered a second Scotch. 'You still look ropey,' he said, sizing Bognor up, 'so I'll forgive you and for absolutely nothing, free, gratis and no strings attached or punches pulled, I will tell you that this afternoon you followed Brother Aldhelm to the house of the wife of Mr. B. Strudwick, M.P. You don't have to tell me. I know.'

'How?'

'Because you asked our jovial host here about Mr. Strudwick's car, because I observed you from my artist's chair earlier today belting off to the Land-Rover like a demented cat, and because I know that the Strudwick woman has got her sexual claws into the unfortunate Aldhelm. Satisfied?'

'How do you know?'

'Observation. Chatter. Intuition.'

'Who else knows?'

'Who else cares?' Xavier grinned. 'A few of us. Not many. Not that bitch Anselm, thank God. And . . .' He was serious. 'For God's sake don't let him guess. There's nothing wrong with Aldhelm. Just for now one person getting the push is quite enough.'

They drank on in silence. Then Bognor asked him about his drinking companion. For a moment he thought Xavier seemed flustered, but it was only a moment and he was feeling absurdly light-headed.

'Brother Hey talks too much,' said Xavier. 'It's true that . . . from time to time I regale a young friend with a pint of shandy and a round of Mr. Hey's succulent sandwiches. But where, I ask myself, is the harm in that?'

'Who?'

Father Xavier smiled. 'At times,' he said, 'I feel you are a remarkably poor detective. Be more oblique. More stealthy. I'll leave you to find out for yourself. There's no point in making things too easy for you. You must work for your living.'

'I am,' said Bognor, with feeling. 'Believe me, I am.'

Xavier claimed a sermon to prepare, and Bognor, who wanted to make another attempt on the mystery of the secret cupboard, needed more sleep. They left together.

'Retreat tomorrow,' said Xavier, as they strode through the dusk.

'All going ahead as planned?'

'So I believe. Vivian picked some up from the station late this afternoon. The appalling old Bishop arrives at crack of dawn tomorrow.'

'How many people?'

'About fifteen or sixteen. You'd have to ask Barnabas for the exact number. Anselm's in a terrible state because he's quite sure the *News of the World* are going to try and sneak one of their reporters in dressed as a retreating visitor. Not a bad idea at that. How much do you think they'd pay for my story?'

'Quite a bit for the whole story.'

'Yes,' said Xavier, 'I suppose they would. For the whole story.' They said good night.

This time he woke when he'd intended, at midnight precisely. He switched on the light and read the text on the wall, 'He that loveth his life loseth it; and he that hateth his life in this world shall keep it unto life eternal.' It depressed him. His head nagged and he felt hung-over. He'd also been dreaming. What about? He forced himself to concentrate and remembered with a slight shame that he had been dining expensively and to excess with a naked Mrs. Strudwick. If he was becoming the victim of his frustrations already, what could it have been like for poor Collingdale?

He got up and washed, then walked carefully out of the hut. It was quite unlike the night before. There was no need for a torch because the moon was bright and shone from a cloudless sky illuminating the silhouettes of the buildings and the line of the hills to the south. He could clearly see each one of the Pleiades and the Milky Way for once lived up to its name. There were no lights from any of the rooms and no noise. From the middle distance of the hillside a fox barked raspingly, to be echoed away on his left by an answering dry animal cough. He waited with his breath held for an owl to hoot, and was rewarded. That meant good luck.

This time he was not going to be caught. He slid almost professionally along the side of the buildings, pausing as before at every corner and in every doorway, to look about him. Whereas before the exercise had been futile, tonight it was easy to see for yards. If anything had moved he would have spotted it. Besides, there was an incentive. Last night he had not expected trouble—certainly not physical assault. Tonight nothing would surprise him.

One door short of the honey-store he paused for a last look round and slipped the metal rule from his pocket. He peered about him for a full minute. A sudden movement made him swing round, and he clearly saw a large rat freeze for a second, staring at him before squeezing into a hole behind a drain-pipe. With almost exaggerated stealth he moved to the honey-door itself, waited a moment as before, and pushed. To his surprise it again gave under his pressure. He opened it gently and stepped inside closing it after him, then stood inside the room, pressed hard against the wall to get his bearings. It took him a second to get accustomed to the new light; but it was not as difficult as it might have been because there was a thin light coming from all round the cupboard door, as there had been the night before. The room was unchanged. Just honey and trestles. He peered anxiously for the sight of a potential assailant waiting in a shadow, but satisfied himself that there was no one there.

To be doubly sure he moved round the room rather than across the middle, still hugging the wall. It took him several minutes to get to the cupboard door this way, but the pain in his head reminded him that caution was worth while. Once there, he put his ear to the crack and listened. There was noise.

Oddly, perhaps, he relaxed. Although he was increasingly aware of the sinister or at least debauched undercurrents of the place he was still conditioned to think of the brothers as harmless, extrovert, God-fearing souls from whom he had nothing to fear. At that moment he should by rights have had a clear picture of Collingdale face down among the potato plants and of Batty Thomas lying wet, cold and bloody by the well-side. Instead he felt at ease because he knew what he was going to meet: smiling homely religious men who wished no harm to any man. Despite this unwarranted complacence, he took one final look behind him and round the room. There was no one there. He bent down once more and heard again the low murmur of human conversation and found the sound oddly reassuring. He put his left hand round the handle, his left shoulder to the door, drew a breath, turned and pushed. The door swung open and he found himself in a small room illuminated by a single swinging naked bulb.

Four faces looked up at him, blankly, surprised, resigned. Immediately opposite him at the far end of the table was Father John, staring at him myopically, mouth half open with incomprehension. On either side of him sat Brother Barnabas, his misty thick glasses turned to him in a similar expression of surprise and disbelief, and Father Simon, his sparrow-like features twitching mildly as he tried to grapple with the implications of the intrusion. The fourth man sat with his back to Bognor, but as he had entered he had spun round to face him. Bognor recognised the swarthy, unintelligent, countryman's face of Brother Vivian.

In his hands each man clasped a number of playing cards. In front of each was a glass and a number of matchsticks. In the middle of the table were two bottles, one unopened, the other almost empty. Against the walls were two buckets, a length of hose, a large blue packet, some bags of sugar and a wine rack containing several dozen more bottles. Bognor assimilated these details and turned back to the four faces.

'Good evening,' he said, and then, because he could think of nothing appropriate to ask, he added fatuously: 'Are you playing poker or whist?'

Father John was the first to regain some semblance of composure. 'Since you ask,' he said, 'we are playing a form of poker known in this instance as "Chicago". Usually we play stud. I'm afraid,' and here he indicated the matches, 'that the stakes are not as high as those to which you are most probably used. Otherwise we would ask you to join us.'

Father Simon was less urbane. 'Oh dear,' he said. 'How very embarrassing. I don't think, John, that that sort of thing makes anything better.'

Barnabas went scarlet but managed to say 'Hello'. Only Vivian remained totally silent.

Bognor continued to stare. John and Simon sat on wooden chairs with backs, Barnabas and Vivian had to make do with orange boxes. The table was rotting slowly and covered in peeling lino, the walls, once whitewashed, were grey with grime and cobwebs, the atmosphere was as damp as the Boot's. He leant over Vivian's shoulder and took the almost empty bottle in his left hand, drew it back and held the neck to his nose. It was disgusting. One quick inhalation was enough. He wrinkled his nose and returned it to the table. 'So that's where the honey goes.'

'Very perceptive of you,' said Father John. 'Why are you here?'

Bognor found this disingenuous. 'You can surely answer that,' he said petulantly.

'Yesterday,' said Father John, 'you assured me that you were no longer pursuing professional inquiries.'

'I did admit to a lively personal curiosity,' countered Bognor, 'and when you were so reluctant to let me in on the innermost secrets of your honey store, I came back to have another look. And that was when someone—one of you I presume—hit me hard on the head. That, of course, was you, Brother Vivian. How do you do. We haven't met formally. Now what on earth made you do an anti-social thing like that?' He suddenly felt in a strong position, and his diffidence diminished.

Brother Vivian glowered.

'He didn't mean it,' said Brother Barnabas. 'It was a mistake. I mean he was late that night and he came in and he found you listening at the door and he was carrying his spanner from the van and, well, he hit you. You can't blame him. It might have been anyone.'

'We did try to make amends,' said Father Simon. 'I know it was the most distressing accident, but I bathed your wound myself, and we put you to bed, and we washed your clothes and got them dried out. I assure you there was absolutely no personal malice involved. It was purely accidental.'

'If you hadn't been so nosy,' said Father John, 'you wouldn't have got hurt. It's your own fault. If you choose to prowl around private property at the dead of night you've only yourself to blame if you get hit on the head. Anyway. Now you're here sit down and have a glass of mead.'

Bognor accepted the proffered orange box and, more reluctantly, the mead.

'It's a new one this year,' said Father Simon. 'There's an infusion of tarragon. Rather special.' He was silenced by Father John, who clearly wished to retain the chairmanship of this meeting.

'Let us assume for the sake of argument,' he said, 'that you are still genuinely and professionally concerned about some aspect of recent events here at Beaubridge. Let us further assume that for reasons best known to yourself you wish to conceal this concern from members of the Community. Ergo . . .' he paused, 'ergo, you are compelled to adopt unorthodox methods, and to follow any suspicions which may present themselves. By so doing you stumble upon circumstances which have no bearing whatever on the events with which we are all familiar.' He sipped with an old man's gentility at his mead, and Bognor suddenly realised that he, and probably all four of them, were at least slightly tipsy. He took a sip himself. It was unbearably sticky and sweet and the tarragon gave it no bite or edge, but it was still a strong drink.

'How long do you let this stuff ferment?' he asked.

'Whole business takes about nine months,' said Brother Barnabas. 'Not bad, eh?' He laughed nervously.

Father John continued: 'And so we find ourselves in such embarrassing circumstances as this. It is at least arguable that you were compelled to investigate the matter of the locked door. It is surely not in dispute that our nightly rendezvous are of no relevance to the deaths of our friends and colleagues.'

'I don't see why not,' said Bognor, trying to look knowing. 'One deceit can easily lead to another. It's an ideal place for plotting. And since on your own admission one of you attacked me viciously last night you are clearly prepared to stop at nothing to protect your secret. Or very little.' Bognor pondered inwardly: One or other of them might have committed murder; might have connived at the passing on of secrets; but in itself he feared that this bromide Hell Fire Club was a self-contained irrelevance. Like the Strudwick-Aldhelm liaison it was an end in itself. A dead end. Or maybe not. He wished he could be certain.

'That doesn't follow,' said Father John. 'If as you seem to suggest there were two murders then they were both done in cold blood. In your case the attack was unpremeditated and justifiable. And when we found out who you were we went to considerable trouble to alleviate the extent of the injuries.' He opened the second bottle of mead.

'Rosemary,' whispered Father Simon. 'A tried favourite. You'll like it.'

'How long has this been going on?' asked Bognor, for the second time that day.

'I've been making it for over twelve years now,' said John. 'And Simon and I have been drinking it for almost as long. Our brothers here entered later. It was they who suggested the cards.' He looked censorious, and quickly became even more prim. 'There's nothing against it, you know. Nothing in the rule. Our Lord drank. If I didn't think that Anselm would be very upset by the idea I would press it on him more fervently. I did suggest to him years ago that it would be more desirable and more lucrative to export our own individual brands of mead rather than just honey, but he insisted that it was sacrilege. And I'm afraid that when the Abbot convinces himself of an idea there is no changing him.' Bognor tried the rosemary mead. It was an improvement. Still too sweet, but not *as* sweet.

'If,' he said, 'I were to tell Father Anselm what I have seen here tonight, all four of you would have to leave the Community.' There was a silence. The four men stared morosely at the table and the bottles. Brother Vivian spoke for the first time.

'Doesn't follow,' he said.

'No,' said John. 'It doesn't follow at all. I agree that it's perhaps irregular. But we don't gamble for money and everything else is entirely above board and would scarcely be noticed in a less strait-laced community. Considering that we are a modern foundation the rule here is extremely strict.'

'Father Anselm,' said Bognor, 'would demand your resignation.'

'He could demand away,' said Barnabas. 'He wouldn't have mine.'

'They're entirely right,' said John. 'In the last resort, of course, we would appeal to the Visitor or conceivably to Convocation. I don't happen to believe that Father Anselm would choose to make such an issue of it. Particularly in view of the rather parlous situation Beaubridge finds itself in at this moment. Nevertheless . . .' He smiled at Bognor in a pathetic attempt at ingratiation. 'It would be preferable if nothing were said to Father Anselm. Particularly as it would seem to serve no useful purpose.'

Bognor looked from one to the other. He would like them to have pleaded a little more. His head had ached desperately for over twenty-four hours now and he wanted some comfort.

'I don't know,' he said. 'Apart from any infringement of your rule, which I admit is an internal affair, I could have been killed last night.'

'Well, I for one,' said Simon, 'am very sorry about that. I think we all owe you an apology.'

The others chorused agreement, Barnabas with enthusiasm, John and Vivian with markedly less.

'I accept that.' Bognor was happy to appear magnanimous. 'But I just can't promise. At the very least I want a lot more co-operation from you than I've been getting in the past.'

Vivian looked particularly surly. 'Should have finished the job,' he muttered. 'One more bang would have done it.'

Father John resumed his chairmanship. 'Don't be infantile, Vivian. Apart from being unnecessarily vindictive and totally impractical, it's not getting us anywhere. Everyone's cards,' he gestured stagily at the remains of the night's poker, 'are on the table. Mr. Bognor here is threatening us with exposure unless we collaborate. Correct?'

'Co-operate, not collaborate,' said Bognor. This was more satisfactory.

'A nice point,' said John. 'What do you want from us?'

'For a start,' said Bognor, with a flash of inspiration, 'I want a list of every person who has been on a retreat here during the last eleven years. And I want it by breakfast tomorrow.'

There was an almost tangible sigh of surprise and relief. 'Is that all?' asked John.

'I don't know yet. I might want more. I'll tell you in the morning. In any case I shall certainly want a great deal more helpfulness than I've had so far.' He drained his mead, and coughed, then scraped back his orange box. 'Well, thank you, gentlemen,' he said. 'That's been most enlightening. And now I'll leave you to your game.'

Outside in the moonlit courtyard he could have cried with frustration. Yesterday he had had two mysteries and with them the prospect of some meaningful discoveries. At the end of today he had solved both and in doing so solved nothing. And then there was the maddening way Erris Beg had told Camberley everything he had wanted to conceal from him. That was bad enough. But for Camberley to go and tell Anselm . . .

Tomorrow he would embark on a different tack. He was not going to be deflected. He would stick rigidly to his brief and disregard the most suspicious behaviour unless it related specifically to murder or espionage. He groaned. How could one know?

He reached his room and undressed. Somewhere along the passage a man was snoring. It didn't worry him. Nothing could disturb his sleep even if he was still left with the same eight suspects that he'd had when he arrived. Tomorrow, he resolved, as he drifted into unconciousness, he would start to discover the link in the chain. If he couldn't find the guilty friar he could surely discover the guilty retreater. Then after the week-end he would confront Brother Bede. Dimly, as his conscious mind yielded to a confusion of naked monks playing poker by the banks of the River Cherwell, he remembered that Brother Bede was the only man who could have spied for all that time and done both murders. The memory brought a smile to his lips as he too began to snore.

* * *

'Retreat', as far as Bognor was concerned, was exactly the right word. The Retreat represented the high spot of the Friary's life. For the brothers it meant a period of devotion, sacrifice and abstinence, a time in which one's thoughts focussed exclusively on God. There was no room during a retreat for any but the most essential considerations. It was like school 'ginger weeks' when a normally severe military routine had been exaggerated to absurdity: cold baths were taken twice a day instead of once, one had to get dressed in three minutes, not seven, and dirty shoes were punished by a beating, not merely extra lines. The presence of the peppery and newly aggrieved Bishop of Woodstock introduced a further element—that of the annual inspection. Under his rigorous scrutiny everyone's essential holiness would have to be impeccable and evident.

He was musing drowsily at seven o'clock on

Saturday morning when Brother Barnabas entered with a cup of tea and some sheets of foolscap.

'Wakey Wakey, rise and shine,' said Brother Barnabas in an unconvincing demonstration of joviality.

Bognor regarded him beadily. 'I should have thought you might have a hangover,' he said.

Brother Barnabas smiled wanly. 'To tell you the truth,' he said, 'too much of that stuff leaves you a bit queasy the morning after.' He drew out the 'eee' of queasy, giving it a sonorousness that made Bognor feel quite ill himself. He drank some tea.

'Is that my list?'

'Yes. Father Simon and I spent a lot of time working on that. Luckily a lot of the names are the same, so we've used abbreviations. Otherwise it would have taken all night.' He handed Bognor the list. There was a lot of it.

Once Barnabas, who was one of the most difficult men to get rid of he had ever encountered, had actually left him to his tea, he began to scrutinise the list properly. Much of it was a waste of time. Entries like 'Party from Sherton School' or 'Delegation of African Bishops' or 'Archbishop's Commission on Divorce Law Reform' were surely irrelevant to murder and espionage, though in view of the story so far it would be cavalier to dismiss them too quickly. He blanched at the idea of African bishops becoming involved and took a pencil with which he swiftly crossed out all the seemingly impossibles. It still left a great many names. The Community, it appeared, organised some half-dozen formal retreats a year, but that took no account of those visitors who came to stay on their own without benefit of organisation. He went through the list again and began to pick out some recurring names. Again a few, like the Bishop of Woodstock himself, seemed unlikely and he crossed them out too. He was reducing the list quite fast.

There were some surprises in it and he began to see that a Friary was not such a bad place for espionage, after all. It reminded him of a call girl's diary in which respectable M.P.s and industrialists, family men all, would recur with remarkable frequency. There were several such people in Brother Barnabas's pages who had at various times visited the Friary in order to recharge their spiritual batteries. All of them could have passed on information of interest, but none of them had been with quite enough regularity to make them the professional agent for whom he was looking. He put the pages on one side and went to breakfast.

It was a silent meal, like every meal on a retreat weekend, and he had ample opportunity to look round. As yet only about half the visitors had arrived. There were a couple of clergymen in shiny grey suits with fraying dog collars; one or two young men with intense faces and very short hair who looked as if they might be joining as postulants before the week-end was over; a Benedictine monk, presumably on an exchange visit; a mousey old man in a sports coat with leather patches who must have been a schoolmaster; and a very young man with straggly hair wearing a T-shirt which bore the legend 'Michigan State University'. Bognor wondered if he was a friend of Brother Bede. It did not look very promising material.

After breakfast he sought out Father Simon and got a list of all those who were on this week-end's jaunt. They had unaccountably been left off.

'Not a frightfully exciting collection,' said Father Simon, twittering over his rimless spectacles. 'Except, of course, for the Bishop. I confess the Bishop does rather frighten me. I suppose you could say he puts the fear of God into me . . . ha ha.' He laughed very nervously and scratched the back of his head.

'Oh yes,' he said. 'And there's one late addition. Our Mr. Jones. Apparently he didn't think he'd be able to get away, but he changed his mind at the last minute. A very cultivated man Mr. Jones, though I wouldn't have thought an exceptionally Godly one. But then there's no telling, is there?'

'No,' said Bognor.

Father Simon blushed and looked reproachful. 'I do hope,' he said, 'that we are all going to be able to let bygones be bygones. Is your head better?'

'Not much,' said Bognor, and returned to his room and a further study of the lists. For a while he continued with his deletions and then when he had reduced the catalogue to more manageable proportions he switched over to a positive approach. It was possible that the contact would not be present this week-end. It depended very much on whether someone's nerve had been lost. He suspected that it hadn't and that a handover would be made, just as it had been every year for the past eleven. He took this week-end's list and compared it with the lists of eleven years before. There were three of the same names: two clergymen and someone called Wilfred Mortimer. He checked through the years to see how often Mortimer cropped up. The total count came to seven. That made Mortimer a distinct possible. That is if there were more than one carrier involved: seven years Mortimer, four A. N. Other. He went back to the original list and decided he couldn't bother with the clergymen. If they were the two he'd seen in breakfast they couldn't be less likely. However, he circled them with pencil and put a query by their names. Mortimer he underlined with another query.

He read the eleven-year-old names again and

was about to move on to the following year when he checked himself. What had Father Simon said? Oh yes. Jones. And there on the original list was one Edward Jones. What an exceptionally ordinary name! Suspiciously so. He felt a twinge of excitement and checked himself. No, he would not allow his intuition to betray himself into any more cul-de-sacs. He underlined Edward Jones and turned over a page. Brother Barnabas had carefully given each year its own page. Halfway down page two he found E.J. He underlined it again and turned over. There, a little nearer the bottom this time, were the same initials. Again he drew a single sharp line underneath and moved on. With mounting eagerness he continued this methodical progress through all eleven pages until after the final neat crisp line had been drawn, when he put down the pencil, and looked up at the sepia picture.

'Thank God!' he exclaimed with blasphemous enthusiasm. 'At last we're getting somewhere.'

It didn't take him long to find out. For the next hour or so he busied himself making careful notes. Under each of his eight names he wrote a short character sketch with additional observations about alibis and motives. Under Brother Bede's name he left a lot of space. That worried him. If Brother Bede was the guilty man—and he was the only one that he could see with the requisite triple opportunity—why had the man Jones come down for this week-end? If indeed Jones was the spy. Perhaps it was bluff. If Bede were guilty he must realise by now that Bognor had singled him out as the only man who could have passed on messages in the honey and killed twice. In which case what better way of throwing off pursuit than by getting oneself sacked and out of the way, and then making sure one's contact arrived in the Friary, and appeared to hand over information to someone else?

It was plausible and it would explain Mr. Jones's last-minute decision to come. Bognor pursed his lips. If Jones turned out to be a red herring he would become suicidal. He put on a jacket and started off to attend Sext. The Office represented the formal beginning of the Retreat and by the time it began everyone would have arrived. Brother Vivian was meeting the morning train at Woodstock, the Bishop was coming by car and so were a few others. He quickened his pace as the bell started to chime more insistently, nodded to Xavier, Simon and Anselm, who were standing in a silent group outside the chapel door, and found a seat in the second row of tubular-steel chairs.

He knelt for a moment in stylised prayer and then sat up and looked round. The choir stalls in front of him were the same as usual. He ran his eye up and down both sides sitting facing each other with arms folded across their chests, eyes raised in apparent contemplation of the stations of the cross. He faltered briefly at John, Barnabas, Vivian and Aldhelm, the only four suspects in the chapel, and again at his first acquaintance, Brother Paul. Once more he was struck by the boy's familiarity. He thought for a moment but couldn't place it. Suspect Bede was in South London. Suspects Anselm, Simon and Xavier still waiting outside. He looked back up the left-hand line and then started as he noticed something unusual. Beyond the furthest friar, and almost on top of the altar, was a heavy wooden chair with arms and a high carved back which he hadn't seen before. In it, under a panoply of golden crosses and shining vestments, sat a hunched purple-veined figure with massive grey eyebrows.

Bognor recognised the Right Reverend Bishop of Woodstock.

He shifted his gaze to his fellow guests in their metal and canvas chairs. They were, as Father Simon had suggested, an undistinguished lot. He wondered if the old man with the leather-patched jacket was Mortimer. If so, he could surely be dismissed. The two clergymen were also rabbits. The youth with the Michigan T-shirt was too young to be Jones, though he was the only one to look remotely possible.

From the belfry above, the bell slowed to a

final regular clang which meant that there was only a minute to kick-off. He opened his hymn-book, as advised, at Mr. E. H. Plumptre's Hymn 604. It was a sturdy processional. He rather went for processionals. Just as the bell stopped its chiming the pianist struck up and everyone stood. Considering there weren't above sixty people there, all told, the noise was formidable. His three remaining suspects, Anselm, Simon and Xavier—odd bedfellows if ever there were—entered in step as the congregation bellowed out 'Thy hand O God has guided' with the thunderous voice of the old Bishop clearly audible above the marginally more restrained utterances of the rest of his flock. Bognor, for once, was participating with such abandon that he failed to notice the small elderly man in the pepper and salt suit until they reached the refrain.

'One Church!' sang Bognor lustily, oblivious to the tap on the arm. 'One Faith! One Lord!' It was only during the gap between verses that he looked up and saw the man smiling at him and mouthing 'Excuse me'. He pressed back and allowed Mr. Jones to pass. Not, of course, that his real name was Jones.

'Thy heralds brought glad tidings,' he went on. 'Glad tidings' indeed. He had recognised Mr. Jones immediately. Mr. Jones was a very senior civil servant indeed. Permanent Under-Secretary at the Ministry of Technology, no less.

Bognor was ecstatic. A triumph at last. Jones's real name was Gaymer Burton. He was flashy, brilliant, and Simon was entirely right in suggesting that he was not the most obviously godly of men. None the less, he seemed to know the tune. He was singing as enthusiastically as Bognor himself.

From now on Bognor would have to watch everything Burton did. It was too much to expect him to permit himself to be seen handing over a bulky envelope in full view. On the other hand, there were so few opportunities for speech during a retreat that he must give himself away simply by his conversation. The service moved on to the 119th Psalm, beginning, as was customary at Sext, at Verse 81 and continuing all the way to 128. Bognor joined in, pondering occasionally on the odd phrase.

'I am become like a bottle in the smoke,' he sang, and wondered what it meant. It wasn't until he reached the curious words 'thy commandment is exceeding broad' that he glanced again at Burton and noticed with surprise that he was singing the words without recourse to his prayer-book. And by the look of him getting them right.

'Show off,' thought Bognor, his natural jealousy getting the better of his excitement.

*           *           *

If he had thought the job of catching Burton out was going to be easy he couldn't have been more wrong. For a start Burton had been given, as an old and evidently valued friend, a room in the farmhouse. During those many hours in which solitary meditation was required a number of people could have visited him. Ideally Bognor would like to have camped on his doorstep. It was not possible.

At meals Burton seemed at pains always to sit next to someone different and the same thing happened at the seminars which were organised throughout the two days. At these Burton—or Jones, as he was studiously described—was brilliant. Where most of the friars were pedestrian and the visitors more so, Burton excelled. Only Anselm and the Bishop exceeded him in knowledge; only Xavier came near equalling him in wit and argument.

Whether the subject under discussion was 'Transubstantiation', 'The Efficacy of Prayer', or in one memorably charged encounter 'Christ in a Secular Society: the role of the Christian in a Changing World', he was, to Bognor, insufferable. His erudition and overall mastery of the problems posed by Christianity in general and contemplative Christianity in particular were such that at times Bognor found himself thinking that here was another red herring. At times like this, in an admittedly heretical sense, he prayed for faith and at all times he watched and waited for a slip.

The moment at which such a mistake might come, he decided, was at Confession. It was traditional during these week-ends for the more senior and respected friars (not just the ordained ones) to hear Confession. This was done not in the ritualistic fashion of the Roman Catholic Church in a curtained kiosk and whispers, but in broad daylight, and, as it was summer, out of doors. At selected times of the day everyone would promenade in their courtyard and on the lawns, in pairs or alone. Each couple was given a wide berth so that a certain privacy could be preserved and nothing overheard. It was a perfect way to hand over verbal secrets, though Bognor was convinced that whatever was being passed on was written down, since detailed plans were almost certainly involved. However, he watched each confessional avidly and was again frustrated by Gaymer Burton's brilliance. He treated the confessionals as an impartial belle of the ball who wishes to give no offence to any of her many suitors.

At the first such session he spent a full half-hour engrossed with Father Anselm, and Bognor, eager for this particular scalp, began to make plans. But just as it seemed certain that was a special and suspicious relationship,

Burton executed a graceful pirouette and shifted his attentions to the more abrasive preaching of Father Xavier. It was the same at subsequent performances. Whereas the doddering Mortimer and the two clergymen and the young man in the T-shirt tended to stick with one partner deep in intense searchings of the inner soul, Burton flitted about from one friar to another, gracefully and gently cutting in on other people's conversations, spending enough time with each man to make it seem polite and not quite enough to indicate favouritism, before moving on once more.

On Sunday morning, after a particularly virtuoso sequence of Burton's, Bognor retired to the Boot in disgust. There unsurprisingly he found Father Xavier deep in his Scotch. He was, however, interested to find that he was not alone. There with him, being corrupted, as Xavier had said earlier, with a pint of shandy was young Brother Paul.

'I would have thought,' said Bognor, 'that during a week-end of such significance you might have managed to stay away from the bottle.'

'Can't,' said Xavier a shade irritably. 'I'm surprised you've managed to find time to take your eyes off the devastating Mr. Jones.'

'What's that supposed to mean?' Bognor found Xavier altogether too perceptive. It unnerved him.

'You've been sniffing around him all week-end as if he were a bitch on heat.' Father Xavier dragged on his Perfectos Finos. 'You know Paul, don't you?'

'Yes,' said Paul. 'You gave me a lift your first day here.'

'That's right. I'm sorry to see you in the fleshpots.'

'It's only shandy.' Brother Paul seemed aggrieved.

'I didn't really mean the drink,' said Bognor. 'I meant him.' He nodded at Xavier, who affected not to hear. Mr. Hey who had been engrossed in farming talk, finally came across and asked Bognor if he wanted his usual. Bognor bought usuals for himself, Mr. Hey and Xavier, and offered Brother Paul another shandy. He turned it down.

'So what do you suspect Brother Jones of having done?' asked Xavier. 'Do you think he's from the *News of the World*?'

'He didn't manage much if he is,' said Bognor. It was perfectly true that none of the Sunday papers had followed up the story of Brother Bede's expulsion with more than a few lame paragraphs. Anselm had obviously been both ruthless and plausible.

'Can't stand these retreats,' said Xavier.

'They're artificial,' said Paul.

'Yes,' said Bognor. Conversation flagged. Xavier seemed distant, Paul taciturn. Bognor remarked on it and Xavier said he was having trouble with his sermon. It was important because it was for Evensong, and the Bishop would be there.

'Theme?'

'I have a text with which I begin and with which I end,' said Xavier. 'As is the manner with sermons. It's a convention. Makes them tidier.'

'And the text?'

'It's apocryphal, like a lot of the best sayings. "Forsake not an old friend; for the new is not comparable to him; a new friend is as new wine; when it is old, thou shalt drink it with pleasure." Ecclesiasticus IX. Ten. Know it?'

'No.'

'Oh. Pity. I bet your friend Mr. Jones knows it.' Xavier drained his glass. 'I should think about it if I were you. You might find the odd clue in it. You never know. Right now I must go and polish it up.' He got up to go. Paul left with him and Bognor ordered another drink.

'And another for you,' he said to Mr. Hey, who allowed himself a smile. 'Is that the regular drinking companion?' he asked.

Mr. Hey resumed his normal morose appearance, but then looked with gratitude at his pint. 'Wouldn't call him regular, sir,' he said slowly, 'not exactly drinking. But he's the only other one that comes in here with Father Xavier.' Bognor thanked him.

That afternoon, after a more than usually spare lunch, the Community went for a walk. During retreats hot food was at a premium and the meal consisted of corned beef and a salad, the principal component of which was beetroot. The walk, a regular Sunday afternoon custom, was designed to exercise away the lassitude induced by a more conventional Sunday lunch and, more important, to remind oneself of the essential Brotherhood love of nature. It was led in athletic fashion by Father Anselm, while others more infirm or more dissipated were allowed to dawdle along well behind. But even for the genuinely incapacitated like Father John the walk was mandatory. After three-quarters of an hour the friars and their guests were scattered about the Oxfordshire hills in an untidy straggle. From where Anselm and Bognor and a handful of the fittest stood, not very far from Aldhelm's staddlestone, they looked like grazing Hereford cattle.

They had been silent until then and Bognor had supposed it was part of the ritual: a mute appreciation of all things bright and beautiful. Apparently, however, it was simply because the exertion made speech difficult, for as they rested, panting slightly and gazing down the gorse-spotted incline and across the valley, Father Anselm moved across and put a hand gently on Bognor's elbow.

'Well, my son,' he said, 'and have you been

able to elaborate on your distasteful theories?'

Bognor disliked being pawed around by other men and he disliked being called 'My son'. He stared at the Abbot with unconcealed suspicion, absorbed the tough but feminine face with its prim lines round the mouth and its watery blue eyes and wondered if he was a saint or a Communist agent.

'Up to a point,' he said.

'Ah,' said Anselm, 'I read Evelyn Waugh too. You promised Lord Camberley that you would tell me what was in your mind and what you'd discovered. If you have found something out you must say.'

Bognor considered. If Anselm were guilty he would know precisely who Jones was and he would probably realise that Bognor knew. If he were innocent it didn't matter unless he went shooting his mouth off all round the place. On the other hand, if he was guilty and he thought that Bognor was ignorant about Jones . . . He remembered Camberley and decided to take the risk. Much as he distrusted Anselm he was increasingly inclined to believe him innocent.

'Yes,' he said finally, 'I have found something. It's your friend Mr. Jones.'

'Dear Edward,' said Anselm, almost rapturously. 'So very intelligent. If only he were a little more serious he would be genuinely wise. I often feel he missed his vocation by becoming a schoolmaster; but there it is.'

'He's not a schoolmaster,' said Bognor. 'And his name isn't Jones. He's a senior civil servant who would quite definitely have access to any secret you cared to mention, and his name is Gaymer Burton.' He said this with an air of triumphal self-importance, and stood back to see what effect the revelation would have.

Father Anselm stared out across the valley and his thin fingers played nervously with the white cord at his waist. His eyes seemed mistier than before.

'I've often wondered about Edward,' he said. 'I can't believe you, though.'

Bognor looked down the slope to where a spritely grey-haired figure in shirt-sleeves and sponge-bag trousers was climbing jerkily towards them.

'Here he comes,' he said with a sang-froid he scarcely felt. 'Why not ask him?' They waited nervously for the little man to catch up. The second he did, Father Anselm confronted him.

'Edward dear,' he said, 'Mr. Bognor here tells me that you are not what you seem, that you are someone called Burton, a civil servant. Tell me it's not true.'

The little man was puffed. He looked hostile, but he was too out of breath and too taken aback to say anything for a minute or two. When he did it was to Bognor.

'I've heard quite a bit about you over the last couple of days,' he said waspishly, 'and as far as

I can make out you're an ill wind. You obviously haven't solved whatever you came here to solve and you've simply succeeded in causing unhappiness by busying yourself with domestic trivia. I shall make sure you're reported to the relevant authority.'

Bognor sucked his teeth and hoped he was right.

Burton turned to Anselm.

'I'm sorry,' he said softly. 'I wouldn't have had you find this out for the world. And certainly not like this. It's true, of course. I often think you must realise, but you've never said anything.'

Anselm was looking back at him, hope fighting with his fear of betrayal. 'Why?' he asked.

Burton sighed. 'Because . . . Oh, because I think I needed to retreat in so many different ways. "My soul's calm retreat which none disturb." That's Henry Vaughan, isn't it? So true. I need a real escape from my self, and every year I've found it here. But I want no reminders at all. That's why. There's no deceit. Or if there is it's purely self-deceit. No deceit from you, old friend.'

Bognor found this speech sentimental and unconvincing, but the formula was immaculately calculated. Either that or Anselm was as good an actor as Burton.

'I understand,' he said, placing the inevitable

hand on his shoulder. 'There's no need to explain. No harm is done. Your secret is safe with me.'

Bognor turned away and walked down the hill. All that he'd achieved was to warn Burton that he was under suspicion and to alienate Anselm still further. It was all Camberley's fault or maybe Beg's. Which reminded him. He had better phone the old boy to arrange the return of his Land-Rover tomorrow morning. He stomped down the hill in high dudgeon, passing every one of the friars on their way up and not acknowledging any of their greetings. By the time he got to the phone box his anger had scarcely evaporated. It was Lady Beg who answered. He left a message for Sir Erris to meet him at opening time in the Owl at Woodstock.

There was nothing further he wanted to do at the Friary. He had decided that the answer must lie miles away with Brother Bede. If it didn't he might just have to concede failure and go back to codes. He would make a recommendation for an exhaustive check on Gaymer Burton and suggest that he was prematurely retired. But he only had a year or two to go, anyway, and there wasn't enough evidence for a charge. In all honesty he didn't have enough evidence for anything or anybody. Unless it were the Bishop of Woodstock. A few words in that prelate's ear and there would be some changes at Beaubridge.

However, that was not his brief. He would make his farewells. Listen to Xavier's sermon. An idea occurred to him. Perhaps the old thing would include some cryptic clue. He wouldn't put it past him. Otherwise there was nothing except to attempt to speak to Anselm and get him to take his warnings seriously. That, he conceded, would be nearly impossible.

Xavier's sermon came first. It was good. Exceedingly good. The theme was loyalty to first principles, resistance to change for the sake of change. It was a mellifluous condemnation of the cheap and tatty, the artificial and the new-fangled. It was unashamedly conservative, tailor-made for the Bishop, and left the entire Community, which was not renowned for any adherence to the progressive principles, glowing with self-righteousness. Bognor followed it carefully and found no clues of any sort.

He accosted Xavier after he had finished receiving the congratulations of the visitor.

'What a triumph!' he said as the Bishop rolled unsteadily towards Anselm's study in search of some early evening sherry. 'Can I get you a drink? I won't have another chance, I'm off in the morning.'

'Thank you no,' said Xavier. 'It's left me a bit drained. I'm going to stay at home this evening. The liver's not what it was. But thank you for the thought.'

'Of course, you don't believe a word of what you said.' Bognor was fishing vaguely.

'I regard hypocrisy as my greatest personal attribute,' said Xavier. 'It's the thing I do best of all. Though for once, or rather as usual, you're quite wrong. I believe almost every word I said. Did you find the clue?'

'No.'

Xavier laughed. 'I thought you might not. Never mind, you will one day. We'll see you again before long. Take care.' They shook hands.

His other farewells were more perfunctory. Some he said that night and others he left till morning. Barnabas was, as usual, overcome with confusion, shuffling and curtseying and changing colour as he had on the first occasion they'd met. Both Simon and Aldhelm thanked him profusely and genuinely for not having betrayed them to Father Anselm. Brother Vivian was silent as ever. Father John with an evil smile offered to lend him *The ABC and XYZ of Bee Culture*. With each good-bye he found himself wondering if there would be another meeting under different conditions. Try as he would he still found it hard to believe that one of them had murdered Collingdale.

His corporate farewell he said at Compline. It remained the one feature of the Friary he found wholly rewarding, because the poetry of movement and of words glossed over the manifold shortcomings of the individual. It was Father John's turn to read, and his thin rasping voice gave an extra dimension of menace to the words: 'Brethren, be sober, be vigilant; because your adversary the devil as a roaring lion, walketh about seeking whom he may devour.' For sheer drama the final raising of the cowls and the procession into the night remained the high-spot. He wished as he watched that that could be the final farewell. It was how he would like to remember them.

The ultimate reality, of course, was Father Anselm. He came out to say good-bye by the Land-Rover. He looked pained and penitent.

'I do so greatly regret the circumstances of our meeting,' he said. 'I do trust you will revisit us in happier times.'

'I'd like that,' said Bognor. 'But look . . . Before I go will you promise me one thing?'

The Friar nodded. 'But certainly.'

'I'm not sure,' Bognor said, 'that you fully appreciate how serious this affair is. You must believe me it is deadly serious and the people who are involved in it are ruthless. I know how difficult it must be for you to appreciate that this sort of crime can flourish in surroundings like these, but it can and it has.

'Now that you see what we suspect you too must be vigilant. I can't impress that on you too carefully. If you see or hear anything which alarms you, ring Sir Erris Beg at once. I'm seeing that Inspector Pinney drops by from time to time to keep an eye on things. Tell him if anything strikes you as strange.

'Whatever you do don't try to confront anyone yourself. They may be old friends of yours, but they've killed twice already and I'm afraid they won't hesitate to kill again. Do I make myself clear?'

Bognor was quite impressed with his own seriousness. Father Anselm was wearing his most martyred expression. 'I do, my son. God be with you.' He shook hands.

Bognor leapt into the Land-Rover and revved loudly before letting the clutch out. He had engaged the wrong gear and it stalled. As he turned to wave after a more successful second attempt, his profound sense of irritation was increased still more by the sight of Father Anselm with his eyes closed making the sign of the cross. He wrestled the heavy vehicle round the corner, frowing furiously. If it *was* Father Anselm he had a colossal nerve.

When he turned the vehicle out of the wood above Woodstock, the town was hidden still in a morning mist which floated up from the sewage farm, on the river and obscured everything but a few of the taller school buldings. Although it was almost half past ten, the sun was making scant impression on this unhealthy cloud. It was rather like descending from the rarified sunny atmosphere of the higher Alps to the greyness of the plain. Sir Erris was already *in situ* with a pink gin, and Bognor, still greatly piqued by his behaviour, made him buy another for himself.

'Well, you dropped me in it,' said Bognor.

Sir Erris looked embarrassed. 'Sorry,' he said. 'I thought I'd forestall any trouble from Bert Camberley by ringing him to say everything was under control.'

'And?'

Sir Erris winced nervously at the memory. 'He said that as far as he could see it wasn't in the least under control and that he didn't believe for an instant that his son bumped himself off.'

'So you then told him everything you knew.'

'Not just like that. But I had to tell him something. He got it out of me in the end. He's very persistent and he was very upset and I didn't seem able . . .' Sir Erris coughed into his gin and drank it. 'Why? Did it matter much? I'm sure you've solved it by now.'

'Not quite,' said Bognor. 'I wish you hadn't told him. *He* told Anselm and then Anselm more or less told Gaymer Burton.'

'Gaymer Burton? He was at school with my brother. Arrogant little shit. What happened to him?'

Bognor bought a couple more gins and told him. He also told him about Brother Aldhelm and about the poker school. Sir Erris enjoyed it all. When he'd finished he said, 'Bloody funny. But you're no nearer a solution.'

Bognor demurred. 'I've got some clues,' he said, 'and some hunches. But from now on in I'm disposed to wait. If there's a secret going out with the honey this year our man must make a move soon. And if we don't discover anything in the next couple of weeks we'll pick up Anselm and Simon at Heathrow and do them over along with the honey.'

There was of course, more to the Community than the eight suspects (it had been eight, but Bognor was now forced to add the name of Brother Paul as a ninth half-suspect), and the deaths had impinged less on the lives of other friars.

Luke had scarcely been known to most people and he was not greatly liked; Batty Thomas had been liked well enough but he was no one's bosom companion; Bede had been resented by many and thought to be off his head by most. So the events had not left any huge gaps, and the great majority of the brethren, while conceding that their peaceful lives had received an upsetting jolt, settled back amiably into the old routines.

If anyone had suggested that the soul had gone out of the Community some might have agreed, but the majority would not have noticed.

* * *

As Expo-Brit grew closer the air of expectancy grew greater. For a handful of friars at Beaubridge, Oxfordshire, for Bognor in Whitehall, for Sir Erris in his rural Oxfordshire retreat, for Lord Camberley commuting between directorships and stately homes and All Souls—September 18 had a special significance. By then the waiting would be over.

## CHAPTER SIX

He took a taxi from Paddington to his flat, which, thanks to a moderate legacy from an aunt rather than any generosity from the civil service, was a comfortable bachelor residence overlooking Regent's Park. The bookshelves bulged with reference books, notably numerous bright yellow *Wisdens*, and there were some quite nice water-colours on the walls, left him by the same aunt. The place was a great deal tidier than when he'd left and the char had made the bed.

He knew that he ought to telephone Brother Bede immediately, but for once indolence got the better of enthusiasm and he had a bath. Afterwards, instead of ringing Bede, he rang Monica. He was fond of Monica. She had been his regular girl-friend now for more years than he cared to remember, and as both of them were emotionally lazy but sexually quite keen, the arrangement worked rather well. For some reason she had never moved in, but they both assumed that eventually they would get married, though the subject was never mentioned.

Monica said she'd be round soon and asked if he'd managed to lose any weight, to which he made no reply.

He expunged the memory of Beaubridge in some style. They had a lot to drink and then they went to Lacy's in Whitfield Street with Americans and fabulously expensive marble tiles on the floor. There they had a lot more to drink. They ate a succulent fish pâté made of salmon and turbot and spinach in squares like an edible chess-board and then they had a delicately flavoured sesame chicken which they were too tipsy to appreciate and then they had rich chocolate cake with cream, followed by brandies and a cigar for him, at which she was allowed a couple of puffs. Then they got a taxi back to Bognor's flat where they went straight to bed and made love seriously and conventionally till the early hours of the morning.

At seven-thirty he woke with a head which hurt more than on the morning after Brother Vivian had hit it.

She was standing over him fully dressed with a glass of Alka Seltzer in one hand and a postcard in the other. 'Gotto rush,' she said, handing them both to him. 'Super evening. Really super. I'll ring later.' She gave him a gentle kiss and let herself out.

He drank the Alka Seltzer and smiled after her. It was good to have earned a headache. Then he remembered the postcard. It was postmarked Oxford and marked 'personal' in the top left corner. He studied it for a moment, trying to think who he still knew in Oxford. His tutors were all dead and most of those contemporaries who had entered academia were in Wales, Scotland or West Africa. He gave up speculating and turned it over. The address was All Souls College, Oxford, and it said simply: 'I wonder if you would care to dine with me here on the 17th (the Eve of Expo-Brit). Black tie.' It was signed 'Robert Camberley'.

Bognor shivered. Why on earth should Camberley want him to dine at All Souls the night before the departure of the Expo-Brit expedition? It could hardly be his idea of a joke. Perhaps he simply wanted to interfere, to be in at the kill.

Bognor got up, had a bath and boiled himself an egg. Over breakfast he read *The Times* headlines and then put pen to postcard.

'Thank you very much,' he wrote. 'See you on the 17th.' He reversed the card and addressed it to 'Rt. Hon. the Earl of Camberley, All Souls College, Oxford'.

There was no point in worrying about it. He must exercise patience. From now on he was in for two weeks of tedium which should come to a satisfactory climax. If not he would just have to start all over again. Or more likely Parkinson would give the job to someone else and he would spend the next forty years behind a desk. He wouldn't mind that much.

At one minute past nine he rang the office. As he'd feared, there had been some official anxiety. The Minister wanted a solution. Camberley's visit had upset people. Bognor listened to the complaints and then said he'd try to be in later, in the afternoon. He had someone to see in the morning. Parkinson sounded very unimpressed.

At twenty past he rang a number in Carshalton.

'Doctor's surgery.'

'Could I speak to Mr. Jenkins?'

'*Mr.* Jenkins?' The voice paused. 'This is *Dr.* Jenkins's number.'

'I know. I want to speak to his brother. He's staying there. It is rather urgent.'

'Hold on.' The voice sounded worried and off-putting. 'I think there must be some mistake. I'll ask Dr. Jenkins.' Bognor was prepared for this. They'd almost certainly been inundated with unsuitable calls from the national press. He waited, and after a couple of minutes another voice came on the line.

'David Jenkins here,' it said. 'Can I help you?'

'I'd like to talk to your brother, if I might, please, sir.'

There was another silence. Bognor thought for a moment that he'd rung off. 'Who is that speaking?'

'You won't know me. My name's Bognor. Board of Trade.'

'Board of Trade? Are you from one of the papers? You're not the *Daily Express* again, are you?'

'No, sir, I assure you. I'm from the Board of Trade special investigations department and I'm making some routine inquiries about certain incidents at Beaubridge Friary.' He sometimes feared being obsequious suited him.

'Look, he's not talking to anyone. He's still very upset and under sedation. I'm afraid that speaking purely professionally I couldn't allow anyone to see him. Good-bye.'

Bognor thought for a moment, despondently, and then grimaced. 'Action, Bognor,' he said out loud, and dialled the nearest car-hire firm.

Carshalton took an hour from Regent's Park. It was a leafy prosperous middle-class district in what was described as Surrey but was really just part of South London. The doctor's house and surgery was a large semi set back from the road.

There were lilacs, roses and two tricycles in the front garden and it was called the Willows. Bognor could see no willows.

He went in and rang the bell on the reception counter. A woman in her early twenties, wearing a blue overall, came out through a door marked private. He guessed it was the one who had answered the phone.

'Yes?' she said clinically. 'Do you have an appointment?'

'Yes. With *Mr.* Jenkins. Not *Dr.* Jenkins.'

'I'm sorry,' she bristled. 'There's no one of that name here.'

Bognor put his hand in his pocket and pulled out a card which he handed to the receptionist. 'Perhaps that will convince you that I am not from any of the papers.' She looked at it, puzzled, then straightened.

'You're the one who rang earlier,' she said. 'Dr. Jenkins said you weren't to be let in.'

'He might let me in if you showed him the card,' said Bognor. It worked. She turned and walked out with it, and a couple of minutes later two men arrived. The doctor and his brother, Bede, otherwise known as Michael Jenkins. Bognor was exasperated. There was no problem with Bede. He was obviously willing to talk and he recognised him. Almost certainly Xavier or one of the more astute friars had given him a clear idea of the sort of questions he was asking. The brother, however, was a bore.

He clucked around like a mother hen, demanding to be present at any inquisition, talking about solicitors and sedatives and generally working himself up into a lather. Eventually he agreed to go, provided Bede was questioned on the premises. There was no problem in that, so the two of them were ushered into the drawing room, where they sat in the worn armchairs on either side of the red-brick fireplace festooned with horse brasses.

'I'm sorry about your expulsion,' said Bognor. The young man, he couldn't have been more than thirty, looked strained and tired.

'No need,' he said. 'It had to happen sooner or later. As you've seen for yourself, they're not exactly *committed* at Beaubridge. Not in any very meaningful sense. Not to the extent of actually getting out and *doing* anything.'

'I suppose not. What are you going to do?'

'Apply for a place at a theological college, and then try for an overseas posting. I want to do something relevant.'

'Yes, well, if you want to do something relevant now, perhaps you'd answer a few questions.' This man didn't look to Bognor like a double murderer, and the ambition to be ordained and become a missionary seemed quite genuine. If he was contemplating a quick flight to Bulgaria or Poland he gave absolutely no sign of it.

Brother Bede nodded. 'Sure. If it'll help.'

'It may. You know that I've been investigating Brother Luke's death?'

'Yes. I thought poor Thomas did it?'

'I'm not sure about that. Maybe. Maybe not. If he didn't, then there's no reason for his suicide.'

'Except that he was mental.'

'Perhaps. Then there's another thing. We have some suspicions about honey and the Expo-Brit.'

'What sort of suspicions?'

'Suspicions. It's complicated. The point is that there is only one person who could have been involved in the honey business, and killed Luke, and killed Thomas. And that,' he slowed his delivery for maximum effect, 'is you.'

'That's just not true.'

'Why not?'

'Well, I don't understand about the honey, and I agree my alibi for Luke is no better than anyone else's. But I couldn't have killed Thomas.'

'Why not?'

'I was in the kitchen all the time.'

'You couldn't prove it.'

'There was someone else there all the time.'

'I thought the helpers spent most of the time serving in the dining room? You must have been alone a lot of the time.'

'Not me. No. The only one who was alone at all was Paul.'

'Paul?'

'He was late. Said he'd been having a kip 'cos he felt a bit poorly and he'd overslept.'

'Nobody said anything about that before.'

'Didn't seem important. We were asked to give our own alibis, not other people's.'

'How late was Paul?'

'Not long. Five minutes at the outside.'

'I see.' He got out a pencil and notebook and wrote Paul in large block capitals with a couple of question marks alongside it. He felt unhappy. 'You're certain you could produce witnesses who would say that you spent every second of that lunch in the kitchen?'

'Certain.'

'I'll have it checked, if you'd let me have the names.' He felt the clipped attempt at professional questioning had let him down.

Brother Bede gave him the names of some non-suspect friars, and Bognor made a further note. Pinney could have a word with them on his next visit.

'You're very young to have been at the friary for twelve years.'

'Thirteen,' he said. He did look young in his jeans and sandals and aertex shirt with his hair worn so close cropped. 'I just joined young, that's all. I went on a week-end retreat and I felt a terrific sense of vocation and I joined soon after I took "O"-level.'

'And how long have you been so politically

aware?'

'Always.'

'Meaning?'

'I've always thought the Church was a force for good. I mean, I don't see the point of just worrying about life after death.'

'What organisations do you belong to?'

'You sound like McCarthy. I was a Communist member, but I left after Czechoslovakia. Amnesty International. C.N.D. Nothing else. I'm not really very keen on belonging and most of the radical groups are too atheist.'

'You're not very pro-Russian?'

'I regard myself as a Marxist, so it's hardly likely, is it?'

Bognor shrugged. 'I must go,' he said. 'Thanks for your help. Do you have a passport?'

'No.'

'Good. I'd like you to let me know if you're changing address at any time in the near future. And you might as well know that you're under surveillance.'

Surveillance was a good word. He decided to use it more often; and the passport admonition which had been quite spontaneous and had a pleasant air of melodrama.

Bognor left and drove back to the office. South London was horrible, he thought, as they struggled back through the traffic and along the drab suburban roads. You never knew where you were because it all looked exactly the same: chain stores and lollipop men at school crossings. Collingdale had a neglected wife somewhere south of the Thames. He supposed he ought to call, but it would seem as hypocritical as he felt. His notes spread out on his knees, he tried yet again to make some sense of the case.

It had to be one of those eight men. At least the spying had to be one of the eight. As no man went on the Expo-Brits two years running, it either had to involve more than one spy or the 'spy' got the Expo-Brit friar to act as an unwitting courier. The secret plans could either be hidden in the honey or on the friar.

Logically Luke's murder should have been done by one of the eight as well, but it could have been any of them. The time had been well chosen. The only man with an absolute alibi was Paul. It was curious that Paul's apparently foolproof alibi for the Luke murder should be balanced by his distinctly shaky one for Thomas's killing. The time of Thomas's murder had been less well chosen. Every single person in lunch had a cast-iron alibi. The only possible killers were those who had been in the kitchen, and now Bede had suggested that of those the only real possibility was Paul. Yet if Bede were the culprit himself it was predictable that he should try to implicate others.

If it wasn't Bede you had to accept a conspiracy theory. The most obvious conspiracy was the poker school. Vivian was undoubtedly a potential murderer. There was no reason why he shouldn't have killed Luke. Moreover, both John and Simon were intelligent and complex enough to organise this sort of scheme and to export the secrets. But none of them could have murdered Thomas. It seemed more and more likely that Paul had done that. And yet the idea was ludicrous. There was no motive. He had only been at the friary briefly. He could not conceivably have smuggled secrets or killed Luke. Bognor sighed.

The ensuing days dragged. For Bognor there was other work to be done. Positive vetting had to be supervised. A minor irregularity in the Ministry of Pensions had to be sorted out. He had an embarrassing session with an influential M.P. (not Basil Strudwick) whose mistress was considered a security risk and another with an Air Vice-Marshal whose daughter had vanished in curious circumstances. Parkinson had remained unimpressed with his efforts but had agreed to give him until Expo-Brit. If nothing had happened by then he had said he would break him. Meanwhile his extra-mural activities regained their former vigour. He ate and drank slightly too well and saw a lot of Monica, went to the theatre and spent a week-end in Suffolk with friends. His head stopped hurting and the bruising subsided. Life, in short, resumed its usual pattern. Only one thing marred it and that was the dim realisation that he had failed, even if only temporarily, to solve the agricultural secrets case. Every time the phone rang he expected to hear the alcoholic cough of Sir Erris or the flat midland accents of Inspector Pinney or even the nasal prissiness of Father Anselm. He dreamt about Compline and the stations of the cross; woke once to find himself singing 'All things bright and beautiful' at two in the morning; and less ephemerally was plagued by a series of memoranda from increasingly superior superiors.

The days dragged at Beaubridge too. For Brother Barnabas the coming of autumn was always depressing. His year and his work revolved around the guests who came to visit them and after the last big retreat of the summer the numbers inevitably slackened. He put in a request to Father Anselm for a new bed in Number 17 and he spent many hours scrubbing and washing and generally titivating. There was only Christmas to look forward to now when for the only time in the winter months guests arrived in quantities. Brother Barnabas was not a very contemplative person, certainly no original thinker, and it was one reason for his having chosen the Society of the Sacred Brotherhood. He had understood that it was designed for those who were not as clever as the rest and he had assumed that the friars were more jovial than they had actually turned out to be. In the end he had discovered that the guests were a great deal more cheerful than the friars. They laughed at his jokes. In a way he was a little like a seaside landlady, Brother Barnabas: homespun and simple.

To Bognor, doodling away incessantly with his notebook in his basement office off Whitehall, Brother Barnabas was one of the more pleasant and uncomplicated memories. But he was still on the list of suspects.

The nightly poker school continued as before. For a few nights there had been a slightly heightened sense of guilt; a tendency to jump at the slightest noise; and there had been near pandemonium on the Wednesday after Bognor had left. The lights had fused just as Father John was about to scoop the matchbox with a royal flush. All four players seemed to be drinking more heavily. Indeed Father John, who was responsible for the provision of the alcohol, began to have serious doubts about the quantities he'd made and even talked of rationing.

He too seemed depressed as the nights drew in and the weather grew misty and damp. Whereas Barnabas missed his guests, John missed his bees. They slept in winter, and while Father John could busy himself in the preparation and refinement of honey and mead, it was no substitute for the daily contact with the living bees themselves. There were times when he believed himself to be the only true religious in the place. He would stand of an evening in his habit and sandals, the fine mesh mask over his face, and anyone who happened to be passing would hear a low humming coming from his mouth. Father John, though he would never have admitted it, believed that he could talk to his bees. But in winter there was no point, and he missed them. He busied himself by writing a paper for the *American Bee Journal* called 'Some aspects of the social behaviour of the English honey bee', but his heart was not in it and he became progressively worse-tempered as the days passed. One day he actually struck Xavier with his stick in response to some personal witticism and from then on many of the brothers began to treat him with circumspection.

Bognor, in his notebook, remarked on his undoubted intelligence, his paradoxically waspish temperament, but made grave reservations about his physical strength. A spy maybe, but he was virtually certain that Father John was no murderer.

Brother Vivian, who was morose at the best of times, seemed unchanged and unchanging. He spent more and more time under the bonnet of the van, and on one occasion actually admitted defeat and took it into the garage at Great Ogridge. The garage fitted a new rocker gasket and some sparking plugs, but failed to improve the van's performance or Brother Vivian's temper.

Bognor, trying in vain, now that the wounds had faded, to find the spot where Brother Vivian hit him, marked him down as a man physically and temperamentally equipped to kill. But when he moved on to the questions of motive and opportunity he was less convinced.

Father Simon, the fourth member of the Community's drinking and gambling syndicate, was by no means as downcast as the others. He was greatly looking forward to his first visit to Bucharest and he had a great deal of work to do. The labels which Father Anselm had so curiously rejected had arrived as promised on Monday morning, and he and Vivian had gone in the van to collect them from the Abbey Bookshop in Woodstock. Father Anselm passed them as fit. Father Simon labelled furiously, making himself quite dry and parched in the process. Then he began, with a little help from his friends, to pack the jars neatly into sturdy cardboard boxes suitable for transporting to Rumania. He was a little unhappy about taking honey to Rumania. It smacked of coals to Newcastle, but he had little time to think of that. He spent much time on the telephone to Mr. Rosenbaum, an employee of Lord

Wharfedale's who worked in the publicity department. Mr. Rosenbaum wanted photographs of the entire Community with their bees. Father Simon tried desperately to arrange it. Other employees of Lord Wharfedale telephoned as well, telling him about tickets, cancelling tickets, reserving suites in hotels, cancelling them, and generally making life difficult. Father Simon, who if the truth be known was something of a masochist, enjoyed every minute of it.

Bognor didn't mark him down as a masochist but gave him an alpha beta for intelligence and therefore conceivably for motive. He could only give him gamma for physical ability and gamma minus for the emotional ability to commit murder. Father Simon, he reasoned, could no more have killed a man than set a mouse-trap.

Brother Aldhelm continued to plough a lonely furrow. He was not a gregarious person and he had a strong streak of paranoia. His relations with the rest of the Community were cordial but distant and although few of the friars would have dared laugh at him to his face he suspected that they did it behind his back. His affair with Lena Strudwick moved indoors on account of the weather and the passion seemed to dim slightly with the seasons. However, he still made his regular appointment by the staddlestone and spent most of his afternoons lasciviously on a large brass bed at the Old Manor, Melbury.

Bognor, who had been so enthusiastic in his pursuit of the red 'E'-Type, still marked down the affair as significant, albeit reluctantly. Mrs. Strudwick would have done anything, particularly for sex and money. But if she were the contact it was difficult to see why it was necessary for Gaymer Burton to put in an appearance. Besides which, Brother Aldhelm was not over-blessed with brain.

Which left three. Bede remained in Carshalton reading *Tribune* and the Red Mole and applying to Lampeter and Cuddesdon. It took him time to get over the shock and he was irritated too that his brother had beaten off the press with such effect. He had hoped that he might emulate those who sold their memoirs for vast fortunes, but the scandal had been short lived and his notoriety had not survived the week-end. Relations between himself and his brother were strained, but he had nowhere else to go and his leaving present of five pounds from Father Anselm had been spent already. He went to some demonstrations and meetings, and was followed everywhere by men from the Board of Trade.

Bognor regarded him as an important candidate. Under close questioning from Inspector Pinney, Brother Bede's alibi had not stood up well. Paul, of course, denied being late, and the other two friars claimed that Bede had been on his own at times.

That at least was what Bognor understood. Inspector Pinney's report had been made in longhand and it was verbose. Also inconclusive. It would certainly not have been easy to establish anything in a court of law from the reported statements of the other brothers. They had been too busy running backwards and forwards with bowls of soup, clearing up empties and helping to serve, to notice or remember anything significant.

Xavier seemed to be suffering from anticlimax like the majority of his colleagues. His routine was unchanged. He still made regular excursions to the Boot and he still smoked too many Perfectos Finos. His wit was as acid as ever, but he seemed depressed. A great deal of his time was spent in the library cataloguing. That was the excuse, though there was an unpleasant altercation when Father Anselm came in one morning to read *The Times* and found that Xavier had scribbled all over the section of the sports page devoted to horse-racing. After Anselm had delivered himself of a high-flown monologue on the evils of defacing communal property and of taking an interest in the horses, Xavier simply said, 'I know two things about the horse; and one of them is rather coarse.'

His fortunes in Bognor's notebook had fluctuated constantly. At times Bognor decided that he was too outrageous altogether; then he remembered Guy Burgess and thought again. It was a constant battle between his affections for the man and his emerging professional self.

The same battle was fought over Anselm only the roles of emotion and reason were reversed. Anselm had seemed greatly relieved after Bognor's departure and for a couple of days had been positively genial.

He played squash with his old friend the headmaster; sanctioned the reading of P. G. Wodehouse at silent lunches, and threw himself into the preparations for Expo-Brit along with Father Simon. But after the initial relief he began to look harrowed once more. In the opinion of his brothers, who gossiped constantly about his moods and preoccupations, it was the reappearance of the stolid Inspector Pinney which did it. Anselm had genuinely convinced himself that the whole nightmare had vanished, that there had never been such people as Luke and Bede and Batty Thomas and Bognor; and then in the middle of the morning cocoa break on Wednesday, just as he had been gazing round the yard and thinking how peaceful and contented his children were, he caught sight of Inspector Pinney. The Inspector had said that he had just happened to be passing by and there were one or two loose ends which needed tidying and did he mind if he asked one or two simple questions. It seemed quite innocuous, but it reminded him of the chain of disasters which had disturbed their quiet routine and it made him nervous once more.

Bognor would like to have nailed Anselm as the guilty one; and as he sat cudgelling his mind in the early evening over a brandy at the flat or day-dreaming in a steamy bath, the one man he wanted to convict was always Father Anselm. Unfortunately it wasn't going to work like this and such intuition as he possessed told him so.

'You really think they'll smuggle something out after all this brouhaha?'

'I really think so.'

'And you're prepared to wait and see?'

'Don't have much alternative. Pinney had got some odd details about people's backgrounds and their real names. I shall do some research on that. I've alerted Anselm. He'll be in touch with you or Pinney if anything happens. I want Pinney to drop in every so often to check the place out. And I for my part will ruminate.' He suddenly remembered that Sir Erris was keeping an eye on him. 'Do you think that's right?' he asked.

'Hope so.' They finished their drinks and walked to the station. Bognor bought a set of morning papers, gave Sir Erris his home phone number in case of emergencies and watched him wheeze away. The train was running late, since, as always, they were working on the line and were also in the throes of some incomprehensible industrial dispute. The journey back to Paddington took an hour longer than usual. Although he normally disliked train journeys, finding them tedious and uncomfortable, he experienced a growing sense of liberation. It had not been an enjoyable few days. He remembered the iron bed and the dingy little room and shuddered. He thought of studying the files, but decided against it. There were another two weeks for that.

## CHAPTER SEVEN

The waiting began to stop, unknown to some, on the day before. It was immediately after Terce on Bishop Lambert's day. Bishop Lambert was not a saint of any great stature but he was always dutifully commemorated by the Community. He came from Maastricht and lived in the seventh century, and beyond that no one at Beaubridge knew anything, except that the lesson for the day came from Daniel and was that curious business of the writing on the wall which culminates in the death of Belshazzar and the succession of Darius.

Immediately after Terce on Bishop Lambert's day the sun was still trying to break through a light watery mist and there was a mild confusion in the courtyard as the friars began to set about their morning's labours. Father Anselm stood just outside the farmhouse door clasping his big black bible to his chest and wondering how the Friary would manage in the absence of himself and Father Simon. He was on the point of turning indoors to deal with the morning post when he observed Father Xavier moving across the yard in his direction. He was holding a buff envelope.

Father Anselm had no wish to involve himself with his *bête noire* at that hour of the morning and he turned hastily to avoid him. Father Xavier, however, was not to be fobbed off so easily. He called after Anselm, quite politely, and Anselm, surprised at the placatory tone of his voice, stopped and turned back.

'Father Anselm,' said Xavier. He looked very tired and his manner was uncharacteristically conciliatory. Father Anselm decided to meet friendliness with friendliness. He smiled.

'Yes.'

'I just wanted to say,' said Xavier, 'that I'm afraid I've been a bit difficult and obstructive recently. It's my liver I think, not that that's any excuse. And I just wanted to say I'm awfully sorry about my general manner, and particularly about that episode in the library the other day. I'm afraid I was unforgivably rude.'

Father Anselm was taken aback. 'That's all right, my son,' he said. 'I'm sure it's just as much my fault. I'm afraid I can appear rather intransigent at times. Don't let it concern you. As I remind myself frequently, we must look to the future. Far better plan future happiness than dwell on past sorrows. Or, to borrow from the vernacular, there is no point crying over spilt milk.'

'No.' Father Xavier stopped and looked at the ground. It occurred to Anselm that he was not finding this easy. Humility was not his forte.

'Was there something else?' he asked, meaning it kindly but making it sound patronising.

'There was actually.' Anselm thought Xavier seemed more ill-at-ease than even his apology would explain. 'It is tomorrow that you and Father Simon are off on the Expo-Brit?'

'Yes.'

'And you are going to Rumania?'

'Yes. You know we are.'

'Yes. Well, I wonder if I could ask the most enormous favour?'

'Of course.'

'Well, you know how difficult it is for our brothers in Eastern Europe?'

'Yes.' Father Xavier was making extraordinarily heavy weather of this.

'Well, I have a young friend in Bucharest, a Carmelite. I haven't seen him for ages. I daren't write to him normally. You know what these Communist regimes are like. They open everything and they persecute people with Western contacts.'

'So you'd like me to deliver the letter personally?'

'Well, not personally,' said Xavier, quickly. 'It's only foreign mail from countries like this that they suspect. No, if you just post it when you get to Bucharest, that would be fine.'

'Is that all?'

'Yes, that's all.'

'Well, that's simple, then. Of course. A mission of Christian love and charity. It will help to lighten the burden of participating in such a materialist excursion as an export drive.'

'Thank you.' Father Xavier gave him the letter. 'You won't forget?'

'Certainly not.'

'And one thing.' Father Xavier paused. 'You know what these people are like. Their spies are everywhere. I'd be grateful if you didn't tell too many people you were acting as a courier.'

'Of course not.'

'Thank you, then.' They parted, Father Xavier to the library and Father Anselm to his study. Before he started to examine his post Father read the address on the envelope idly. 'Brother Aloysius', it said, '117 Bde. Georgiu-Dej, Bucharest.' It was really rather touching. Perhaps he had misread Father Xavier. He offered up a little prayer for forgiveness, and put the letter in the top of a basket marked 'Pending'.

He thought no more about it for a couple of hours while he answered some letters, made a couple of phone calls and drafted a sheet of instructions for Father John, who, contrary to some advice, was to be left in charge while he and Simon were away. At about 10.30 Father Simon came in, a worried fraught expression on his face.

'Do you know,' he said, twitching, 'that that frightful man Rosenbaum has changed our hotel yet again?'

'Oh well,' said Anselm. 'It's not that important, just a little frustrating. Providing we have somewhere to sleep I don't see that it's that important.'

'Sometimes,' said Simon, with feeling, 'I think I may be getting anti-Semitic.' He came round the desk and looked over Anselm's shoulder. 'Have you reminded John to say the stations of the cross on Friday?' he asked, looking at the neatly written catalogue. His eye strayed across to the pending tray and took in the envelope addressed to Brother Aloysius. The address had been typed. 'Oh,' he said. 'Who's that from?'

'Xavier,' said Anselm absently.

'That's interesting,' said Simon. 'He has a lot of friends in these places. I'm surprised he never asks to go on a trip.'

'Mmmm,' said Father Anselm, who was

trying to compile some detailed directions about the oil-fired central heating. The tanker was coming next week and he was sure John would be unable to cope. 'Sorry, what?'

'I was only saying that Xavier had a lot of friends in these places. I seem to remember him giving me a letter to a Benedictine in Warsaw four years ago.'

'Yes. Very interesting. Is there anything else? This is complicated.'

Father Simon pursed his lips. 'No, nothing else. It's just odd that he never seems to talk about them.' He went out, slamming the door behind him.

It wasn't until Father Anselm had finished drafting his letter to Father John that he assimilated Father Simon's remarks. He thought about it vaguely as he wandered out for the cocoa break, and wondered if he had seriously under-valued Xavier. It was an unanticipated side of the man's character. He continued in this cheerful vein until he was halfway towards the trestle with its chipped urn when he looked up to see the intrusive Inspector Pinney. He suddenly went very cold.

'You all right, sir?' said the Inspector as Father Anselm stopped and put a hand to his head. For an instant he thought the man was going to faint.

'Yes, thank you. Perfectly. What can I do for you?' Anselm's voice was tense.

'Nothing in particular, sir. I just happened to be passing by. Thought I'd drop in and see everything was O.K. You're off to foreign parts tomorrow, aren't you?'

'Yes indeed.' Father Anselm seemed to have recovered. He offered the Inspector a mug of the weak cocoa and chattered to him inconsequentially and plausibly about various everyday matters. The Inspector left after a quarter of an hour. It had been peculiar, that moment, he thought to himself. Not like Father Anselm. He was usually so well in control of everything. Probably just got last-minute nerves about going off to Rumania. He wondered if he should mention it to Sir Erris.

Father Anselm finished his cocoa and went back to his office, where he sat down heavily and picked up Father Xavier's letter. He sat looking at it vacantly for a good twenty minutes.

Normally he would not have been in the least worried by it. He would have dismissed Father Simon's querulous innuendoes without stopping to consider them, but the sudden reminder of that dreadful week of death and scandal had made him unnaturally suspicious. He turned the letter over. There was nothing on the back. There was, he told himself, nothing remotely peculiar about it. He was just being melodramatic.

At the same time it was difficult to

over-dramatise when you'd had two people murdered under your very nose. He tried to remember what Mr. Bognor had said to him, 'Ring Sir Erris Beg in emergencies', but was this an emergency? Hardly. One of his senior brothers had written a letter to an old friend in Bucharest and asked him to post it. Now where was the emergency in that? He was being ridiculous. In any case, what was he supposed to do? He could hardly go round opening people's private correspondence, particularly when it had been given to him in trust. He returned the letter to the pending basket and went on a tour of inspection.

It was sunny now and although it was a crisp pale autumn sunshine it buoyed him up. He put the business of the letter out of his mind and walked up the lane a little way to see how the tree-felling was getting on. The smell of fresh sawdust and sap pleased him still more and he returned ten minutes before Sext in a state bordering on contentment. He was cogitating quietly in his study, preparing himself for the Office, when the phone rang. It was Sir Erris Beg.

'Is everything all right?' he asked. Father Anselm meditated briefly on the evils of alcohol. Sir Erris's voice sounded blurred, and yet it was only ten past twelve.

'Perfectly, thank you, Sir Erris. Father Simon and I leave at first light in the morning.'

'Oh,' Sir Erris sounded disappointed. He put the phone down. Father Anselm noticed Xavier's letter and felt disturbed again. Suddenly he remembered the policeman's threat. He had said that if the case of the vanishing secrets were not solved, then Simon and he would be apprehended at the airport and searched. That was too absurd. But if they were searched then Father Xavier's letter would be found. Perhaps he should warn Xavier, but no. That was equally ridiculous. He would simply refuse to show the letter to the authorities, to Bognor or anyone else. It was a free country and the letter was private. He left to celebrate Sext.

Afterwards at lunch he sat next to Father Simon. Halfway through, between the fish pie and the prunes, Father Simon whispered to him: 'I happened to mention that letter to Father Olaf. He said that Xavier gave him one last year when he went to Sofia.'

Anselm looked back at him disapprovingly. 'You shouldn't gossip,' he said. 'It's bad for morale and it's wrong.'

'Sorry I'm sure,' said Father Simon. But it worried Anselm. He left half his prunes. Suppose, after all, that the police were right? Suppose that there were a spy in their midst? That dear Edward Jones had brought down some secrets that week-end and given them to Xavier and Xavier had given them to him to post in Bucharest? That would be dreadful. If so, then surely he would have a duty to open the letter? But that would be equally bad. He sighed. He wished life were less complicated.

It so upset him that he stumbled twice in reading the psalm at None. That was very unlike him and it did not pass unnoticed. Immediately after the service two sentences were exchanged between Father Xavier and Brother Paul, which though apparently innocuous, would have greatly interested Simon Bognor, even if he would not quite have grasped the significance.

'I'm not happy about Anselm,' said Xavier, pulling hard on his cigarette. 'Something's upsetting him.'

'Relax, Father,' replied the younger man. 'It's probably just the prunes.'

Bognor, of course, did not overhear the remark and was indeed unaware of what was happening at the Friary. He too was on edge. He had succumbed to temptation and telephoned Sir Erris, but Sir Erris had been able to tell him nothing. He had busied himself with arranging the apprehension of the two friars at London Airport next day, but it was routine work and presented no challenge and was no sort of diversion. That evening he was dining at All Souls and that worried him too. There had to be some ulterior motive for that and if there was going to be some dramatic revelation then it was being left a little late in the day. He lunched in the canteen and wondered whether to drive to Oxford or take the train.

Father Anselm couldn't concentrate that afternoon either. His mind kept wandering. He tried to do a little packing, but nothing seemed to fit into his suitcase properly and he abandoned it till later. He attempted to explain the central heating to Father John, but Father John was being more than usually obtuse, so he just left the paper with him. At half past three he went to the chapel and prayed for guidance, but even then the words failed him. He attempted to formulate a prayer about the invasion of privacy and the opening of mails, but each time it sounded more absurd. He gave up and recited the Lord's Prayer several times.

Afterwards he took a brief walk up the hillside. He remembered the confrontation with Gaymer Burton. What if he had been wrong? If only there was someone other than God to whom he could turn for advice.

Bognor had suggested that he ought to ring Sir Erris Beg, but he would certainly not do that. The involvement of outsiders, and particularly the police, had brought him and the Community nothing but trouble. He would deal with this situation on his own. As far as he was concerned it was a purely internal affair. He watched as a rabbit stood up and peered about it, nose a-twitch, then saw him and ran off down its hole. Perhaps the best thing would be to summon Xavier and ask him to show him the contents of the letter himself. No. That would imply lack of trust and it would be wrong of him to display that.

By six o'clock when he returned to his room the indecision had become agonising. Again he picked up the letter and stared at it, almost as if he expected it to yield up its secret voluntarily.

⋆ ⋆ ⋆

At the same moment precisely, Simon Bognor was sitting in the corner of a first-class compartment, moving gently out of Paddington station. For the umpteenth time he adjusted his bow tie. Then he unfolded his evening paper.

⋆ ⋆ ⋆

Between six o'clock and Evensong half an hour later, Father Anselm had come to half a dozen irrevocable decisions. Twice he had picked up the phone and started to dial Sir Erris Beg. Twice he had actually put on a kettle with a view to steaming the letter open, and twice he had put it in his Gladstone bag with a view to forgetting all about it until they arrived in Rumania.

He was so overwrought that he poured himself two glasses of sherry and drained them both. The alcohol numbed him, but he scarcely felt better, and again he conducted the service badly. The lesson too came as a shock. It was read by Father John in his metallic tones and it had an almost eerie significance. It was the first twenty-seven verses of the fourteenth chapter of St. Mark's gospel. The story of Judas Iscariot's betrayal of Christ. Anselm felt a sickly awfulness as Father John read, 'Verily I say unto you. One of you which eateth with me shall betray me.' What did it mean? It had to mean something. Did it mean that he was about to betray Xavier's confidence? Or that Xavier had already betrayed his confidence? It was a message from above, he was certain of that, but why did it have to be so oracular? He looked hard at Father Xavier to see if he had found the passage significant, but Xavier appeared quite unmoved. He was staring absently at the wall opposite, not even joining in with the prayers. Anselm felt a flush of anger. He wished Xavier *participated* more.

*   *   *

The service ended at seven, at which time Bognor, his nerves steadied by a miniature bottle of Scotch, was standing in the corridor of his train watching the spire of the University Church and the tower in Tom Quad, Christ Church, slide past as the train drew into Oxford station. He looked at his watch. There was time to walk to the college. He got out and paced along the lavatory-like tunnel under the station, past Nuffield and the Royal Oxford Hotel and on towards Carfax and the High. It was ages since he had dined in All Souls and he had a vague memory of an endless procession through a series of rooms filled with food and drink. At least the meal should be good.

* * *

The brothers filed straight from Evensong to supper and Anselm said Grace. It was a silent meal, but there was reading. He regretted having sanctioned P. G. Wodehouse as a suitable volume. Brother Barnabas was reading it and the Yorkshire accents were quite wrong. Wooster, who he had always pronounced like the great cathedral city, became 'Wooooooster' and 'Aunt Agatha' was rendered as 'Unt Ugutha'. The copious laughter of the brothers grated on his nerves as he continued to wrestle with his dilemma. It was made no better by the realisation that he would have to make a decision soon. Tomorrow would be too late. He ate nothing and was relieved to be able to rise and say 'For what we have received may the Lord make us truly grateful'. He had come to half a decision and he knew that it was a trifle cowardly. That was too bad. On his way out he put a hand on Father Simon's shoulder. 'I'd like a word, please,' he said. 'In my room.' Father Simon nodded silently.

Once there he poured himself another sherry and offered one to Simon. Simon started to protest that he never touched alcohol but soon desisted.

'This is very difficult,' said Anselm slowly. 'Indeed, I scarcely know where to begin. But I need your advice.'

* * *

Thirty-five miles away in a quiet panelled room on the first floor of All Souls three other men were drinking sherry. It was a particularly fine Viejo Oloroso, Solera 1830. Bognor had been expecting his host, Lord Camberley, but the presence of the third man was a surprise. It was Gaymer Burton.

Bognor had been the last to arrive and Burton therefore had the advantage of him. The surprise on Bognor's face was all too obvious, but Burton had displayed nothing. Lord Camberley had been patrician and patronising, smooth as mayonnaise. Burton had been suave, diplomatic, but worried with it.

'You two have met, of course,' said Camberley.

'Indeed,' said Burton.

Nothing else was said until sherry had been

tasted and then it was only a tease.

'I won't pretend,' said Camberley, 'that we don't have something important to discuss. But we can hardly do it in front of the entire college. There are conventions. It will have to wait till the port.' Bognor licked his lips. The sherry was superb. He had two glasses before it was time to dine. They seated themselves at eight and started on the smoked trout, accompanied by a fresh chill Muscadet.

★ ★ ★

Father Simon was appalled. 'I really didn't mean . . .' he began. 'I mean I was just chattering . . . I mean if what you're suggesting is true then it's tantamount to accusing Father Xavier of murder. You can't. It's not conceivable.'

Father Anselm drummed his fingers on the desk and looked at his frightened colleague with new resolve. He always derived strength from other people's inadequacy.

'I'm inclined to think,' he said, 'that there is only one thing for it.'

'What?'

'It will have to be opened.'

'You can't. It's not fair.'

'On the contrary. It's the only thing which is fair. Fair to you and me. Fair to the Community. Fair to the police. Yes, fair even to

Xavier. It's the only way.'

'Can I have another glass of sherry?' asked Simon. Anselm pushed the decanter across the desk and looked suspicious.

'But what?' asked Simon, as he half choked on the gulp, 'what if it's innocuous?'

'Then I'll seal it up again.' He went outside with the kettle, glad that Simon didn't know it was the third time he'd done so. It didn't take a second to light the gas ring and the kettle, a cheap old thin-bottomed model, boiled quickly. Within five minutes he had steamed open the envelope. For a moment he contemplated it with apprehension, then he went back into his room and put it open on the desk, but without removing the contents.

'Let us pray,' he said, closing his eyes. 'Guide us we beseech thee, O Lord, that we may do only that which is right in thy sight. That if we err we do so through the error of our understanding and not through evil intent. Through Jesus Christ our Lord. Amen.'

Father Simon, who had long since ceased being surprised at the Father Minister's capacity for on-the-spot spontaneous prayer, echoed the Amen and opened his eyes. For the last time Father Anselm glared at the object of his concern and then in one dramatic gesture put his hand inside and drew out the contents. There were three large sheets of paper, squared graph paper. He unfolded them carefully, flattening them out on the surface of the desk, side by side. Then he stood back and looked at them. Father Simon came round to his side of the desk and together they stared at the letter to Brother Aloysius.

'Oh dear, oh dear, oh dear,' said Father Anselm.

'You'd better ring Sir Erris,' said Father Simon.

They continued to stare uncomprehendingly at the mass of drawings and formulae scattered across the pages.

'I suppose,' said Father Simon, 'I suppose it is what I think it is. I mean you don't think this chap Aloysius is just keen on mathematics or something?'

Father Anselm regarded his colleague with derision. 'Be your age,' he said. 'No, I will not ring Sir Erris. Not yet. This is our own problem and *we* must deal with it. Whatever Xavier has done, it is we who must confront him with it. Then we can decide about the police. But it is we who must decide.'

It was ten to nine. There were only ten minutes to go to Compline. 'Simon,' he said, 'go to Xavier's room and tell him to come here to see us after the service . . . And, Simon . . . say nothing about this to him. I don't want him to suspect. Not yet.'

Father SImon went off, and Anselm sat back, trying again to unravel the secret of the sheets of squared foolscap. He shook his head several times and sighed. Oddly enough, it didn't occur to either of them to feel fear.

★ ★ ★

There had been times, and not so far distant either, when dinners at All Souls had been enormously protracted affairs of nine or more courses. On St. Lambert's Day, however, the meal, though good enough in its way, was neither long nor imaginative. Tournedos Rossini, which followed the smoked trout, were, to Bognor's way of thinking, the sort of thing one got in flash expense account restaurants in stockbroker country. Good stuff at the country club. The Château Montrose, however, was more than compensation.

The conversation, which was what an All Souls Dinner was supposed to be about, impressed Bognor with its brittle brilliance, but he found its lack of humanity distressing. Brother Bede would have found it even worse.

It suited Gaymer Burton, and to a lesser extent Camberley, but Bognor kept quiet. He was amazed that both men, though they obviously had something vitally important to tell him, were able to forget it completely and talk with wit and fluency about everything from the new Rent Act to salmon-fishing. He found it unnerving.

At nine a pineapple concoction appeared and with it bottles of Rauenthaler Rothenberg, Riesling Auslese.

'Very remarkable. *Edelfäule*,' said Burton, and started to talk with his usual irritating grace and knowledge about the manufacture of great table wines.

* * *

Now that his decision had been taken Father Anselm was almost boisterous. He conducted Compline with verve and returned afterwards to his study with all the elation of a public school housemaster who is about to deliver a well-merited beating. He knew now with a perfect certainty who had betrayed whom and yet he felt no bitterness. Only a militant, all-conquering self-righteousness. For three minutes he and Simon sat, waiting in glowing silence, the three offending pages still lying flat on the desk top, as witnesses to the crime. At twenty-five past nine there was a sharp triple knock.

'Come,' said Father Anselm, and Father Xavier entered softly, followed closely by Brother Paul.

'I'm sorry,' said Anselm, with the assurance of might and right. 'I only wanted you, Xavier.' Xavier said nothing. He just looked at the papers on the desk. Then he reached under his habit and pulled out a packet from which he extracted one cigarette. Very deliberately he lit it and blew smoke in the direction of Anselm and Simon.

'How very unfortunate,' he said at length.

Quite what happened next neither Anselm nor Simon ever knew. It was so fast. One minute, it seemed, they were admonishing an erring inferior, and the next they were sitting on the floor securely bound up in white dressing-gown cords (their own and Xavier's and Paul's) with handkerchiefs stuffed in their mouths. It can't have been long because Xavier, who had left practically all the work to Paul, was still smoking the same cigarette.

'You'll be up in time for Terce,' he said. 'They'll miss you at Prime. And by then we'll have gone. I'd love to explain, but there simply isn't time. And, by the way, Anselm, I'm not really in the least sorry about what happened in the library the other day.' He smiled. 'Well. Good night and good-bye.' Simon and Anselm heard the key being turned in the lock and the sound of footsteps walking urgently away. Then another door. The front door of the farmhouse. And silence.

* * *

The atmosphere in Lord Camberley's room was already thick with cigar smoke when he began but there was none of the relaxed contentment normally associated with the aftermath of dinner in an Oxford college. His grey gaunt face with its hooded eyes took on an expression of great seriousness and melancholy. Bognor couldn't help feeling that everything he did seemed contrived.

'I'm afraid,' said Camberley, 'that I owe you an apology, Simon—I hope you don't mind my calling you Simon—I didn't realise until yesterday that this would be the case, and I'm sorry that my apology and the information that accompanies it should be so belated . . . However . . .'

He turned to Gaymer Burton, who was sitting well forward in his chair, eager and nervous, toying with an eight-inch Cuban cigar which was several sizes too big for him. 'I think, Gaymer, that it would be best if you told Mr. Bognor the whole story.'

'Yes. Absolutely,' said Gaymer. Bognor studied him closely. He was undoubtedly nervous and the nervousness was undoubtedly genuine, but there was still something phoney. 'Well . . .' he started, 'I'll try to be reasonably concise. The other day, after we met at the retreat at Beaubridge, I bumped into Lord Camberley here and naturally commiserated with him about the terrible business of poor Thomas. Anselm had told me that in his view it was quite definitely suicide, so I was most surprised when Lord Camberley told me this was quite without truth. He also told me why . . . In some detail.'

Simon wished he understood other men's minds. Burton sipped more port and continued. 'I was upset and, of course, concerned. Both for personal and for political reasons. It seemed to me to be distressing on both counts. And naturally I gave the matter a great deal of thought over the next few days.

'Now you'll think me terribly naive and silly when I tell you the next bit. But it's so naive and silly you will just have to believe it.' Bognor noted inwardly that he would believe anything of Gaymer Burton, but not naivety or silliness. 'Anyway, it suddenly came to me, and why I didn't think of it before I can't imagine. But . . .' He *was* very nervous. 'But, as you know, I've been going to Beaubridge for many years now.'

'Eleven,' said Bognor unnecessarily.

'I hadn't kept count, I'm afraid,' said Burton irritably.

He drank more port and picked up the interruption. 'Eleven years ago—if you're right and that *was* the year of my first visit—one of my colleagues gave me a letter to pass on to Anselm. He claimed he was an old friend but he hadn't for various reasons been able to see him.'

'What reasons?' asked Bognor.

Again Burton was irritated. 'I don't know. I

don't make a habit of prying into the private affairs of my colleagues and friends. I suspect, if you must know, that it was something to do with my colleague's wife. I suspect. I don't know and I don't happen to think it's relevant . . . . anyway, as I was saying, he gave me a letter and I passed it on.'

'Why didn't he just post it?' Bognor was anxious to make sure of the details.

'I don't know. He may have posted letters as well as giving one to me. I suppose when he heard I was going down to Beaubridge he thought he'd save the stamp. I simply don't know.'

'Sorry. Go on.' Bognor resolved to interrupt more tellingly in future.

'Well, to cut a long story short, the same thing happened every year from then on. A few days before the retreat my friend gave me a letter for Anselm and I passed it on without giving it a second thought. Until, of course, Lord Camberley told me this dreadful story about secrets. Then suddenly it all clicked into place.'

'I see.' Bognor, with a blinding glimpse of the obvious, realised that one of his strongest cards in this case was the way everyone underestimated him. 'Can you tell me the name of your friend?'

Burton flushed, and appeared embarrassed. 'I'm sorry,' he said. 'At this stage I don't think

I can tell you. I will. Later. But I would like the chance to talk to him first. The important thing, though, is that Anselm must be the courier.'

'So you see, Bognor,' Lord Camberley had slipped back easily into the habit of calling him by his surname, 'I'm afraid . . . horribly afraid . . . that I misled you about Anselm. I find it inconceivable that he should have done anything so evil and carried on this deceit for so long. But in view of what Gaymer has said there is no other possible explanation.' Lord Camberley rose and dispensed port from the decanter. 'I only hope this news doesn't come too late.'

'No,' said Bognor. 'Happily not. As you know, the Expo-Brit doesn't leave till tomorrow at noon and I've arranged for Father Anselm and Father Simon to be picked up at the airport. No doubt we shall find the incriminating letter and that will be that.' He paused and drank. 'As you know, sir, I've had my suspicions of Anselm since the very beginning.'

He didn't believe Burton's story. But, on the other hand, if they did find a secret letter in Anselm's habit tomorrow it would be difficult to disprove it. 'I wonder,' he said with assumed simplicity, 'why he should have killed your son?'

Camberley looked at Burton. 'We agreed,' he

said, 'and it's a small consolation, that although he directed it, he must have "hired" or "ordered" an assassin.'

Bognor nodded sagely. 'Because he'd seen your son talking to me and he knew that your son had seen him killing Brother Luke.'

'Quite so,' said Camberley. 'Tell me again. What precisely did Thomas tell you?'

Bognor thought for a moment. He had always realised that there was something important there, muddled up with the gibbering about the Royal Family. 'Nothing conclusive,' he said. 'There was something about seeing someone who shouldn't have been there.'

Even as he said it Bognor suddenly realised. Christ, he'd been an idiot! Burton was droning on, but Bognor only half heard him. 'It's obvious,' he said, 'Anselm never went near the vegetable garden. He wouldn't soil his hands with that sort of work. That was what Thomas was trying to tell you. Only you didn't recognise it.'

Bognor tried to conceal his elation. That wasn't it at all. The only person in the entire Community who had a real alibi, who had actually been miles away from the Friary when it happened, was the person who was the most likely murderer of Thomas. The man he and Sir Erris had picked up on the road. He had invented the one alibi any one would accept without question, then waited in the vicinity of the Friary until he got his chance, committed the murder and kept well away for another day. Only Batty Thomas had spotted him. That was what he had meant about the man not being supposed to have been there. Bognor's mind raced. He mustn't let Burton or Camberley think he didn't accept their theory *in toto*. Camberley, he reasoned, must be simply a dupe. The death of his son had thrown him off balance. He must somehow get Burton to give the rest of the secret away. If he could go on managing to appear stupid it shouldn't be hard. Nor, on previous performances, should it be difficult to look stupid.

'What about motive?' asked Bognor, hoping it wasn't too much of a googly. If Burton thought he was such an idiot he might not have done his homework. He sneaked a searching look at the man. Burton had definitely relaxed now. The dinner and the port were taking effect as well. He was off guard. Bognor felt grossly insulted that anyone should think so little of him.

'Motive?' said Burton superciliously. 'I've thought about that. It's too silly. In fact the whole thing is too silly and . . . jejune. Or would be if it wasn't so tragic.' He only just remembered his host's bereavement. 'No,' continued Burton. 'I'm afraid it's the same old story. He was a passionate anti-Fascist when he was up here before the war. It was so fashionable then to be passionate about Spain and the Nazis and so on that you don't expect anyone's obsession to endure. Well, I'm afraid that Anselm's passions persisted. He never grew up. It's as simple as that. Whereas most of us assumed that he had effectively channelled his anti-Fascism into Christianity, it seems that the first love of Marxism or whatever it was never really died. Extraordinary, because he's no fool.'

Burton was now well into his stride. He seemed to believe that he had won a victory and was prepared to chance his arm still further. The combination of port and over-confidence, ably assisted by his natural arrogance, was leading him into excess. Bognor was certain he was going to over-reach himself. Camberley sat very hunched and heavy-lidded.

'I must say,' he mused gloomily, 'I can't understand how I can have been wrong for so many years.'

Burton warmed to his theme. 'Heavens,' he said, 'you weren't the only one! I mean, Anselm was so good; so saintly; so without ambition and side. Perhaps, in a way, those are his problems. But it's no wonder none of us saw through the deception. If, for instance, it had been a more suspect member of the Friary.' He paused and appeared to pick a name at random. Bognor was incredulous. This was either stupendous double bluff or he was giving the whole game away through sheer blind arrogance. 'Take Xavier for instance. He's a dreadful old rogue in many ways. He was a passionate Communist in the thirties. He smokes and he drinks and heaven knows what else. *But*, when all's said and done . . . he's probably—well, demonstrably now—a better man. "Better" in an absolute sense than poor Anselm.'

Bognor tried to appear totally impassive. If Burton thought for an instant that Bognor retained a vestige of intelligent suspicion he would clam up again. However, it seemed there was no stopping him. For a hideous moment Bognor even wondered if he was telling the truth.

'It's purely incidental, I admit,' said Burton. 'But I've always felt that Anselm was inclined to discriminate against Xavier on very superficial grounds. Now, as we see, it's clear that appearances can be very misleading. I, for one, have always been inclined to take a charitable view of Xavier. After all, the dreadful business of his wife must have left a permanent scar.'

It was coming. Bognor was certain of it. At any moment, with the merest prompting, he was going to give something away; something that would unwittingly put Anselm and six other major suspects in the clear and at the same time implicate the guilty man. Bognor couldn't afford to prompt himself. It was too risky, so he was immensely thankful when Camberley came to his aid.

'Wife?' he said. 'I'd no idea. I didn't think . . .'

Burton should have stopped then. Normally perhaps he would have done, but by now nothing at all could prevent him.

'Not many people have. She was Polish, married already, of course. Might, I think, have loved him genuinely. It was wartime. No one ever really knew who was employing her or why. Some people say she died in Belsen and some that she's still alive in South America. I don't know. It's all in the past, but it explains his eccentricity. And then her leaving the son. I never know if it was a blessing or a curse, it always . . .'

'Son?' Once more, fortuitously, it was Camberley who asked the question. Bognor, still groping, thanked him silently and almost forgave him for previous follies and indiscretions. Perhaps the old boy had not been as easily hoodwinked as he seemed. However, this time Burton checked himself, even though the question came from someone he treated as an ally.

'Yes,' he said slowly. 'I thought that as he . . . No. Forget I ever said it. It's a betrayal of a personal secret. I'd forgotten the steps that . . . never mind. As I was saying, you could hardly be blamed for not recognising Anselm's deceit.'

He prattled on, trying to undo the harm, but it was too late.

The moment he'd said 'wife' something had stirred in Bognor's subconscious; the second he'd said 'son' it emerged. It had been a major effort of will for him not to shout out when he saw it. Now he knew why Paul's face seemed so familiar; why he had an uneasy feeling that he'd met Xavier somewhere before. An age difference of a quarter of a century plus a lot of living and a lot of whisky had not totally camouflaged the family likeness. They were father and son. It explained everything. Xavier was the spy and Paul the assassin. The motive was filial piety. He'd solved it.

Burton was drivelling on. Bognor tried to work out if he realised how much he'd given away. The man was nervous again, but, by the look of him, more nervous of Camberley than Bognor. He wasn't giving him a second thought. He looked at his watch. He could be at the Friary in under an hour.

He got to his feet. 'Well,' he said, 'I must thank you both. You've been most helpful. Luckily it doesn't change our plans, but I'd like to be at the airport myself, so I think I'll aim for the next train, if you don't mind.' They shook hands and Lord Camberley rang for a taxi. Trivial pleasantries were exchanged, Bognor offered thanks for the meal, accepted another cigar and was unable to tell if Burton was still anxious. It no longer mattered anyway.

*         *         *

Lord Camberley and Mr. Burton would have been surprised to know that three minutes later Mr. Bognor's taxi was speeding, not towards the railway station, but down the Woodstock Road.

*         *         *

Father Xavier and Brother Paul arrived in the bar of the Boot breathless. Mr. Hey raised his eyebrows.

'Later than usual tonight, Father,' he said. The bar was as empty as it normally was. Only the toping cowhands stood at the far end with their pints.

'Yes . . . George, I want you to do something for me.'

'Of course. Always do something for an old pal. You having the usual, are you? And the boy?' Father Xavier nodded impatiently.

'Yes,' he said. 'But we're in a hurry. Look, George, I've never let you down, have I?' Mr. Hey thought for a moment.

'No,' he replied. 'Can't say you have.'

'Not over money?'

'Never over money. Certainly not.'

'Good.' Father Xavier pushed his already

empty glass over the bar and asked for the refill. 'Look, George.' He was almost whispering. 'Will you do a cheque for me? Now?'

''Course. How much?'

Father Xavier paused and then said very softly, 'Hundred and fifty?'

'Hundred and fifty?' Mr. Hey whistled.

'Shhh.' Xavier leant further across. 'I'll give you a cheque, and the money's there, I promise. It'll be through in a couple of days. Promise.'

'But I don't have it, Father.'

'Oh, come on. Can't you see it's important? It matters.'

'You must be joking. We don't take a hundred and fifty a month, let alone a week. You know that.'

'Come on, George. Under the mattress. You've told me.'

Mr. Hey's eyes widened. 'I couldn't. It's the wife's. She'd slaughter me.'

'George.' Father Xavier's voice was rising dramatically. 'I have never,' he said, 'asked anyone a more important question in the whole of my life. Never.'

Mr. Hey registered growing amazement. An hour had been reached by which he had generally consumed several pints of mild-and-bitter and tonight was no exception. He struggled, recalled the two deaths at the Friary and the policeman from London, and asked Father Xavier, 'Not in any sort of trouble are you, Father?'

'Of course I'm in bloody trouble,' said Xavier. 'Why the hell else do you think I'd ask?'

Mr. Hey nodded and screwed up his eyes. 'Back in a tick,' he said. Xavier lit another cigarette and waited. Shortly Mr. Hey returned with a black tin money box from which he withdrew a quantity of pound notes kept together by an elastic band. Deftly he counted out a hundred and fifty of them and passed them across the bar. Father Xavier presented him with a cheque and agreed to a final Scotch.

'There's one other thing,' he said, still talking conspiratorially. 'Young Paul and I have been called away rather suddenly and we're without transport. You don't have any thoughts?' Mr. Hey considered. He was deriving a lot of vicarious pleasure from this. He wondered if there would be a reward.

'What's wrong with the Friary van?' he asked.

'Just,' said Xavier, 'that Brother Vivian wears the key round his neck at all times, and he might not let us borrow it.'

'Not easy,' said Mr. Hey, sipping carefully and smacking his lips. Then he suddenly said, 'No. Tell you what, though.' The two men were leaning so far across the bar that they were practically rubbing noses. 'Can you ride a motor-bike?'

Father Xavier turned pale and choked slightly on his drink. After a moment he said, 'I haven't touched one for over twenty years. Used to own an old Norton.'

'Well, there's a bit of luck.' Mr. Hey smiled gleefully. As far as he was concerned this was turning into a splendid game. 'Now, you see Gilbert?' He glanced furtively down the bar towards the two farm labourers. 'He's the tall one.' Father Xavier nodded, and the landlord continued, 'Well, it so happens he rides a bike and I have a mind it's an old Norton. Always brings it down here in the evenings. Parks it round the back behind the gents'. You couldn't miss it.'

'What about Gilbert?' asked Xavier. 'He'll miss it.'

'Couple more pints and he won't remember where he put it,' said Mr. Hey. 'He's been in here since half six. Always gets pissed after he gets his wage packet. They say he knocks his wife about a bit. Doesn't look the type to me, though.'

Xavier smiled at Mr. Hey. 'You've been a great help George,' he said. 'I don't know where I'd have been without you. I don't know when or even if I'll see you again. But I'll be in touch.' And, so saying, Xavier ushered his young accomplice out of the Boot and round to the back of the pub.

The good-bye saddened Mr. Hey briefly, but he was not a man for nostalgia or regrets, and he had not known excitement like this since the night Mrs. Rideout came in and threw a bottle of Guinness at her husband. He would enjoy seeing the look on poor Gilbert's face when he heard his old Norton making its getaway. Mr. Hey felt like celebrating, so he poured himself a large Scotch and settled down to wait. He was just beginning to get worried, forgetting that the two friars might well decide to use the gents' before setting off . . . when there was the staccato cough of a petrol engine being started. It faded in a wheeze and the three drinkers all glanced up. Gilbert strained his ears and looked concerned.

'Hey!' he said, not moving. There was a moment's silence, then another kick, another cough, an instant when it seemed the engine would die again, then a few seconds of half-hearted splutter as it ticked over indecisively and finally a gathering crescendo as the throttle was applied. The noise grew to an impressive roar, faded slightly before it moved. There was a skidding, a brief halt near the front door, and then another rev before it powered away down the road. The three men rushed to the door and were outside just in time to see the rear light of Gilbert's Norton as it took the first bend in the lane, already doing at least sixty.

* * *

Bognor sat in the back of the taxi and sucked his Havana in a mood of utter elation. Bognor's first case, he kept telling himself, was ending in triumph. He pictured the scene at Beaubridge when he arrived. Himself, the intrepid, incisive and utterly original sleuth, arriving in the dead of night, knocking on the Abbot's door. The Abbot, in long white nightshirt, emerging sleepily, his eyes widening in revelation and alarm as Bognor revealed the ugly truth, the tramp across the chill courtyard to the killers' cells and the final dramatic confrontations. 'Father Xavier . . . the truth is out. You and your son will have to accompany me . . .' He exhaled another lungful of heavy smoke and imagined the telephone calls. One to Parkinson and one to Sir Erris. The utter incredulity of both as he gave them the news, laconically and coolly. 'The Beaubridge file is now closed,' he would say. 'I suggest we breakfast tomorrow at Woodstock police station where I and the accused will pass the night.'

He was so carried away by these euphoric imaginings that he scarcely noticed the motor-bike, as it came round the bend on the wrong side of the road causing the taxi to swerve violently. 'Hooligans,' shouted the driver, waving a fist at the bike's rear light as it swayed away, bearing its two riders towards

Oxford and beyond.

* * *

The first few miles had been pretty hairy. The old bike was rusted up and the tread was going on the rear tyres. Xavier couldn't see much either. He had no goggles, of course, so he had to use a pair of dark glasses. As it was dark, anyway, it didn't improve matters. Besides, his riding was as rusty as the bike itself.

They had a series of near misses, including Bognor, but by the time they'd filled up with petrol at the self-service station on the Bellingham roundabout he was beginning to get some confidence. It was like swimming or Serbo-Croat. Once learnt, never really forgotten.

So far, he calculated, so lucky. They had a good start and a hundred and fifty quid, legitimately acquired, in one-pound notes. If the old machine kept going they should do the rest within two hours, easily. There was plenty of dual carriageway now and he'd stick on the M40 to Wycombe and then cut across to the M4 at Maidenhead. He hoped the hell there'd be flights. There'd be no way of checking. But if they could be out by eight or at the latest nine they should be perfectly safe. The two men talked little. Contingency plans had been half formulated for ages, though they had never expected to be forced to leave in quite such a hurry. Nevertheless, ever since Xavier's espionage had begun, Gaymer Burton on his annual visit had brought fresh passports and visas as well as his smuggled secrets.

As he filled the tank, Xavier said crisply, 'You go first I'll check out with Burton. RV at the Bristol in Prague. The cellar bar, six-thirty to seven. If I'm not there in three weeks forget it.'

The road from Bellingham was perfect for motor-cycling in the small hours. He experienced an increasing access of confidence and noticed with pleasure that the boy behind him was beginning to relax and move with him and the bike, no longer braced against the sway as he had been for the first few miles. There were bends in the road, but not too sharp. He let the bike dip to almost forty-five degrees as they rounded them, hardly slowing at all. On the double 'S'-bends he allowed a double sway, first to the left, then to the right. It was like riding an animal. His movements became more and more fluid and the speeds crept up and up. They did Woodstock to the other side of Oxford in nine minutes. Father Xavier smiled widely. He wished he could see better.

* * *

There was a full moon that night, and Bognor

could see round the Friary as clearly as on the night that he'd discovered the poker school. That time he had tried to be silent and unobtrusive, but now he could be as noisy as he liked. It was, after all, Simon Bognor's hour of triumph. For a moment he stood at the entrance to the courtyard, savouring the situation, then he clumped aggressively across it, past the well, into the farmhouse, and to the door of Father Anselm's room. Once there, he knocked loudly three times and listened.

There was a light on inside, which was curious even to Bognor, who at that moment was past curiosity, but there was no reply. He knocked again and this time was rewarded by a strange muffled sound. It seemed to Bognor that it was a voice, or even voices.

'Father Anselm,' he said loudly, 'please open. This is Bognor of the Board of Trade.'

Again he was answered, but quite unintelligibly. 'Oh, really,' he said aloud. 'This is absolutely ridiculous.' Since he was getting nowhere at all he decided to go out and look through the window to see what was happening. He had an uneasy feeling that all was not as he had expected. Outside he pressed his nose to the lighted window and let out an indeterminate sound of utter amazement as he saw Father Anselm and Father Simon bound and gagged and sitting on the floor. At once his elation deserted him. He had been foiled.

Stepping back from the window, he tried to think clearly. He had better rescue them. But how? He needed a key. Or could he force the lock? He had no metal rule with him, so it had better be a key. From where? Who had keys? The guest master. He'd better find Brother Barnabas.

A few minutes later the two Fathers, Brother Barnabas and Simon Bognor were standing in the Abbot's room with glasses of sherry in their hands. All four, for different reasons, appeared quite distraught and all four were talking at once. 'They can't have got far,' said Bognor. 'They've no money, no transport, no friends, no nothing. They'll be hiding in the woods.' Suddenly he had a nasty hint of intuition. 'No friends,' he repeated. 'No friends . . . not true, not true at all . . . Mr. Hey of the Boot.' Shouting which he fled the room, leaving the friars in a state of aggrieved confusion.

Down at the Boot he found another bizarre scene. It was after closing time, but in the bar Mr. Hey, two cowhands and a strange woman he took to be their landlord's wife were gathered in varying stages of intoxication and hysteria.

'It'll bounce . . . It'll bounce!' Mrs. Hey was shrieking, tears staining her face as she pummelled feebly at her husband's shirt-front.

One of the cowhands was sitting in a corner slouched over a half-empty bottle of Scotch, muttering obscenities, while the other sat beside him with an arm round his shoulder attempting apparently to console him. Mr. Hey remained silent under his wife's assault, though from his appearance it seemed that speech was physically beyond him. He was hardly able to stand.

'What on earth?' said Bognor feebly.

Mrs. Hey turned on him. 'Everything!' she screamed. 'Every last pound note, everything. And Gilbert's motor-bike. Why, why, why? He's mad.' Whereupon she returned to beating her husband, who was now collapsed on the bar, apparently asleep.

Bognor turned round and stepped outside, where he drew a deep breath of chill air. After a moment he had made a decision. It was his case and nobody else could help now. He was on his own. He must simply give chase.

* * *

Father Xavier and Brother Paul had made sensationally good time. There had been an anxious moment on the Oxford bypass where Xavier had only just managed to cut in front of an articulated lorry as the road reverted to two-lane traffic. Also his dark glasses tended to mist up. But as they bombed down the tunnel which leads from the M4 to the main terminal buildings at Heathrow Xavier noticed with satisfaction that it was only midnight. He slowed to an unobtrusive thirty and parked Gilbert's Norton in a dark corner of the park outside the No. 2 European terminal.

'Well played,' he said, patting her affectionately on the saddle and the two men marched swiftly inside.

The cavernous building was almost deserted. Little huddles of sleeping passengers lay about on the benches. A very few uniformed hostesses and air crew walked busily; others sat lethargically at desks.

Xavier had not been inside the airport for ages. He was dismayed to find it so huge and so empty. Despite the fact that their habits had been left behind and that they were in conventional, if scruffy, civilian clothes, they looked conspicuous. It would be better by about seven o'clock when the rush started, but if by any frightful mischance there was a search on before then, it would be difficult to evade capture.

'I hope there are some early flights,' he said to his son as they mounted the stairs to the main arrival and departure boards. 'I want you out as quickly as possible.' Paul, who led the way, shrugged.

'I'd like us both out fairly quickly,' he said.

The departure board was not encouraging. A B.E.A. to Paris was about to take off, but there was little else before five.

'That looks good,' said Paul, who was more

used to reading boards like this. Xavier had missed it. It was a LOT, Polish airline flight to Warsaw at 1.55.

'Right,' said Xavier. 'This is where we split up.' He handed Paul seventy-five pounds and the two embraced briefly.

'See you in Prague,' said Paul. 'Good luck.'

* * *

Bognor arrived at Heathrow almost two hours after the friars. His driver had gone fast, but was unwilling to take serious risks. As they came out of the tunnel and swung right towards No. 2 terminal, Bognor noticed an old four-engined propeller-driven plane shaking past the main buildings and clambering up the bright night sky above the airport. To his fevered imagination there was something sinister about it. He sucked his teeth and prayed for luck.

The question, really, was where to begin. He went to the girl on the B.E.A. desk and showed his card. 'I want a quick summary of all European flights out before 9 a.m.,' he said.

The girl produced a typewritten list and he scanned it swiftly. There were three likely ones. The 1.55 to Warsaw, 5.30 B.E.A. to Prague, and seven o'clock TAROM to Bucharest.

'Have you had a couple, male, booking on any of these three flights?'

'You mean recently?'

'This morning.'

'I'm sorry, sir, no. We've only had two bookings this morning. It's unusual. Most people book further in advance.' She smiled nervously.

'Two bookings?'

'Yes, sir. They were made independently.' She consulted her records. The names, thought Bognor, would mean nothing. They'd hardly travel as Father Xavier and Brother Paul. And the passports would be faked as likely as not. He wished he had some support.

'Do you remember them?'

'Yes, sir. There was a young man, in his early twenties, who seemed rather agitated. And then an older man with dark glasses. He only booked on about twenty minutes ago.'

'Which flights?'

'The young gentleman was on the 1.55 to Warsaw, sir. And the older gentleman . . . One minute, sir. Yes, he was on the 5.30 to Prague.'

'What do you make the time now?'

'Just after two, sir.'

'Do you know if the 1.55 to Warsaw got away on time?'

'Hang on, sir. I'll check for you.' She dialled an internal number, but Bognor sensed that it was useless. He knew that the clumsy old plane he'd seen as he drove in was the 1.55 to Warsaw. It couldn't have been anything else.

He felt depressed. It was going to be Xavier alone, without his son. He wished it had been the other way round, because he'd become attached to the old boy.

The girl replaced the receiver and smiled a neat plastic smile.

'Yes, sir. The 1.55 to Warsaw left on time.'

'Thank you.' He turned and walked upstairs. He had two alternatives. He could sit in the exit channel round about five when the flight was called and pick Xavier up as he came through. Or he could go and look for him. He weighed the alternatives. The trouble with waiting was that Xavier might spot him and change tickets. There was nothing to stop him changing to a flight anywhere else in the world and by the time Bognor had realised that he wasn't going to Prague he would have wasted three hours. By that time, too, the airport would have filled up.

He looked round the empty halls. The cleaners were in, sluicing down the marble floors, waking up the unfortunates who were lying on the benches. Bognor felt tired looking at them. He walked over to an automatic vending machine and bought a coffee.

If Xavier chose to spend the next few hours sitting out in the concourse he'd be easy to find. It was conceivable that he would, since he presumably didn't expect a hue and cry until the friars had noticed all those empty places at Prime and Matins. On the other hand, Xavier was worried by now. Surely he must realise that his behaviour had been cavalier. Bognor wondered what clue there had been in the sermon the other day. It would be interesting to find out.

He finished the coffee and looked blankly at an Italian family complete with grandparents and three young children. The youngest appeared to have wet itself. There was a lot of confusion and the harassed mother carried the screaming infant off through the lavatory door marked with the word 'Ladies' and a diagrammatic picture of the female form.

Bognor reacted to the sight with what he considered professional acumen. The most obvious place for Xavier to hide for three hours was in the gents'. He could sit in there reading a good book and no one would disturb him. It was not a happy thought. Bognor did not relish a detailed tour of every lavatory in London airport. Instead he decided to start on an inspection of the more obvious places. It would be silly to waste time in lavatories and then find Father Xavier sleeping openly and casually on a public seat.

There was a lot of ground to be covered. Bognor walked slowly along the main floor, his footsteps echoing through the emptiness. At the far end he stopped and listened to the tannoy saying, 'Alitalia announce the departure of their flight 235 to Rome and Naples.'

Suppose Xavier had managed to change his ticket and slip on that? He turned round to walk back, past the bank of telephone kiosks, when he stopped again and sniffed. There was a smell. He sniffed again. There was disinfectant from the cleaners and another less easily definable one which was just people *en masse*. Or the remains of people *en masse*. But there was something else. Very close. He sniffed more deeply. It was a familiar smell and it was coming from below. He looked down at the floor and let out a grunt of recognition before bending down to pick up a smouldering cigarette stub. It was more than a stub—almost half a cigarette. Perfectos Finos.

He ran his eye down the telephone kiosks and saw what he had, typically, missed before. There was a light on in one and one only. He could only see the back of the man, but he recognised immediately the thickening body in its stained old canvas trousers and silk shirt, with its grizzled hair and bulging neck. He went across and very softly opened the door.

'Excuse me,' he said gently. 'You dropped your cigarette.'

* * *

Father Xavier came, as they say, quietly. Indeed, it was the most civilised arrest. He appeared surprised to see Bognor, but only mildly.

'I'd been talking to Gaymer Burton,' he explained later, in the car. 'He seemed to think he'd been wildly clever. Didn't react very kindly when I told him he was a conceited little prick. Still, I didn't expect to see you so soon. You're only two hours late. Not that it made any odds with Anselm's prissy silliness. I must say that I didn't expect his curiosity to get the better of his prudishness. I thought he might experience the odd pang. No more.'

'But you must have realised I'd have him searched?'

'Knowing you, you'd have forgotten. Anyway, we'd still have scored. I doubt whether you could have proved that Gaymer was other than a dupe. And Gaymer would have sworn that he gave the letter to Anselm, not me.'

'Gaymer Burton's word against Anselm's.'

'Not only that, Anselm would have been caught with the plans on him. That wouldn't look good.' Father Xavier drew heavily on one of his incriminating cigarettes. 'I think given a little more luck and a little more modesty from Burton we might have pulled it off. Do you have a drink, by any chance?'

'Sorry,' said Bognor. 'Something else I forgot.'

'Anyway,' he said, 'the boy got away with it.'

'With murder maybe,' said Bognor,

seriously, 'but not with the secrets.' Xavier looked at him incredulously.

'My dear boy,' he said, 'we *always* take a spare copy. It just means that they go to Father Stanislous in Warsaw this year and not poor Brother Aloysius. Luck of the draw.' And he drank again very fully.

They had passed the Heston service station and the road had risen up above London on its concrete stilts. There were still a lot of questions.

'What about the clue in the sermon?' asked Bognor.

'Forsake not an old friend, for the new is not comparable to him; a new friend is as new wine; when it is old, thou shalt drink it with pleasure.' Father Xavier recited it with his eyes closed. 'In certain respects,' he said, 'you've conducted this investigation in a manner which verges on the intelligent. At others your lack of original insight is heartbreaking. It's not even as if it is a difficult or complex clue. It's ludicrously simple. You should have twigged when that fool Burton was talking about Anselm's motives. They're the same as mine.'

Bognor was too tired to unravel it. 'I'm sorry,' he said, 'you'll have to do it for me.'

'Oh Christ,' said Xavier. 'All it means is that I became a Communist when I was nineteen and a friar when I was thirty-eight. The reasons for becoming a Communist were perfectly valid thirty-three years ago and they have not changed in any essential. My reasons for becoming a friar were more complex.

'My little annual espionage was something I concocted with Gaymer. We'd been aware of each other's sympathies since before the war, and the idea struck me as droll. It was also some compensation for dropping out. I agree it didn't put me in the Fuchs-Lonsdale class, but I've done well enough. Anyway, I wouldn't entirely accept dropping out. For all its shortcomings Beaubridge has many of the better characteristics of the Communist society. And as you have observed, I haven't been unduly concerned with the aspects I don't care for. To be frank, I've almost become fond of the life religious. But it is a secondary allegiance. In other words, my old friend is Marxist-Leninism; my new and less vital friendship is with my sacred brethren and all that.'

'Are you trying to tell me,' asked Bognor, 'that you joined the Friary simply so that you could smuggle out trade secrets?'

'That's crude. Like so much post-war British thinking,' said Xavier, chuckling. 'But broadly correct. Wouldn't have missed it for anything.'

'But,' said Bognor, very slowly and deliberately because he was thinking out loud, and finding the process difficult, 'that means that you joined the Friary specifically to get secrets to your ideological comrades. But when you joined there was no Expo-Brit, much less any Beaubridge involvement in it.'

'Ah.' Xavier patted Simon on the knee. 'It was no problem to get Beaubridge involved. They fell over each other trying to get the glory. Persuading Wharfedale Newspapers to start Expo-Brit was, I concede, a little more taxing.'

'Oh, come on.' Bognor wished he were in bed. 'You'll be telling me next that you put the *Globe* up to it yourself, and that Lord Wharfedale is a member of the Communist Party.'

Father Xavier turned and with one hand ruffled Bognor's hair, as if he were an idiot child. 'My dear boy,' he said, 'that would be fearfully indiscreet. If I ever say anything like that, don't believe a word of it.'

★ ★ ★

Cool shafts of afternoon autumn sunlight filtered softly through the ilex and sparkled on the two silver goblets below. Between them, on a small table overlaid with a crisp white cloth, was a bottle of Dom Perignon beady with condensation formed from its ice bucket, which was elegant, Georgian and, typically, uninsured. Three days had elapsed since the apprehension of Father Xavier and the escape of Brother Paul and they had been filled with paperwork and awkward questions. It was the first chance Bognor had had of relaxing, and he had cheerfully accepted the Begs's invitation to stay, on the sole condition that at no time did they venture to within ten miles of Beaubridge.

Sir Erris had been delighted with the champagne and insisted that it would only be ready to drink after a testing round of croquet. Which was why the first bottle sat, chilling and unbroached, under the ilex. A few yards away Sir Erris yet again struck his opponent's ball fiercely into the roses, and said sorry.

'I still think it's a pity about Gaymer Burton,' said Sir Erris, when Bognor was back within earshot. 'He'd have got his "K" in the next birthday list.'

Bognor shrugged. He couldn't summon much regret. Burton had been told that his resignation was required within twenty-four hours and that no decision would be taken on charges for a few days. He'd been found in bed the next morning with an empty bottle of aspirin and another of Tallisker malt whisky on the table. There was a careful and precise letter to his solicitor, and another for his brother. Bognor's first reaction had been that it was a waste of Tallisker, but he never said so. It would have seemed unduly callous—except perhaps to Xavier, who would have enjoyed the remark.

'I didn't terribly care for Burton, you know,' said Bognor, and smiled, to take the edge off the cliché. 'But I'm sorry the boy got away. He's the sinister one; and the one who did the killings.'

'Have you found out more?'

'Not much. Poor Xavier's still being grilled. They're putting him through it, but he's not saying very much. Apparently they got their claws into Paul years ago, and Xavier never really objected. After all, with his beliefs he was more than happy for the boy to join the party and go on jamborees to the East. Then he went to East Germany for three years—to the university in Leipzig—came back and said he'd like to live with his father for a bit. Nobody at the Friary knew anything about the relationship. It would have been merely temporary, of course—his stay as a brother. It's ironic too. I think his employers wanted him to bolster Xavier and just find his feet before starting on some really hot industrial work outside. Then he lost his nerve and started killing people; which is what he was trained to do, of course; so they've only themselves to blame.'

Sir Erris stooped briefly over his mallet and hit his ball firmly through the penultimate hoop.

'It . . . er . . . took you a long time to work it out,' he said. 'You could just have questioned everyone who'd ever been on Expo-Brit.'

Bognor tried to achieve a cannon, but the

range was too great and an unexpected slope in the lawn took his ball away towards another flower-bed.

'I suppose so. But then I'd have alerted the guilty party and scared them off. It was you who suggested I should go slow.' To be absolutely honest the idea had never occurred to him.

Sir Erris made the final token stroke and watched his ball gently nudge the multi-coloured pole which represented the end of the game. Bognor congratulated him wryly and they shouldered mallets and made for the champagne. 'The Strudwicks,' he said, opening the bottle with a flourish so that the cork narrowly missed his host, 'have Bollinger. But I wanted to be different.'

'Quite right,' said Sir Erris, watching with quiet anticipation as his guest poured the golden frothing liquid into the goblets. Then he raised his, and extended his arm in a southward direction, pushed the felt hat back on his head and said, 'I propose a toast.' He paused to make sure that Bognor was going to participate, and then declaimed, 'The Bloody Brethren.'

Bognor drank. 'The God botherers,' he said, 'especially Father Xavier.'

Away to the south, across the green valley turning slowly brown, and over the hills of downland pasture, the objects of their toast were assembling for Evensong. Father Anselm stood, as was his wont, just outside the chapel door with his big black bible and watched as his now sadly depleted flock hurried across the yard. He assumed a world-weary smile and inclined his head in an understated greeting as they passed him: Father John more bent and arthritic than ever; Brother Barnabas still preserving at least an outward jollity; pinched, worried Simon; silent, surly Vivian; and the rather similar, though more intelligent, Aldhelm. Father Anselm sighed as the bell changed its rhythm. He wondered what secrets these men hid. He hoped sincerely that he knew and understood them rather better than others. He sighed again and opened his bible. Luke, Batty Thomas, Bede, Xavier and Paul. All gone. It had been a most distressing period in his life.

He turned and entered the building. It was comforting to see the ranks of homely brown lined up in their choir stalls beneath the stations of the cross. By the time he reached his position near the altar he felt happier and more confident. Even charitable.

'Let us pray,' he intoned. 'Let us pray for our brothers so newly departed that the Lord our God may have mercy upon them, now and for ever more.

'Let us pray for our Brother Luke.

'Let us pray for our Brother Thomas.

'Let us pray for our Brother Bede.

'Let us pray for our Brother Xavier.
'Let us pray for our Brother Paul.'

And after each individual name there floated back the immensely heartening response of his Community at worship. Like an echo, strong and confident of a continuing future, the plain masculine chant.

'Lord have mercy upon him, Lord have mercy upon us, Lord hear our prayer.'

Photoset, printed and bound in Great Britain by
REDWOOD BURN LIMITED, Trowbridge, Wiltshire